Praise for *Girls They Write Songs About*

'This excellent novel – strange and artful, full of texture and feeling – reads like a *Sentimental Education* for our time; and I am so glad that a talented woman has written it.'

Vivian Gornick, author of *Unfinished Business*

'Razor-sharp… With deftness and candor, Bauer tells a moving and thoughtful story of how desire and ambition change over time and how to make sense of the messiness of carving out a path and life of one's own. A smart and beautifully rendered portrait of two women's lives.'

Kirkus (starred review)

'Gimlet-eyed… [Bauer] questions the choices women are forced to make as they age, and the way those decisions unite or divide them. [She] offers no easy answers nor pat conclusions, and her layered tale is all the stronger for it.'

Booklist

'Finally, a book that stirs up the fire, hilarity, heartache and powerplant energy of female friendships. Remember how it felt to be young and invincible in New York City? Remember the friends who showed up at your gorgeously gritty apartment bearing new and sparkling worlds? *Girls They Write Songs About* carries the giddy, smart, shouted exuberance of free young women right up and into the questions that haunt us as we grow: how, oh how, did I get here?'

Samantha Hunt, author of *The Unwritten Book*

'*Girls They Write Songs About* is the instant feminist classic our generation has been waiting for – a profound and perfect book about girls raised to believe they can be anything but who as women learn the truth: every choice requires sacrifice, and freedom isn't free. Carlene Bauer – a Kate Chopin for the 21st Century – brings a fiercely funny, exquisitely brave, vibratingly intellectual voice to a world of bar flirtations, I-love-this-song enthusiasms, envy, ambition, and regret. I'm giving it to all my friends because I love them and I love this book.'

Ada Calhoun, author of *Why We Can't Sleep*

'I lost myself in this exquisitely written story of two women finding their place in New York. Carlene Bauer has created characters so authentic, so honest and so complex that you will feel you've known them for decades. Bauer tackles the interplay between friendship, feminism, motherhood and creativity and, as great writing should, leaves her readers not with answers but with lingering questions... *Girls They Write Songs About* is wise, witty, atmospheric and layered – I absolutely loved this book, and I am desperate for my friends to read it.'

Katie Allen, author of *Everything Happens for a Reason*

'Humor and feminist passion power *Girls They Write Songs About*. Charlotte, the book's narrator, a 'self-questioning mystic trapped in a late capitalist body' forges a new family of intense female friendships and kinships with beloved dead female authors. A riot grrrl anthem of a novel, one that celebrates female longing, accomplishment and sisterhood while never forgetting the high stakes of our internal struggle to respect ourselves.'

Darcey Steinke, author of *Flash Count Diary*

ALSO BY CARLENE BAUER

Not That Kind of Girl

Frances and Bernard

Girls They Write songs About

CARLENE BAUER

MAGPIE
BOOKS

A Magpie Book

First published in the United Kingdom, Ireland and Australia by Magpie Books,
an imprint of Oneworld Publications, 2022

ISBN 978-0-86154-469-1 (Hardback)
ISBN 978-0-86154-522-3 (Trade paperback)
eISBN 978-0-86154-470-7

Text designed by Songhee Kim
Printed and bound in Great Britain by Clays Ltd, St Ives plc

Oneworld Publications
10 Bloomsbury Street
London WC1B 3SR
England

Stay up to date with the latest books,
special offers, and exclusive content from
Oneworld with our newsletter

Sign up on our website
oneworld-publications.com

FSC
www.fsc.org

MIX
Paper from
responsible sources
FSC® C018072

Girls
They
Write
songs
About

1.

Rose and I moved to New York to be motherless. We moved to New York to want undisturbed and unchecked.

And what did we want? We wanted to be seen as an overpoweringly singular instance of late-twentieth-century womanhood. We wanted fan mail. We wanted to be worshipped. We wanted lives full of purpose and free of regret. True daughters of the second wave, we were counting on work to get us there. We thought that if we worked hard enough we would one day, and on time, stand exactly where we hoped.

But we were neither selfish enough nor selfless enough to become heroines. And even though she and I are no longer speaking, it makes me happy to think and write of that *we*.

Once, on my twenty-sixth birthday, we ran out on the bill at a very expensive restaurant. When I realized that our waiter's shift had finished and our table in the corner had been forgotten in the Friday-night frenzy, I said *Let's make a run for it*, and we stood up from our chairs and walked out. All the while looking at all the handsome, burnished people with money, looking at them as if they were rings in a jewelry case, as if they were lives or faces we might buy for ourselves one day, realizing that maturity, too, was its own kind of money, and yet still feeling reckless and regal, because we were free and no one could buy us.

Another time: the two of us, riding the Staten Island Ferry for no other reason than it was unseasonably warm in March, meeting two elderly women with winking eyes and fanny packs, one with a cane and one wearing a sun visor, who said, as we sped away from Manhattan, white waves pounding behind us, waves as white as their hair, *You two must be sisters, the way you're laughing.*

One night, at a friend's bewilderingly ostentatious wedding, we charmed the bartender into giving us each a bottle of Veuve Clicquot as revenge on such ostentation, and we ran out of there with coats flying behind us—coats we'd bought for fifteen dollars each on the street in the West Village, castoffs from the lives of long-dead old ladies—clutching those green bottles to our chests as we hopped into a cab. New York: getaway cars everywhere, whenever you needed one.

On yet another night, summer, at a birthday party, we danced ourselves into cramps so painful we walked barefoot out onto the sidewalk, shoes crammed into our handbags, and hobbled one block to a Duane Reade where we bought flip-flops and then hobbled another five blocks to the subway. *Let's get old in exactly this way*, I said, as we clutched at each other's arms and crept toward the entrance to the R train.

Rose and I, true daughters of Long Island and New Jersey, loved a diner: it was democracy in action. We were sitting in a booth at the Red Flame, a diner we loved on Forty-Fourth Street, a diner that's still around, and a family of French tourists, who had been sitting a few tables away from us, wearing trim down jackets, eating what looked to be shrimp scampi, sent a bottle of white wine over because they'd heard us arguing over Godard. Rose was trying to tell me why I should hate him and I was trying to explain why his misogyny didn't bother me. You could have those kinds of conversations back then. We drank the whole bottle with our grilled cheese-and-tomato sandwiches and fries and declared that we'd had way worse at book parties.

When the Red Flame goes out, Rose used to say, *we're leaving New York.*

One night we left work too late to see a band in the East Village, and I remember Rose saying *Well, we missed it. We missed U2 at Red Rocks, we missed Billie Holiday at the Blue Note. Napoleon, Sid Vicious, Martin Luther King, Muhammad Ali, Moses. May of '68 and July of 1789. We missed it! All of it!* I had to sit down on the sidewalk on Avenue B I was laughing so hard.

I think of that all the time: *We missed it! All of it!*

2.

When Rose and I moved to the city, living in Brooklyn meant you had to commute to Manhattan in order to have a good time. Tokens were still the only currency accepted by the subway. *The New York Times* printed their photos in black and white, and there was no such thing as the Style section. Coffee cost less than a dollar. You could smoke in bars. Tower Records still stood at the corner of Broadway and Fourth Street. The most important machines at work were telephones, Xerox machines, faxes, computers, and printers. If you needed to temp you could still sign up, like your grandmother did, with a Kelly Girl service, and some of the Midtown offices they sent me to had IBM Selectrics sitting out on the desks like old horses nodding off in their stalls, and I can still hear the warm hum they radiated between words, and the clicking of the cylinders as you pulled the paper up and out of them. The Strand was a dump. Other places were dumps, too—dumps or near-dumps, like McHale's and the Subway Inn and Rudy's and the Holiday Cocktail Lounge—but the Strand stands out at the moment because I was in there the other day marveling again at the heaps of branded merch that now greet its guests and contrasting that place with the one that used to smell of dust and the funk of its unwashed cashiers. We drank at night in dumps; ate in near-dumps. Sat in vinyl booths patched up with duct tape; pissed in scrawled-up, paint-peeling, rust-watered bathrooms. Nobody minded or cared. That's how you knew you were not in the suburbs.

Everyone has their own New York, and this was ours.

Rose and I met in 1997 at a music magazine we used to refer to as WKRP. On my first day, as she led me down a cramped hallway back to my cubicle, through a gauntlet of offices blasting music from behind closed doors, I apparently wondered aloud: *And where are the adults?* Rose always said that's when she knew she liked me. Rose, of course, scared me a little. But she didn't scare me as much as the girl with an office at the end of the hallway—Tracy, the managing editor—who was actually sleeping with musicians we loved, Bikini Kill be damned. Since Tracy was doing all of this while earning a master's in psychology from CUNY, however, you couldn't call her a groupie. You wouldn't dare call her a groupie, because she'd tell you to go fuck yourself and ask you how much fun you were having over there in your saddle shoes. Tracy. She wasn't tall, but bony and angular enough to make you think she was, and her black hair, chopped into a bob, gleamed blue, just like Veronica's did in the Archie comics Rose and I later discovered we were both addicted to as kids. Tracy's official title was managing editor, but her true value lay not in wrangling copy, but in wrangling all the talent for the magazine's annual music festival. No one knew where Tracy lived or where she'd come from, although someone thought they'd heard it was Forest Hills. Someone once said that she didn't even graduate from college. Tracy. She drew all kinds of glamour to herself, and seemingly without effort. People wrote songs about her, blew her kisses in liner notes.

Tracy had no time for equivocating bullshit. She wanted what she wanted, and hated what she hated. One night, when we were all drinking after work, the editor-in-chief told us that he'd heard from a friend in a band who sometimes slept with Tracy that Tracy was getting herself handcuffed fortnightly to the bed of a famous writer for *The New Yorker*. Rose rolled her eyes and I said *Nice work if you can get it*, but on the train home we both confessed to wishing we were somewhere in the vicinity of invitations to what we used to call the voluptuous ludicrous.

One morning I got into the elevator with a copy of *The Dialectic of Sex* and Tracy laughed and rolled her eyes. *If I were you I'd stop reading about it and start getting some.* I laughed, too, but weakly. *Philistine*, I thought, and then *Handcuffs* and then *Point taken*, and tossed the paperback in a trash can on the way to the subway that night after work.

Tracy. *Famous Tracy*, the editor-in-chief called her. *Vanilla Nice*, she called him. I remember Tracy at staff meetings, standing by a window in the conference room so she could smoke, her blowing the plume out into the unremarkable skies that stretched over Fourteenth Street. Calling bands *asshats* and dismissing someone's album as *a piece of jizz*.

Rose and I did not become friends immediately, although I'd been aware of her before we met. She'd been writing for the *Voice*, for the *New York Press*, for *Time Out*. But never for the *Times*, I noticed with relief. I'd stare at her byline on the subway or in a bodega thinking *Who is this girl doing my job?* I'd sit on the subway reading her pieces, listening to the voice of a girl that was louder than ink and larger than column inches, I might have written at the time, if I had to review the sound Rose made. A girl unafraid to lose herself in a description of the physical pleasure the music gave her and unafraid of turning lethally bemused when the music failed her. The display, and the confidence it took to put it out there and keep it coming, was infuriating. Rose wanted you to watch and she knew you wouldn't stop watching, and if she hadn't been funny, which meant she was smart, I would have been able to write her off as an attention whore. And that might have been the most infuriating thing of all—not being able to write her off completely.

And then she and I were up for the same position at the magazine—staff writer—but Rose was the one who landed it. I didn't really have the experience to apply, but the editor-in-chief said he liked my sentences enough to want to talk with me.

These pieces aren't very strong argumentatively, said the editor-in-chief, at the interview. Karl: blond hair shaved very close to his head, heavy black eyeglass frames, bitten cuticles, combat boots cracked from use. He was not an eighty-five-year-old man, as his name suggested he might be. *But they are lively.*

I see, I said. No one had ever suggested that my writing was lacking in any regard. And he had a resume in front of him that tallied several awards for writing over the course of college and graduate school. This was yet another encounter with a very particular kind of assertion of authority practiced by many of the young men I'd meet in New York: a routine dispensation of firm, almost acerbic verdicts that made them seem much more unflappably discerning than their twenty-six or so years. They wore used T-shirts and dress shirts and sneakers to work—I almost wrote *school*—and so they performed their adulthood by putting on a suit they thought they had to wear because they were paid to traffic in opinion and taste. You could almost hear them adjusting their rhetorical cuff links and shaking out the cuffs of their rhetorical trousers before they gave you their take.

You want to write, he said. *But can you edit?* He took four pages of copy off the middle of his desk and handed them to me.

I took out a pen, plowed through the copy, gave it a once-over, and handed the pages back to him quicker, I think, than he expected, or so the look of slight surprise on his face suggested.

The next day he called to tell me that he'd given the job to a writer whose byline he'd been seeing all over, a writer whose voice was already fully developed, and who had more experience, all of which meant he wouldn't have to spend time training her to write a profile. He was calling to tell me this, he said, because he didn't want to make me sit around wondering what had happened and why. The sincerity made me almost pity him rather than mind that I was being rejected. And then he called a month later because Rose, the writer he'd hired, needed more editing than he'd imagined, some other editor of his had just quit to run a record label in Chicago, and would I mind helping him out for $25,000 a year? *Maybe you can write, too*, he said. *We'll see.* I did the math on the back of a Brooklyn Union Gas bill lying next to the phone and said yes.

It was very easy work. The magazine, like most magazines, was nothing more than a mosaic made up of rewritten press releases, despite several of us trying to write sentences that could potentially be cited in other people's think pieces. And since most of my coworkers just wanted to leave at five to collect the free drinks and free drugs that came with the job, they took my edits easily, smilingly, often letting me rewrite pieces outright if they were a big enough mess. *You do it*, Tracy told me the first time I asked if she might take another stab at a piece. *You're smart enough to make sure I don't sound like an idiot.* When I wasn't rewriting pieces, I pushed punctuation around, uprooting colons and semi-colons and planting them where they needed to be. I was weeding a garden, and I found it soothing. When I'd gotten my bearings I told the editor-in-chief I could turn myself into the managing editor Tracy was too busy schmoozing to be, and with his blessing I drew up schedules, sent out reminders via email, walked around with a clipboard, and beaned people with it playfully when they said they needed another day, another hour. I was impersonating a person with a career, which amused me. And after the psycho-logical torture of graduate school, the piecework felt like a much-needed convalescence. I thought I might vacation at the magazine for a year—which became two.

Karl Orson Schroeder. Or, as it appeared on the mast-head: Karl O. Schroeder. Native and apostate son of Orem, Utah, descendant of Mormon bishops on his mother's side and gun-toting polygamists on his father's. I suppose he could have had any name, or been anyone in that position, at that time, with those approximate qualities and tastes, and a crush would have gone off within me like a long-buried land mine.

He was the oldest of five and seemed to know something

about keeping a group of people mostly, happily in line. He never lost his temper although he could lower a stone-cold look of warning, pulled his oars harder when one or ten of us, hungover and sleep-deprived, dropped ours, and bought us all beer or pizza to keep us rowing. We might have bitched at his rigor but never too forcefully, because we knew he was right and we were lazy. Karl, from time to time, could be seen through his door reading from John Berryman's *Dream Songs* and James Baldwin's *The Fire Next Time*, as if to ward off the evil spirit of serviceable prose working in the service of capitalist gain. He was an extremely intelligent boy-slash-man from a working- to middle-class family—from what, if he got drunk enough, he called *trash*—and those two biographical coordinates have always worked on me the way a handsome face never could. His weekly emails to the staff were small master-pieces chiseled out of wit, both anarchic and dry, and what I suspected was creeping intellectual boredom.

Whenever I heard the sounds of Rose and Karl walk-ing down the hallway, their laughter announcing their return from lunch, I'd stop typing and sit still, listening to her high spirits tumbling over his measured, but clearly amused, interjections. I eavesdropped on those two the way I'd eavesdropped on Heloise and Abelard for my se-nior thesis: judging them one moment and envying them the next. *Have mercy on me, Heloise*, I prayed, *for I too am a woman who responds not to beauty but to authority*. And then I'd type faster to chase these thoughts away.

Karl was pleased with himself for hiring me, but Rose thought I was her bête noire. Because with Rose it wasn't weeding, it was wondering whether you could get a coherent narrative to grow in rocky, incoherent, and self-dramatizing soil. She must have been able to publish so much, I thought, although I didn't want to think it, because the men who ran the music sections liked the sound of her voice and what it promised: easily aroused availability without demands. I wondered, and I didn't want to think this either, whether Karl had hired her because he was beguiled by that promise, too.

Rose knew how to talk to famous people and could get them to say all sorts of things, could get them, at the end of every interview, to say that they hated interviews but they loved talking to her, which left her with so much material she could never decide what was most important, so she poured it all into the blender and hit puree. Tracy could get you to want to sleep with her, and Rose could do that, sure, but she could also get you to just want to spend hours and hours with her—the more dangerous prospect. So much so that from time to time a publicist would call the magazine and request that Karl do the interview—a request that he would respectfully deny. Karl used to say that he thought Rose was so good at getting inside people's heads he sometimes worried that she'd end up in a cult—or even worse, would found one herself.

I'd email to say I was coming over to her cubicle to give her edits, and when I arrived she'd already be in fighting mode. Her back stiff, her face blank in the even blanker light of the computer, she would not look at me when I talked. She would wordlessly, testily hit the backspace key to erase whole sentences, and select and then delete whole paragraphs—whole paragraphs, when I had suggested maybe losing just the first few words. She knew I was right but had to do something to make it clear to me and to herself that she had been hired for a reason. Standing there trying to talk to her ice-cold face while remaining ice-cold, too—I could not let her break me—was like driving through a slaughtering rain with no exit ramp in sight. I hated it. I'd have to take three walks around Fourteenth Street to shake off all the gritting of teeth I'd done while suffering through her performance. Once it drove me downstairs to the ancient Irish bar across the street that smelled perpetually of bleach, where I sat watching NY1 for two hours while nursing a whiskey.

Karl was shrewd and wise, but not yet wise enough to realize that it was incredibly stupid to have one highly strung, highly intelligent girl tell another highly strung, highly intelligent girl that she needs to stop being herself— for this is what you are doing when you tell someone to cut five paragraphs in order to get to the almighty point.

More often than not, reentering the magazine, coffee in hand, after one of these clashes, I'd see Rose in his office with the door closed—no, what I'd see were her feet on his desk, and sometimes I saw him laugh, stand up from his chair, and forcibly remove her fancy feet from his wire-basket inbox. Rose had a pair of shoes for every day of the week, it seemed. Through his door's window I noted a parade of the following: platforms from the seventies, red snakeskin with brass buckles; black velvet platforms from the forties; white canvas platform espadrilles, embroidered, probably, in Mexico in the sixties, with fuchsia and egg-yolk-yellow flowers, and about six inches' worth of green grosgrain ribbon running up the trellis of her calves.

And when I walked around Fourteenth Street I thought:

Why should she have everything? Why should she attract the attention of famous people and Karl alike?

Do you think Rose and Tracy ever, you know, worry about the consequences of their actions? asked Nicole, one afternoon while she sat on a plastic orange milk crate in my cubicle going over edits, and the both of us paused to watch Tracy walk down the hallway, earrings, hair, bracelets, and black coat of what Rose would later tell me was Persian lamb, jangling and swinging as she strode out of the office on high heels, reading a *New York Post* as she did. Nicole, the editorial assistant and heavy metal enthusiast who'd dropped out of Rutgers to take care of her mother while she underwent chemo, who showed up to work that day with a wreath she'd made of pink and blue silk flowers from Michaels atop her long brown hair, this wreath crowning an outfit of striped T-shirt, jeans, and Chucks, an ensemble she would later wear that night to see a band that sang about death, blood, and charred remains. Nicole! Who had postcards of Pope John Paul II and Ricky Martin tacked up in her cubicle. Who I'd hear talking on the phone to her mother, telling her mother where in the kitchen she'd put the Crisco or baking powder after using it to make chocolate chip cookies for the bands she interviewed. *Ma!* Nicole would say. *It's right behind the freakin' Bisquick! Ma!* We would go to lunch, my treat, and talk about the books she read for her uncompleted senior thesis on Mary Wollstonecraft and England's slave trade. I took her bra shopping at Filene's, and brought her books I thought I'd outgrown. Or she would come and sit on a milk crate in my cubicle—I'd bought a velveteen pillow, pink, from the Kmart on Astor Place, so it would be more comfortable for her—and we'd strategize responses to the boys who were not returning her emails.

Well, I began, torn between wanting to let rip my own resentment and wanting to keep steady for mentoring's sake. I did not finish that sentence, because what can you say when your own heart is held up to yours like a mirror?

Rose claimed she did not like Nicole. Perhaps because she had an irrational fear of catching a worse case of what she already had: an upbringing that had steeped her tongue for too long in salt and vinegar, that had given her the heart of a street fighter rather than the cool, calculating mind one could inherit if one had been to some manor born. The kind of cool, calculating mind that could result from seeing it all, and having it all, before the age of eighteen—school in New York City, camp for socialization purposes in Maine, camp for educational purposes on Martha's Vineyard, Christmas in India, summer in Italy, internships in London—and so could not get too worked up about possibly missing the train to the rest of your life. The kind of mind that had unshakable faith in its own powers. The kind of mind that never had to worry about money, and so could do what it pleased, when it pleased, no matter how unremunerative.

Tracy liked Nicole, and this made me less afraid of Tracy. Tracy had been what we used to call a metalhead when she was younger, and sympathized with Nicole's borderline spastic passion for an utterly uncool genre. You could not say that Tracy saw herself in Nicole—because Tracy herself had probably never, would never, expose her love of anything with the abandon Nicole did.

Tracy appointed Nicole to be the moderator of a panel

during one of the magazine's annual festivals, and I remember standing with Tracy in the back of a conference room in the Hilton on Sixth Avenue across the street from Radio City, smiling with Tracy as we watched Nicole, clutching a sheaf of index cards in her left hand and clicking a hotel pen in her right, leaning in, ready to engage and ready to note. Wearing a dress she'd bought the night before with boots Tracy had lent her, sitting erect and confident, her tightly wound energy appearing in this context like authority and efficiency, shrouded as it was in a black dress and black boots, a suit of armor that I know from much experience helps repel all stray and sloppy thoughts, and helps you fend off the sloppiness of thought in others, a uniform that makes you feel that you have taken the shape of a sheathed knife in watchful, elegant reserve. Nicole, confident because someone had given her the spotlight she needed to grow a little taller. Nicole, making the panelists laugh and provoking them to admit that she had asked questions that had never occurred to them. Which is what every journalist likes to hear: that they have momentarily unseated the expert.

You're kind, I said to Tracy, as we watched Nicole, index cards tucked under her armpit, shake hands and work the crowd.

Please, she said. *I just didn't want to have to moderate a conversation with these yo-yos. I've slept with two of them.*

Yo-yos. The exact word my grandmother used to call out idiot drivers, and this was another reason why I could not be 100 percent terrified of Tracy.

How'd I do? Nicole said, beaming. The crowd murmuring and percolating all around us under fluorescent lights.

Beautifully, I said. I was beaming, too. It felt so very good to deliver a compliment and mean it, to hand it over without jealousy or false cheer.

Can you smell me from where you're standing? she said, holding her arms out by her side and circling them like propellers. *My armpits are soaking wet.*

The Chucks and the flower crowns disappeared after that day, and Nicole began wearing black dresses and black boots, exclusively, to work.

Later that day, in the same conference room: three musicians, two men and one woman, all of them wearing faded, previously used cowboy shirts. The men had thrown theirs on top of new jeans whose hems were artfully fraying; the woman had tied hers over a black slip dress that had probably been someone's actual lingerie. The woman's songs—I knew I should like them because they were trying to get me in touch with the eternal feminine that lived in the dark and could communicate only in howls, and a lot of people did like them, a lot of people loved them, but to me the howls just sounded like preening—like one woman's advertisement for herself, and for the healing powers of anal sex. No thanks. One of the men, the more handsome of the two, was causing a bit of a commotion at the time because, after spending most of the last decade annihilating American hypocrisies over two-minute punk songs, he'd just released an album, mostly acoustic, on which every song was named after a girl: Amy, Aimee, Jessica, Heather, Stephanie, Dana, Michelle, and Lori. (The hidden track: Andrea.) The names seemed like a cruel joke about the inescapable banality of a certain kind of girl, and how that certain kind of girl was a symbol of the inescapable banality of a certain kind of American life, and there was a lot of discussion about whether this was an anti-capitalist critique or straight-up misogyny or both or who cared. The songs themselves were sometimes cruel, but they were crammed with images I wished I'd come up with, and it reminded me of why I did not listen to Bob Dylan—was it a compliment to be looked upon so long by him, to have riled him up to blistering, Shakespeare-grade poetry with your essential mutability, or was it plain old humiliation? But the hidden track was so beautiful it made me forgive the possible cruelty.

I want to talk about this guy's record, said the woman, after everyone had been seated and before Rose had even had a chance to make the introductions. She leaned into her mike and cast an intense and mischievous look down the table. *I can't tell whether it's a mean stunt or what.*

I'm sorry you feel that way, said the minor commotion, whose robotic intonation made it clear he was ironizing that phrase and its worth as a communication tool.

I laughed in spite of myself. Other people in the audience did, too. So did the woman. Angela.

You're such a cunt, Josh, she said, still laughing.

Josh was grinning like crazy. I looked at Rose, who was also grinning like crazy, clearly delighted that an altercation between lesser deities had broken out on her watch. I looked at the other guy in the cowboy shirt—leaning all the way back in his chair, stretching out his arms way over his head, and scrutinizing the ceiling as if none of this was happening. I looked at Nicole, sitting next to me. She had buried her face in her hands.

I'm sorry, Rose—that's your name, right? the woman said. *This is your party, you host it.*

Yes, said Rose. She faced the crowd. *My name is Rose,*

19

Rose Pellegrino. And I'm so happy to be here and to have a conversation with these musicians, whose work I've loved for such a long time. A conversation, an interaction, an encounter, a bar brawl, whatever.

Everyone laughed—the guests and the audience both, the tension that had been in the room dissipated, and it all seemed under control for about forty-five minutes, until Rose and Josh began openly flirting with each other.

So love songs, said Rose.

It's the whole point, said the guy who was not Josh. *Every musician I ever admired tried to say something about okay, yes, existence in general, and I'm pretty sure that coming of age after punk made it harder to talk about having tears in your beer, for a lot of reasons, some good, some bad. But what I mean is that even when I wasn't writing about a girl I was still, you know, writing like that girl was watching, or, you know, might be watching. The thing doesn't have to be about love to be about love, if you know what I mean.*

He's right, said Josh, who seemed a little stunned, if I had to guess, by the fact that someone he usually felt comfortable writing off had bested him through this completely spontaneous and completely sincere attempt to cut through the crap—his own and ours. But because you don't get to be a minor commotion without needing the spotlight like a drug, Josh had to find a way to upstage this guy.

Josh leaned into the microphone, arms crossed in front of him. *Let's say I'd just met you*, he said to Rose.

Rose smiled.

And maybe I wanted to get your attention somehow, but I didn't want to come on strong. So maybe I'd write a song where I'd say, When she puts her mascara on she doesn't need a mirror.

He had seen what Nicole and I had seen—Rose, out in the hallway just before she had to go on, in the middle of a crush of people, back against the wall, head tilted back, flicking the wand once, twice, on each set of lashes, tossing the tube of mascara back in her bag, blinking, and then wiping her index finger under each eye—left side, right side—to remove any smudges. Said Nicole, on our way into the room: *If I tried that I'd totally poke my eye out.*

And then, he said, his voice just a bit softer, as if there was no one else in the room but him and Rose, as if night had fallen and he was calling her with his last dime, *I'd send it like a letter and hope you heard it.*

Goddamn, said a woman sitting next to me.

That's not a tribute, said Angela, *that's a hit and run.* She was sitting back in her folding chair, nowhere near her microphone, but everyone could hear her.

Then what would you want me to do? said Rose to Josh.

This is stressing me out so bad, Nicole whispered to me. *I gotta get out of here. Let's go.*

We can't, I whispered. *We're in the middle of the room. We'd become part of the show.*

Rose is gonna get herself murdered.

Good, I said. *She deserves it.* The words hopped out of my mouth like a hot coal from hell. I might have even hissed them. Nicole's eyes widened, and I felt awful for letting my mask slip.

It's up to you, said Josh. *You have all the power here.*

Then Angela spoke. *I'm having trouble deciding*—and then she broke off. The room's attention swung back to her.

Rose, she said, *I'm having trouble deciding whether you're actually smart, or just ballsy and hot.*

I'd been wondering the same ever since I'd met Rose.

Ballsy? said Angela. *Or do I just mean mouthy?*

I've heard worse, said Rose. She did not appear bothered.

I don't think you have, said Angela.

Karl had materialized at the front of the room, I noticed, and was now standing off to the side by the doorway, arms crossed, staring, ready and waiting, it seemed, to wrestle all of these people and their egos to the ground. I noticed Rose notice him.

Let's talk about music, said Angela. *That's what I came here to do.*

Is that really what you want to talk about, said Rose, *or is that just some line you know you need to throw out so we know you're serious and have ideas when you're not busy taking it up the ass?*

Oh my God, I said out loud. Nicole had been chewing extremely hard on a pen cap and I heard a piece of it crack off in her mouth.

You're a cunt, too, said Angela, who was smiling again, wildly happy to be back in the position of stirring up shit.

Josh tried to get a handle on the situation. *I think—*

Don't rescue me, said Rose, holding up her hand like a stop sign, not looking in his direction at all, still staring down Angela, who was still smiling.

Karl walked up onto the stage, unhurried but determined, and picked up a microphone. It was 4:59, he told the audience, and there was another panel due in here any second, so we'd have to wrap this conversation up. He thanked everyone for coming, told the guests he really appreciated the time they spent with us, put the micro-phone down on the table, and made a signal for the sound guy to start some music. And stood there until everyone on the stage had made their way off. He touched Rose's arm as she passed but she kept walking.

I still did not know whether or not Rose was smart, but I saw that she was tough in a way that appeared rooted in something like real courage and, what's more, had ap-plied that pressure to a woman who claimed to be acting on behalf of femalekind but was really just interested in making messes wherever she went, and that kind of thing could only serve to liberate one woman—the woman mak-ing the mess.

That was a Friday. On Monday Rose threw a fit in her cubicle because I suggested that maybe she was putting words in a famous musician's mouth. *How can a person be this much of a goddamned stickler?* she shouted, and when I think about it, I may have suggested such a thing because I wanted Josh to be the unicorn eating out of my laughing maiden hands, because I wanted Karl to reach out for my arm as I walked away from a battlefield, because I wanted to be onstage with an audience hanging on my every word. And maybe Rose burst into flames because she had neither fucked Josh nor definitively trounced Angela, and Karl had pulled the plug on her show. I said nothing, just let her rage, and stared at the black-and-white publicity shots of musicians, particularly the shot of Johnny Cash, who, Rose claimed, once read out a verse from a Gideon New Testament as a blessing to her, until it seemed like she had exhausted her store of indignation. I fantasized, as Rose punctuated some point by slamming the heel of her hand down on her desk, once, and then twice, about being able to go home soon, where I could eat a shitty mass-produced chocolate chip cookie the size of my face while reading *Anna Karenina*.

Karl overheard it all, as did the whole staff, which I could care less about, because it had been Rose who'd lost control, and on my way back to my desk, he motioned me into his office. Then motioned me to close the door. We stood facing each other.

You're a good person, Charlotte, he said.

I don't know what earthly good that's doing anyone, but thank you, I said.

What can I do?

Give me the rest of the day off?

He laughed. *Deal.*

And money for dinner?

He took his wallet from his back pocket—he still wore one on a chain, a hardcore-kid habit that Rose and I would later affectionately mock—and fished out two fives.

Thank you very much, I said. I didn't leave. I wanted more words from him.

Come out with me tonight? he said. With something that sounded like panic, but also like now-or-never, head-for-home-plate, hop-on-the-bus-before-it-pulls-away-into-traffic hope.

Won't you want your money back? I said, because I was panicked, too, and thrilled, and had to paper it all over with meaningless speech.

He shook his head as he pawed over his desk to find something. A piece of paper to write on. *Meet me here at seven thirty*, he said, now confident, now back in control, scrawling an address down while I tucked the fives into his mug of pens and pencils.

On my way out I saw Rose in Karl's office. He'd left the door open just enough for sound to leak out as I walked past. *You want what you want too badly*, he said. He sounded annoyed, frustrated. *You're going to scare it away, you know?*

My coat, as I made for the elevator, swung like Tracy's, propelled by feelings of mild triumph and slight vindication. Because of course what he'd said to Rose would never apply to me.

When Karl sat down across from me at the Bemelmans Bar, he slipped a used paperback in my direction while asking a white-jacketed waiter, who had alighted at our table, for two gimlets.

Lost Illusions? I said. *Gimlets?* I wanted to laugh but I couldn't because laughing was really just a defense against my envy of Karl's swift and sure exercising of his critical faculties, his tastes. His confidence.

Two classics that deserve higher profiles, said Karl.

I've read this in French, I said, looking in the front flap to see who had owned the book before me. *For Elaine*, the cobwebby hand of an elderly person had written. *Christmas 1980.*

Is that a joke? he said.

No. Is that an insult?

He laughed the way I'd heard him laugh with Rose. It was a stoutly unselfconscious burst of approval that ran counter to his seriousness. The sound happened and disappeared so quickly it made you wonder what you'd actually heard.

No, Charlotte. You make a lot of jokes, and I—

The waiter stood there with our drinks. Karl explained that his first boss in New York, his first mentor, had given him a copy of the book, and he thought I might appreciate how contemporary it felt. He'd given Rose a copy, too, he said.

Rose, I said. I wished I hadn't.

Karl's expression: curious, amused. He waited for me to say more, and when it became clear I wasn't going to, he raised his glass. *To you, Charlotte Snowe, and your formidable work ethic.*

I raised mine. *Well*, I said, *no one's ever allowed me to be mediocre. Or lazy.*

Same here, he said. *But don't you think that* you're *the one not letting yourself be mediocre?*

I drank, trying to steady my shaking grip on the delicate martini glass; he drank, and stared right at me. It seemed that Karl was delivering me the supreme compliment of focus—that he was staring at me the way I'd stared all my life at paintings and oceans. I steadied my hand and stared back.

I believe in geography the way some people believe in astrology, he said, after we had set our drinks down on the table. *Where did you grow up?*

I opened my mouth but Karl spoke again. *No, wait.* He was shaking his head, looking at his knees. *There's a better question.* He looked up. Sergeant Pepper *or* Pet Sounds?

The Kinks Are the Village Green Preservation Society, I said.

Karl smiled as if he'd found a hundred bucks in his coat pocket.

We talked for three hours. Three hours in which we'd each had one drink more than we'd promised ourselves, and by the end of it he'd written the titles of three books I'd mentioned across the top of his right hand. Three hours in which I came to understand that the self-seriousness was the armor of a young man who, like myself, came from people who did not overly value, and might even be suspicious of, the mind, and so had to erect an impregnable shell to protect what no one around him seemed to hold dear. Karl. Whose father no longer talked to him because this oldest of five no longer believed. Whose family did not understand why New York. *It's as if my sisters think I'm still on my mission and I'm coming home in a month*, he said. Whose fellow missionary, when he was stranded in Bolivia for his requisite two years, once woke Karl up in the middle of the night by choking him, and was subsequently sent home, where he was diagnosed with manic depression, leaving Karl to wonder what kind of God would allow that much torment to visit a soul. Whose mother used to write to publishers if she noticed too many typos in the Agatha Christie books she checked out of the library for his brothers and sisters. Whose youngest brother once had to use pliers to pull a fishing hook out of the inside of Karl's right forearm—*Let's take a look*, he said, unbuttoning his cuff and rolling up his long black cotton sleeve to show me a scar that looked like a tiny raised wishbone, and then, *Oh, while we're here*, he said, and pointed to another scar hovering above it, the remains, he said, of a botched attempt at self-tattooing with a sewing needle and some India ink he'd stolen from his high school's art room.

It appeared that the brailled flesh was trying to spell out *Jenny*.

In return I turned my right cheek toward him to show him the three currently empty holes in my ear—my souvenir from high school art room days, I said.

When I turned back to face him his head was in his hands.

Should you go home? I said. I put my right hand on his left knee. *Do you need to throw up?*

He took my hand off his knee, turned it over, and looked at my palm like he wanted to drink that, too.

Then the check came, and Karl, almost immediately, became businesslike, avuncular. Out came the wallet, the shuffling of cards, receipts, pens. I realized I was drunk not just on gin and sugar but on my own powers of charm. *I will win you like a prize*, I thought.

At around midnight we walked out to Madison Avenue, stood side by side outside the entrance to the hotel, and stared down into the tunnel made by Seventy-Sixth Street as it ran toward the blackened park. I made a number of immodest wishes on the taxi lights and the streetlamps and the scant number of stars in the sky as we continued to stare straight ahead into the dark tunnel.

You're an A-side kind of girl, he said. *Get home safe?*

I rode the subway wishing on faces, shoes, fluorescent lights, maps, tiles, on the cheeks and noses of children asleep in strollers, and on my own clasped hands, which turned the wishes into a prayer. Wished for the rumble underneath us all to be a sign of happy upheavals to come.

Early the next morning, Rose appeared in my cubicle. Large cup of coffee from the cart on the corner of Fourteenth Street gripped in black-leather-gloved hand, blond hair piled on top of her head, some curls still wet, some curls not, a huge woven red scarf wrapped around a gray wool coat, vintage, with brass buttons, and leather boots in a color I'd call burgundy but she'd call wine. I was begrudgingly appreciating her formidable sense of style when she spoke.

Last night I had a dream that you and I were at the Barneys Co-Op sale fighting over a dress. She took a sip of coffee and watched my face. It seemed that she was waiting for me to explain this dream to her. Did Rose really not see that it was an expression of the anxiety she felt when I questioned her choice of words or the veracity of her facts, because when I did I forced her to question who really owned her stories, and by that extension whether she had any talent at all?

Since I couldn't say any of that, I said this: *You know, I don't wake up every morning thrilled to contemplate all the ways in which I can ruin your day.*

It's like you forget there's a human girl who wrote the sentences, she said. *You never give me even one compliment to soften the blow. You just show up and start telling me where my slip is showing and where my stockings have run.*

She could have been me, talking about my mother. *Rose*, and it tumbled out of me without thinking, *you could be a great writer if—*

If what? Someone had said what I was about to say to her before, I could tell, before she'd fallen into her sea of helping hands, and she didn't like being reminded of it.

If you started at some point before midnight and read back over what you wrote before you hit send! Take your sentences seriously. *Take your audience seriously. Limit yourself to one cliché a piece instead of ten. You're in this incredibly privileged position—don't make us think we could do your job better!*

Is that what you think? Do you think you could do this job better?

I didn't answer.

And where have you been published?

Nowhere.

Do you want this job?

I interviewed for it but didn't get it.

Confronted with a fact that would have certainly wounded her had it been her lot, she appeared to soften.

But I learned that I actually don't want your job, I said. *Musicians are rock dumb, and I have no interest in wasting my mind in the celebration of their talent when I should be sharpening my own.*

Rose laughed. *They are rock dumb*, she said. Pause. *I like your shoes.*

I looked down at my Doc Martens. Wing-tipped Mary Janes left over from college, inflexible black leather, with ridged rubber soles, which I made myself wear even though they hurt, because I'd bought them in London and spent a lot of money on them.

I don't think you do, I said, *but I appreciate the gesture.*

She sighed. *I keep meaning to find some other less trivial way to bond with other women, but nothing works as well as a compliment on your clothes.*

In my other life I was Elsa Schiaparelli, I said.

Oh that's funny, Rose said, more to herself, a note taken, than to me.

I stood up and held out my hand. She smiled wide and

shook it, and I smiled, too, relieved and very pleased, but a little scared, too, because Rose of course might be crazy, and then she turned and strode down the hallway. I rested my hands and forehead on the top of my cubicle wall, still pleased and relieved but also exhausted, and feeling that I didn't want to do anything much because I'd already achieved quite a bit for the day.

3.

We officially became friends that evening, on the train ride back to Brooklyn, when we discovered not only that we were both scared of Tracy—I said *scared* of Tracy but Rose said she was *kind of scared*, just so I knew who was in charge here—but that we were both enraged by that Rolling Stones lyric about American girls wanting everything. Rose was impressed by my reading of the situation, which referenced Isabel Archer and Daisy Miller, and I was impressed by Rose's reading of the situation, which referenced Margaret Sanger and Emma Goldman. *But,* I said, hesitantly, *ultimately our rage is impotent, because I suspect Mick Jagger knew the truth that all our women's studies classes refused to acknowledge, which was that all the raised consciousness in the world couldn't prevent—*

Rose interrupted me with a laugh, and said: *Oh my God, no. Dude didn't get blown by some Pan Am stewardess. That's what that's about. End of story.*

A picture of what Rose and I looked like, taken at Coney Island, on the boardwalk, beach and gulls in the background, in the summer of 1998, the year we became friends: I'm wearing a baby tee that says *Girls kick ass!* under denim overalls, barefoot, my pair of red suede Pumas in one hand, cat-eye glasses, my red-brown hair cut in a bob like Tracy's. Rose is wearing a red zip up polyester mini-dress, formerly a waitress's uniform that had come with a name tag—Brenda—still pinned to the front, and silver Doc Marten boots. Her curly blond hair, bleached platinum, is caught up in a topknot in a red bandanna and she is striking a James Bond pose in front of me, one knee down on the boardwalk, gun pointed off camera. Later I would refer to outfits like the one I'm wearing there as examples of an unfortunate tendency to drift toward clothes that made me look like your kid sister the garage mechanic, and Rose will, even later than that, tell me that though she protested at the time, she saw what I meant.

The guy who took the picture drove us to Coney Island that day to decide which of us he wanted to sleep with. He told me, while Rose was off buying us beer, that I'd probably have more luck finding men who wanted to fuck me than I would trying to publish books. He told Rose, while I was off buying us tickets for the Cyclone, that she'd probably have more luck trying to publish books than she would trying to find a man who could take her level of crazy.

Rose is beautiful, that guy said, while Rose was off buying us beer. *But you're a good person. If I could live another life in addition to this one, you'd be the one I'd marry.*

You mean, I said, *in the life after this one, where you're actually talented?*

He laughed, loudly, and I think sincerely. He was too confident to care that I'd insulted him. It was not unattractive.

We were twenty-five.

What did we want?

We wanted the guy who took that picture in Coney Island to write a song about us. And he did—or he might have. Rose was sure he had us in mind when he wrote a song that started with the line *Two girls, one freckled, one curled*. I remember driving us to Long Beach that summer and playing the advance copy of that guy's record and hearing that line and thinking, *Am I crazy to*—and then Rose started cackling. *We won!* she said. Now we both were cackling. And then Rose again: *That prick!* The windows down, the wind tearing our hair apart, the heat of the day a drink we could not get enough of. *Well*, I said, after a few bars went by, *that could be anybody*, demurring out of habit, and Rose said, *Yeah, but we're not just anybody*.

Some more of what we wanted, which we talked about in bars, so many nights in bars, that first year we met: I told Rose that I sometimes thought I could die when I knew that I had lived nearly every line that Joni Mitchell had written and sung on *Blue*. Rose said she thought she could die when she knew that she'd lived every word written or sung by Aretha Franklin on *I Never Loved a Man the Way I Loved You*. I told her that I knew I could die also when I had written myself out of the fear that Joan Didion would laugh if she were ever introduced to any of my sentences. Rose said she knew she could die when she had written something as good as *In Cold Blood*. I made fun of her for owning Sarah McLachlan's *Fumbling Towards Ecstasy*, and she made fun of me for owning the Weezer album, but we both agreed that "Box of Rain" was the only Grateful Dead song worth shit, and that we'd been in love with Sting for one album too long. *But what were we supposed to do?* said Rose. *Get it up for Axl Rose?* I told her that sometimes I wanted to be Wendy Darling, wanted to be responsible for these Lost Boys in bands we saw coming through the office, wanted to be bedded among their absurdity and mess, wanted to be enthroned in a high-necked nightgown, above their absurdity and mess. Rose nodded. She said: *In college I'd have met one of these dudes in a band and said, Fuck you and your bullshit, I've got my own stuff to do, but you know, now*—and then she remembered that in college she'd almost had a one-night stand with someone who had been busy making rock history, as they used to say, when we were children. *Rose*, I said, *I feel the need to say maybe fuck you and your bullshit!* And she laughed. *I guess*, she said, *I am into your bullshit if you are old enough to be my father.* Then I laughed, and nodded, and didn't say much, because as a feminist I felt I wasn't supposed to admit to wanting to be seduced by an older man. I did, though, mention that I first learned what erotic feelings were the first time I watched *The Sound of Music* on television, and watching Captain von Trapp blow his whistle at the bottom of the stairs made me feel uncomfortable that my parents were in the room with me—I mentioned it because I wanted a laugh, and I got one. *Yeah!* Rose said. *Me too!* And said that she remembered feeling the same exact thing—but then started worrying about what Anne Frank would think of her for being turned on by an Austrian. *Anne Frank was my Joan of Arc*, she said, *until I read Hannah Arendt.* Then, to see just how closely aligned we were on the subject, I brought up Mr. Bhaer, the German professor Jo falls in love with at the end of *Little Women*. We learned that in the summer of 1983, both of us ten years old, Rose and I—she in her twin bed in Port Jefferson, Long Island, and me in my twin bed in Somers Point, New Jersey—separately but together came to the conclusion that while we too thought we should of course one day marry professors who were older men, Mr. Bhaer was much too old. Laurie was too pretty, too foppish, too flimsy a foil for Jo, we knew, but Mr. Bhaer was grotesquely old. Too old and too bearded, per the illustrations in our respective copies, to be contemplated as a suitable match for Jo, who was our once and future self.

The first thing I did when I learned Rose was pregnant was to track down the exact copy we'd owned as girls. Grosset and Dunlap Illustrated Junior Library edition, first printing 1982.

What did we want? In childhood, Rose wanted the love of one man and the praise of the world; I wanted the praise of the world and the love of one man. We could see traces of adventurers in our ancestry, but no full-blown cases. No one had escaped the bonds of familial or economic duty fully enough to have both love and fulfilling work—that was the fairy tale the two of us had raised ourselves on, that work would set us free. Rose had great-uncles who would have tried out for the Dodgers if only they hadn't gotten their girlfriend pregnant; I had great-aunts who would have gone to work in New York City as secretaries but for their dying father and a fear that they'd end up as single women living in boarding houses. Our family trees were groaning with missed or ignored opportunity. So we had taken it upon ourselves, in our respective twin beds, in the 1980s, to achieve glories and freedoms our female relatives had never dreamed of. We had read, in our respective twin beds, that you could have a maiden aunt, circa 1908, who worked in a factory and organized

her fellow working girls to demand what would later become known as the weekend, or, if it were circa 1947, you
could have a maiden aunt who taught French, and spent
her vacations traveling the world when the world was still
shrouded in danger and mystery, or if it were circa 1966,
you could have a maiden aunt who became a nun and
shortly thereafter went to jail for plotting to burn down a
draft office.

Rose joked that she came from Italians who were too
sad and lazy to join the mob or the church. I joked that I
came from Irish potato farmers who came to America and
farmed laundry and appliance repair. My father managed a
plant that cleaned clams on the Jersey Shore. Rose's father,
who died in a motorcycle accident when she was five, had
managed a lawn-care business started by his uncle. And
both of our fathers escaped being drafted for Vietnam
because they'd signed up for the National Guard early
enough. Rose's mother was a hairdresser who gave haircuts
in her basement and did hair and makeup for weddings
when she wasn't working at a strip-mall salon that, as Rose
liked to say, she presided over like Madame de Staël. My
mother helped keep books for the plant; she also altered
prom dresses, wedding dresses, and suits for all occasions
on a Kenmore sewing machine in our basement.

Rose and I loved each other because we were relieved
to finally find a friend who understood what it was like to
want so much for yourself it hurt—and who understood
that real heroines don't let on that it hurts, they shut up and
do the work. A friend who knew what it was like to love
your family but to want another family created out of the
authors you have decided are your truest relations, and to

try to live up to what the famous dead, unrelated by blood, had asked of you. What it was like to have known even before you learned the word existed that you were a feminist, but to be raised by women who were never impelled to take up that label and in fact sometimes disparaged it. What it was like to be the first person in your family to graduate from college and how that could make you feel like a changeling; like an alien; like a prodigy one day and perennially late to class the next. What it was like to have read so much, and wanted so much, that you could sometimes ride a subway feeling distended with hope and intent as you'd finish a book, and then look up at all the people sitting around you and get what felt like the bends trying to reconcile the want that book had stoked in you with the chaos of the world in front of you, the world as it was.

We did not want children.

I have zero interest in getting involved in a power struggle with a two-year-old, said Rose, in a booth at O'Connor's that year.

Same here, I said. *I don't want to trap some unsuspecting human in a psychodrama that'll go on running even after I die.*

Say that again? Rose rummaged in the bag that sat next to her and fished out a pen.

I did, and she wrote it down on the back of a damp Sam Adams coaster.

Rose and I would never have said that we had unhappy childhoods, but they were shadowed childhoods, because we knew, or thought we knew, that our mothers were unhappy, even though Rose's mother and grandmother and aunts worked it out so that she would never have to see the worst of her mother's grief if they could help it, and my mother and grandmother and aunts hid all their true feelings behind jokes and food and alcohol and housekeeping. Still we sensed that there were clouds hanging over the women who raised us, and it made me quieter than I should have been, made Rose louder than she should have been, and left us both determined never to be mothers. To be a mother meant to die inside, constantly, so that everyone else could live. No thanks.

My mother had no blood to bleed, or so I believed, nothing to say or sing or else she'd die. Rose believed the same of her mother. We didn't run around saying that we would die unless we wrote, however, because we did not come from people who would put up with that kind of nonsense.

Sometimes I think that growing up puzzled and shadowed by our mothers' sadness did as much damage as if we had grown up without mothers at all. Not knowing what our mothers wanted from their own lives and what they loved sent Rose and me off into the world a little blind and a little lame. Because we did not know these things, we imagined ourselves the first women on the moon, shot out of a void into more void, which made us more susceptible than most, perhaps, to the notion that we had to constantly labor to make it new, like Ezra Pound said. And even more frequently I wonder if Rose and I might not have been feminists as much as girls who possessed a deep horror of becoming their mothers, which as I type tempts me to ask whether there's any other kind of girl, and if, because of when we were born, we just happened to run into a body of literature that we could raid at will for the fuel needed to keep running away from home. If I wanted to condemn us,

I could say that our feminism was almost purely personal—nothing but a tool for self-empowerment—and hardly ever political. I could blame us for being more interested in finding the right word than fighting for the rights of others, and for being content with an education that left us with the impression that cultural representation mattered as much or more than economic equality. But if I don't want to condemn us, I don't want to celebrate us by counting the ways in which we did try to improve the lives of all women, and all people, and either way I'd be giving in to the voices in my head that demand I legitimize my existence by desiring exactly what others desire.

Another night that first year we met, I said that I hated how sometimes being a feminist seemed to mean never having questions about feminism, that there was a party line as immutable as the ones drawn by Communists and the Catholic Church. Said Rose: *I know, I know. But you have to speak your mind about where you think it's wrong. What would Anne Frank say?* I laughed. *I'm serious*, she said. *I mean, it's crazy, but I always, well, no, I used to, ask myself, what would Anne Frank think of me if she knew I was wasting—*

I finished her sentence by quoting the last line of Mary Oliver's "The Summer Day."

Rose cackled. We hated that poem. Too much Morrissey on my part, too much N.W.A. on hers. Too much children of the children of the children of the Depression. *God, I hate that poem*, she said, *but I love you for hating it with me. Anyway, so, yes, what would Anne Frank do if she knew I was wasting my precious freedom of speech worried about what the fuck other people would think?*

Rose and I might have been a little bit better at hating what we hated than loving what we loved.

Rose and I didn't want to be rich—at least not when we were twenty-five. We wanted to have enough money to buy used books and vintage dresses; we wanted to be able to buy turkey sandwiches at a bodega when we were drunk at 2:00 a.m. on a Saturday, and then bagels and the Sunday *Times* when we were hungover the next afternoon, and not have to think about it. We wanted to save money to travel. So I got us jobs moonlighting as cocktail waitresses at a bar in the East Village. One night, in December, while I'd been reading and waiting for Rose to show up, the bartender mentioned they were losing two of their Friday night waitresses. I volunteered us both on the spot, because Rose and I had both waitressed summers and school nights.

Rose and I, standing across from each other in that crowded bar, backs against the wood-paneled walls, holding our trays against our chests as patrons squeezed by, exchanging identically elated smiles: benevolent presiders over loves at first night. Rose and I sparkling under red lights, because of the tiny fake pearls covering every inch of my ice-blue lamé minidress, and the silver sequins on the white tulle skirt of hers, both dresses bought for ten dollars each, fished out of cardboard boxes full of vintage clothes outside Canal Jean Company on Broadway before our first night on the job. That dress of mine lasted four shifts. It shed and scattered its tiny fake pearls over the floor of the bar and the floor of the subway and the floor of my apartment. Years later, I'd keep finding those plastic beads under the couch and in the corner of my closet. A votive candle on a table set Rose's tulle skirt on fire, burnt most of the front right off, but she continued to wear it with glittering pink fishnets and old Capezio dance shoes that she'd painted silver. Rose called her look Cancan Girl Just Sprung from Bellevue; I called mine Arthritic Former Figure Skater on a Bender.

A digression: Rose and I once followed Lou Reed up Broadway into Canal Jean Company and hid behind a column while we watched him look through a rack of used sport coats. At one point he looked up at us and said *Are you following me?* and I said *Yes* because I was too stunned to lie and Rose was too stunned to say anything at all and he nodded, no big deal, said *Just checking*, and went back to perusing used sport coats. *Give Laurie our love*, Rose said on the way out, and he either did not hear us or ignored us.

New York. Or maybe I mean: Lou Reed. Same diff, to use a phrase beloved by Rose's mother.

Lou Reed, Rose used to say, with dream in her voice, and sometimes apropos of absolutely nothing, *Lou motherfucking Reed*.

At the end of the night at the bar, sitting on stools counting our tips and eating cheesecake the bartender ordered from Veniero's three blocks up. Cheesecake. I don't know why, and we used to beg for him to order burritos or falafel, but the bartender, who came from outside Nashville, used to tell us to hush now and let him get the diabetes like the kind what killed his pawpaw. That bartender. Our first night ever in that place, I asked if they had any nuts. *You're looking at them*, he said, motioning out to the crowd. Rose always said he liked me, I always said she was crazy, and if he did like me, he never did anything about it, probably because he had a girlfriend finishing up college back home, and the bartender, we guessed, was no younger than thirty-two. That jukebox, which the bartender tended like a garden, planting and weeding, weeding and planting—he removed "Walkin' After Midnight" when he thought I'd played it one too many times. That jukebox, that bar, where I first heard Johnny Cash and June Carter sing "Jackson." The heat of the light coming through the smooth glass, warm and bright like a fireside, while I fed it with dollars, snow blanketing the streets, silencing the East Village, sending all the children home. That jukebox gave me an education. Memphis Minnie, Skeeter Davis, Sister Rosetta Tharpe, Kitty Wells, Loretta Lynn. Better the jukebox than that bartender.

Walking to the subway one night that year, back to Brooklyn after a reading in Manhattan, I felt compelled to confess to her that at one point I had certain thoughts about Karl. I did not want to hide anything from Rose, and I told her so.

That's brave, she said.

We walked a block in silence and then she spoke.

I did, too, once, she said. *But I am now of the mind that he and I missed our chance. It would never have worked. Karl's too good for me, for us, for anyone on earth.*

She sounded sad—so sad I wondered if something had actually happened between them. But she did not seem to want to talk about it, and neither would I, if Karl had judged me and found me wanting. I changed the subject and leaned into the mere reporting of fact.

I saw him eating a hard-boiled egg for lunch yesterday, I said. *One egg. Just one. He didn't even salt it.*

Rose laughed, and I relaxed a little bit more. *Oh, God.*

His one egg. And his exactly three shirts and exactly two pairs of pants from Galaxy Army Navy.

We walked another block. *I think he thinks I'm too much.* Now she sounded even sadder.

Well, I like you.

I like you, too. You're teaching me that women can actually be friends.

Rose! I stopped, but she laughed and pulled me on. *Who on earth have you spent your life hanging out with?*

Self-hating punk chicks who think it's uncool to talk about your feelings. Rich bitches with serious self-esteem issues who mistake my bossiness for replacement mothering. Anorexic kleptomaniacs who steal not just your shoes, but the thesis for your senior thesis.

Ah. Drama queens and sociopaths.

Yep. I—oh, I don't know why I couldn't find one good female friend. I guess I'm supposed to say I didn't really want one.

The way I'm supposed to say I didn't have a boyfriend in high school because I didn't really want one.

Don't ever leave me, she said, and I linked my arm in hers—just like Anne and Diana did as they walked along the Lake of Shining Waters, just like Betsy and Tacy did as they entered the halls of Deep Valley High, just as girls across centuries have done, as they walk streets and sketch dreams—knowing that in doing so I'd made a choice.

4.

My father liked to say, approvingly, that Rose was a real pistol. My mother liked to say, approvingly, that Rose had her head screwed on straight.

Rose's mother, the day she met me, stood on the stoop of their house as we approached the front door with her arms stretched wide as her smile and said *Let me give you a hug!* Dressed like Rose at rest: a big men's shirt over leggings, only with much fancier flip-flops. Her deep red pedicure and a life's worth of gold rings shone in the sun. Ann Marie.

My mother, the day she met Rose, sent her back on the train with a grocery bag filled with a jar of homemade dill pickles, half of the pound cake she'd made for dessert, and a newspaper cone full of hydrangeas from the backyard. And a large bag of Herr's potato chips, because Rose, having met them, would not stop eating them.

Rose's house was warm, neat, filled with framed pictures, plants, pillows, and Yankee candles. It was the house Rose had been born in, a house that was spotless but still nestlike, despite new carpets and highly polished old furniture. Like a place you could sink down into in the middle of the forest—or maybe that was just the wood paneling in the kitchen, full of potted plants, giving me that impression.

Said Rose of my home, which was also spotless, but with newer furniture and far fewer knickknacks: *There is a serious draft in there and I am speaking metaphorically.*

Rose and I reading a week's worth of the *Inquirer* together on my parents' couch while it rained one Saturday afternoon, Rose falling asleep in the corner of the couch and my mother arranging an afghan over her, wordlessly, before moving on to some other task. My mother, later that evening, as Rose and I sat at our kitchen table, photo albums spread out before us, bending down to kiss the top of Rose's head, too, and saying, *Goodnight, girls.* My mother: her short frosted blond hair, her tanned freckled hands, her tiny gold hoops, her polo shirts and pleated khaki shorts, her tanned knees. My mother: brisk when she was not at rest, and when she was at rest impervious.

That first summer Rose and I became friends, we spent as much time as we could at the beaches where we'd grown up, spent as much time introducing the other to the slice of the Atlantic that we'd loved. When she came to Somers Point, Rose got the Jersey Shore experience that she'd spent her childhood longing for: roller coasters, bumper cars, iron-on T-shirts, boardwalk flirtation, funnel cake, pizza, water ice, soft serve. Rose loved walking the boardwalk slowly, the two of us being at the zoo and of the zoo at once, making up stories about all the faces we passed.

Rose loved flirting with the teenage boys who served us slices of pizza and large lemonades on the boardwalk. *Take a number*, I said one afternoon, when one of them asked what we were doing later, and Rose laughed, loudly. *Take a number*, she said, as we walked away. Repeated it as we walked and ate our soft serve, walked the boardwalk

and let the light and the haze wrap us in an almost immo-
bilizing gauze. *Look at this one*, she'd say, as a sweet tiny
pumpkin of a face came toddling into our vision. *Look at
this one*, she'd say, as a dog waddled or trotted toward us.
Or: *This guy*, if she saw a man whose self-regard clearly out-
stripped the objective rationale for it.

My mother taught Rose how to use her wrist to reli-
ably, unerringly flick a Skee-Ball into the fifty-point ring—
taught her the same way she'd taught me, standing on
Rose's left side, kneeling slightly, her right hand bracelet-
ing Rose's left wrist with her fingers, my mother narrowing
her eyes and adjusting, just so, as if she were cracking a
safe. *You and your mother have the same exact face when
you're pitching a Skee-Ball*, Rose said, during one visit. And
then she did an impression: mouth shut, screwed up, brows
furrowed, a gaze that could perform laser surgery.

You're kidding me, I said. Because I was sure that my
mother and I were nothing alike.

*You and your mother both tap your finger on the table in
the same exact way when you want to make a point*, I said to
Rose during a visit.

I've never noticed, Rose said, but I knew she was lying.

I loved going to Jones Beach with Rose and her mother
and drinking spiked iced tea from a thermos and eating
the antipasto her mother had packed that morning. Sitting
in chairs or lying on blankets while reading *Newsday* and
the *Daily News* and talking trash about Rudy Giuliani and
people's ill-behaved children. *You're too nice*, said Rose's
mother, laughing, when she noticed I was reluctant to talk
trash about people's ill-fitting bathing suits. Rose's mother,
in the evenings, teaching me how—or as she said, teach-

ing me the right way—to make sauce with fresh tomatoes and basil while Rose sat outside on top of a picnic table listening to a Mets game on the radio and smoking, using a Diet Coke can for an ashtray. *Rose Angelica my love*, said her mother, *either you put that out or I'll put it out for you.* Sitting with Rose's mother on the couch on those evenings, watching old movies, Rose's mother impressed by my knowledge of the actresses and actors who had peopled the films of her and my mother's youth.

In these contexts, it was difficult to picture Ann Marie shouting so loud Rose saw the spittle or throwing plates and knives at the wall, as she was said to have done when Rose was fifteen, sixteen, seventeen, eighteen and intent on escaping the house, intent on dressing in weird, unfeminine ways that angered Ann Marie, who could not see the Doc Martens and Manic Panic for the phase that they were, could not see that there might be things other than mothers making Rose angry, could only think that all of it meant she was going to lose Rose forever the way she lost her husband forever, and so raged at Rose so much it turned, said Rose, *my heart into an empty freezer.*

Rose's mother, not unlike her daughter, liked to do things her way. During visits I'd ask if she could show me how to make gnocchi or biscotti, items I was pretty sure I'd spend my whole life only ordering in restaurants, and while we would start out in tandem, side by side with utensils and aprons, after a half hour I'd be elbowed—nicely!—out of the picture. She'd take a knife or a pile of dough away from me—nicely!—to show me one thing, and my hands would never touch that knife or dough again. She could not give up control of a task, and so I'd always end up leaning against the counter, drinking a cup of coffee, learning by watching, and asking questions about their family.

Rose and I spent hours lying together on our respective beaches talking and staring at the ocean as if it were television. At some point, if the water allowed, I would go for a long swim. At other points, Rose would fall asleep, or I would fall asleep, one or the other always awake keeping watch on the water.

We also loved to sit at our respective kitchen tables, after our parents had gone to bed, with family albums and shoeboxes full of photos, a bowl of popcorn, and a bottle of wine between us, listening to whatever records were available to play on the stereo. Earth, Wind & Fire's *Spirit* at Rose's house and *Ella in Berlin* at mine. Rose and I discovered that we shared an inexhaustible appetite for scrutinizing photographic records of the clothes that other people's grandmothers wore, of the Christmas gifts that people attacked, unwrapped, and then abandoned, of poses in scantly vegetated and obviously freezing front yards. Figures trapped by style, sealed definitively off from the present. Staring at the past in order to commune with it, to try to know its contours through its uncomfortable shoes and elaborate hairstyles, to learn how to salute it, forgive it, and be on guard against it all at once.

To this day, if you showed me pictures of Rose's aunts Mary, Gina, and Teresa, I could tell you which was which, and who their first loves were, and Rose could tell a Peggy (my mother) from a Linda from a Suzanne from a Carolyn (my aunts), and which Beatle they preferred. I could still tell you the name of the streets her grandmother and mother grew up on—Ridgewood Avenue and Keswick

Place—and she could I'm sure still tell you the name of my father's first girlfriend and the priest who coached his football team. Father Anton.

I don't think I'll ever have another friend who was as sincerely interested in my family and their vicissitudes as Rose. That kind of interest in another's family, no matter how unremarkable the gene pool, is the mark of someone who has been wounded, stymied, beloved, beguiled, betrayed, and stonewalled by their own. The mark of writers and historians. They're the first facts we have to gather; the first gaps we have to fill with our imaginations. The primary instance of primary resources and the failure thereof to tell the whole story. And that kind of attention to—reverence for?—another person's first facts is a form of love.

On Labor Day weekend that first summer we were friends, we pulled up to Rose's house and found a man sunning himself on a chaise lounge atop her carport roof. A man, tanned, muscled, and no doubt baby-oiled, wearing bright red swim trunks with a nautical-looking rope tied in a bow at his waist, holding a reflector, proudly but effortlessly, under his very Roman nose. Slicked-back black hair, highly visible black eyebrows. Ray-Ban aviators. Boxer's or swimmer's build and tortured, prominent features.

Oh no, said Rose, as we pulled up to the house.

Did your mother get herself a boyfriend? I said, leaning forward in the passenger seat to get a better look.

I'll explain this later, she said, as she put the car in park.

Later as in twenty minutes from now, or twenty years from now?

I love you because of your quick wit but please be quiet so he doesn't hear us, she said.

Ma! she shouted, as we entered the house. *Ma!* No answer. Her mother had already left for the weekend. A church retreat. *Oh no*, said Rose again. *You stay here*, she said, and headed outside. I stood at the window nearest the carport to watch.

Uncle Jimmy? she said. Glass and distance muffling her voice. One hand on her hip; the other, still holding on to keys, shielding her eyes as she looked up to the roof. *It's Rosie. Why aren't you at the beach?*

Too freakin' crowded, I heard him say. *Wanna come up?*

I got a friend here. Rose, slipping into dialect. *We're going to the beach. Does my mother know you're here?*

No answer. Then his voice: *You bring a guy to the house?*

When Rose came back inside every muscle, from her face to her feet, seemed to be inhabited by what I'd call a full-body grimace, and she held herself in that traction for the next few hours. Even at the beach. The sun could not fire her ice, and I stared out at the water and waited for her to talk.

Okay. So. He's my father's brother.

What? Rose!

I know.

You never, ever mentioned him.

I know. She paused. *Why would I mention I have an uncle Jimmy? I might as well legally change my name to Angela Red Sauce.*

Her uncle, after high school, stole money from the pizza place he was working at because he'd gotten a girl pregnant and wanted to help her get an abortion, but she performed one herself and then died. He kept stealing money, enough to get himself caught and sentenced to one year in prison. After he got out, during which time his father, too, had died, and his mother—his mother, Rose and Ann Marie thought, died because her youngest son had been sentenced to prison—he thought about going to school for forestry, Rose couldn't remember, but it didn't stick. Rose's mother let him live with them that year, the year he got out, because she remembered the boy not the man, the boy who used to pick her up forty-fives from Sam Goody, disco and soul forty-fives that he knew his brother never would, the boy who used to watch the Mets while letting Rose fall asleep on his chest, and once her mother came into the living room and found Rose on his lap, face up like a tiny bug, having slipped from his arms onto his knees and not to the floor, thank God, the boy who used to fix his mother's radios and his mother's blenders out in the mad scientist's laboratory that was his mother's second kitchen, used to play guitar, at least for one summer, in his mother's second kitchen, and then Rose's mother kicked him out when she found him having sex with some girl on her brand-new couch, the couch Rose and I and her mother sat on to watch *From Here to Eternity* and *Days of Wine and Roses*. *To this day*, said Rose, *I don't know whether my mother was royally pissed because this was a sin against God or a sin against her living room*. He found a job driving a UPS truck, moved out. There was a marriage, a drinking problem, an anger problem, a divorce, a UPS truck crashed into the window of a 7-Eleven. A girl pregnant somewhere, maybe Florida, but they never met the girl or the child. Now he lived in an apartment at the top of an old friend's house in Bay Ridge, working as a baker at a Polish whole-sale bakery in Williamsburg. Her mother refused to let him into the house. It killed her, but she refused to let him into the house.

Occasionally Jimmy would drive out to Long Island and sun himself on the carport the way he did before he went to prison, the way he did before Rose came along. In the summer, Rose said, usually. And because he did not technically set foot *in* the house, her mother turned a blind eye. Mostly.

You know when you go to Williamsburg and you see those drunk Italian guys shouting outside that Irish bar, the one with the stained-glass panel over the transom, the one that's all the way down by the river? That's my uncle.

I had seen those men, and Rose's ache became an ache in me.

I wish I didn't love him, she said.

On the way home from the beach we stopped to get veal and ricotta because Rose had decided to make her uncle some rollatini. *I'm telling myself it's for you,* she said.

I get it, I said.

Did I see Jimmy on the roof of your mother's carport on the way to work or was I still hungover? said the man weighing the veal.

You were hungover.

Gotcha. The man smiled. I noticed he piled more veal on her order after he turned off the electric scale.

I sound exactly like an Angela Red Sauce, said Rose, starting up the car. *Why are you friends with me?*

Because you sound like somebody upholding the virtues of the northeastern middle class.

And that sounds like what exactly?

Like somebody constitutionally averse to bullshit and performance.

Rose laughed, loudly. *Let us go with that. Thank you.* Then, as she swung into traffic: *I'm putting him on an eight ten train.*

Her uncle, when Rose introduced him to me, reached out his hand and said, *Well fuck me if you're not the second coming of Eileen Healy, class of 1981.* He had topped his bare chest, bare feet, and swim trunks with a straw fedora, and despite this peacock feather of an accessory, his grip—on both my hand and his short, sharp, tightly wound masculinity—instantly, mortifyingly made me want to get in the back seat of a car with him and make out. While also thinking I wanted to call the police and tell them somebody's stray, cross-eyed pit bull was pissing all over my lawn. I could only imagine what Rose was thinking.

For Christ's sake, said Rose. *She's my best friend.* Which I did not know until that very moment. We did not use those terms for each other, finding them too redolent of the playground.

While Rose and I cooked dinner, Jimmy went out to the driveway and shot baskets. *Should we put aprons on to complete this retrograde charade?* I said. She laughed.

Who played basketball? I asked as we chopped.

My dad did, she said. *We used to play horse out there with Jimmy.* The metal backboard sounded as if it were taking a beating; it sounded like most of the shots were going in. I looked up and stared at her uncle's back and shoulders. I poured myself a glass of wine and downed it too quickly.

That's a good idea, said Rose, and did the same.

After we'd set the table, Rose stood, one hand on the frame of the back door, the other pushing the screen door open and out, one foot behind the other, and said: *Dinner's ready*. I knew without being told that her mother had probably held that pose and said those words in just the same way, because whenever I stood at a kitchen sink for longer than two minutes, or set food down in front of my father, I became similarly, instantly possessed by my mother's posture and inflections.

At dinner, despite having put on a brand-new-seeming Hawaiian shirt for the occasion, Jimmy did not present like someone who'd crash a UPS truck into a convenience store and steal from your register. He opened the wine, poured us glasses, served the two of us before serving himself, said he'd do the dishes afterward. It was as if he knew his job was to tend the warming fire that Rose and I had created by making the meal—knew that was his job, and was enjoying it. He had excellent table manners—although, shame on me for assuming he wouldn't. He asked questions about how Rose and I met, where I'd grown up, asked Rose what she was up to in New York, if she'd found a boyfriend yet.

Good, he said, when she told him no. *No one's good enough for you. We're all a bunch of fucking assholes.*

How 'bout you? he said, turning to me. As if ready to fight, or to flirt. *You got a boyfriend?* I blushed and stared.

If you were any quieter, he said, *I'd have to organize a search party for your tongue.*

In response, I stuck out my tongue, and he laughed. Rose laughed, too.

I like this one, he said to Rose.

Rose asked him what he'd put in his freezer this winter.

He hunts deer, she said to me by way of explanation, *and used to try to figure out ways to make it so I'd finally eat it.*

The closest I ever came was venison sausage, he said. *On a grandma pie.*

You hunt deer? I said. With too much surprise in my voice.

What, you think I'm too much of a mook to like trees? Sitting back as if ready to judge or be judged. To fight and to flirt.

Actually, yes, I said.

She's not the first, said Rose. *Don't act surprised.*

You college girls know jack shit. But he was grinning.

That's true, if we're talking about life in prison, she said.

All right all right, and he put one hand up to stop her from going further.

But not even then, I said. *We read the paper.*

Oh you do, said Jimmy.

So comeoncomeoncomeon, said Rose, grabbing him by the knee and tugging it back and forth, *tell us what you caught this winter and what you did with it.* And she was grinning, too.

Like Rose, her uncle knew how to tell a story. About Orange County and the collision, one November weekend, at a rest stop off the Palisades Parkway, of the out-of-control wild turkey population, obese and clueless *Star Wars* re-enactors, incompetent cops (*Although consider the source,* said Rose when he reached that point in the story), and a Range Rover full of what he called cider-donut hunters from the city, who'd pulled into the rest stop to breastfeed their toddlers. Like Rose, her uncle knew how to time a joke, how to throw a voice, how to skewer self-importance. Like Rose, like her mother, her uncle liked to hear himself talk, but never went on in a way that made you want him to stop talking—the flow of words never swelled over the banks into pointless digression. And as I listened I realized that I might be able to marry someone who'd never gone to college, as long as they knew how to tell a story at a table; as long as their words could become electric with verbal intelligence. As we sat and talked I thought Rose would probably say she too could fall victim to the same, and I worried a little for both of us.

Tell Jimmy, said Rose to me, *about the deer you ran over in high school and how that Piney woman with an eye patch ran out of the woods, bow and arrow in her hands, and told you and your friends that you were going to help her skin that deer right there on the side of the road unless you paid her a hundred bucks because she'd been after it all morning and what you'd done was poached her dinner.*

You told the whole freakin' story, Rose! said Jimmy. *What the hell kind of friend are you?*

We continued laughing and talking until Rose left the table to get us more water and while her back was turned and my eyes sought the time from the clock over the sink—10:15—Jimmy put his hand on my knee.

The hand was a tongue that licked at my ear while a ringing inside my ears grew louder. I wanted: his fingers to move closer, his fingers inside me. Wanted him to come inside me while I lay on my back on the concrete outside. I jumped up from the table, which made Rose turn around, and all the plates and glasses clattered and wobbled. A wine glass dropped to the floor and burst into pieces. Jimmy, still seated, took a sip out of his as if it were sunset on the deck of a Cunard liner passing Antarctica.

I'm driving you to the train, she told him. *Now.*

You asshole, I said to Jimmy, but I didn't really mean it, and he knew it. He took one more drink, stood up, and smiled at me on his way out of the kitchen.

Go! said Rose, slamming her hands on his shoulders and heaving him into the living room.

I cleaned up the glass and then headed upstairs to shower. When I came out of the bathroom I heard the refrigerator open and close, and when I reached the bottom of the stairs I saw Rose sitting at the kitchen table, staring into the distance, two full glasses of wine in front of her.

She raised her face to mine. It was tired and sad. She pushed one of the glasses toward me.

I'm sorry, she said.

Please.

A person should never think they know better than their mother, she said.

Then let's kill ourselves right now, I said.

Will you tell me something?

My face burned again. I nodded.

Would you have let him—

I nodded.

We're all doomed.

Shut up, I said.

You're not the first friend he's swooped in on like that.

I sat down at the table.

I don't want to share you.

You won't have to. I promise.

Don't ever leave me, she said.

It had become our version of *I love you. Don't ever leave me* or *I hate everyone except you* or *What is wrong with everyone?* or *You're the only person I can stand to talk to right now.*

Why don't we go see my parents tomorrow? I said.

Set your alarm and get me up, she said.

In the car, somewhere on the Long Island Expressway, I began a sentence with the word *Why* and Rose said *Later, I promise.*

That Sunday, I asked my father to take us clamming, because I thought Rose might need some time on the open seas with someone of the male persuasion who was given to saying very little when very little seemed exactly what was required. Someone to block our view of the Jimmys and make us realize how puny were the Karls. Someone to make us feel that we were talking behind the backs of all the women with babies, with husbands, with money to make or houses to clean. If only for an afternoon.

You two are quiet, said my father, once we'd reached a spot on the bay that he'd deemed suitable. *You guys are usually going off like a couple of firecrackers.*

The water lapped at the side of the boat.

Big city getting you down? said my father.

Give her the rake, I told him.

I had never before seen Rose in the act of trying and failing, but it seemed that watching her try to drag the bullrake through the sand to drag up the clams might qualify. I almost had to turn away. It was strange to watch my friend, who moved through the city with five thousand flourishes, confront some physical limitations out in what you might call nature. But she kept plunging and maneuvering and grunting.

Rose has a hard time giving up, I said to my father, who'd sat down next to me after showing her the ropes.

That's why you two are friends, he said.

On the way back to shore we passed a boat with the words *Scared Money Never Wins* painted along the craft's backside. Two people sat in the hole: a woman whose sunglass lenses were as big and black as Jackie O's and a man in a captain's hat with no shirt.

I'll bet you anything that guy's scared crapless one hundred and ten percent of the time, said my father.

Rose laughed for the first time that day. Too hard and too long, probably, but I understood why, and I felt a great deal of love for my father just then.

I like you two, he said, as we ate burgers and drank beers at the oldest bar in town, the wood of the booths dark and soft, scarred by pens and knives and boredom and drunkenness, while a Phillies game droned in the background on three separate screens.

Rose excused herself very quickly to go to the bathroom. After about two minutes I went to check on her, and when I opened the door to the ladies' room I heard sniffling, heard a blowing of the nose. I turned back around and headed out.

She okay? said my father.

There was a line.

There are five people total in here, he said, giving me a look.

I shrugged.

My father took a bite of his burger, I took a bite of my burger, and we watched the baseball game.

Then my father said: *I've had friends, but I never had a friend like Rose. I couldn't open up to people.* He did not seem to be speaking out of regret.

I think she's grateful for you, I said. Instead of saying what I wanted to say, which was: *I'm grateful for you.*

Settle down, said my father.

Rose let me drive us back to the city in her grand-mother's Buick. We didn't talk much but instead ruthlessly searched the dial for the perfect hit of well-known sound.

You know what it is, about your father? said Rose, when traffic had rolled to a stop just outside Elizabeth. To our right, beyond her rolled-down window, beyond the refiner-ies, the city stood shrouded in a pink and tangerine haze. *He treats you like a worthy opponent.*

We sat a while in silence. The sun contracted to a tiny glowing dot. We were no closer to the exit.

Said Rose: *Did you ever drive by the house of a guy you liked, just to see if they were there? Just to be where they might be?*

Never, I said.

You're Charlotte and I'm Emily, she said. *Brontë, I mean.*

Who else would you have meant? And you're Laverne and I'm Shirley. But just to be clear: This doesn't mean you're privi-leging your wild tempestuous nature over my plodding realism, right?

Rose laughed. Sometimes her laugh was as rapid and prolific as gunfire, as rapid and prolific as her typing. *No, no! It's just—you're a little more pragmatic. I wish I were.*

I hope one day I'm not pragmatic at all.

That's what I'm hanging around for, she said.

5.

Because Rose and I had become so close, I didn't think it was right for me to keep editing her. I asked Karl if he could take over that duty, and he did. He became our editor, then, in more ways than one: he became a force shaping the myth we were building.

Lock up your interns, he said to us one night, after watching the two of us arrive late to a party and saunter up to the bar where he'd been waiting.

Said Rose: *Marry us, Karl.*

I am *a Mormon*, he said. *I mean, was.*

We do love you, I said. *We'll never be able to work for anyone else. You've ruined us, with your good manners and your work ethic and your inspiringly fascistic insistence on everyone taking a lunch hour.*

I think you two have ruined me, he said.

I know we did, I said.

Who else is going to ask you every last thing about your three sisters and your two brothers? Rose said. *Who else is going to care so deeply about where you went to breakfast after temple?*

Karl, smiling, drinking his drink.

On another night, Rose and me telling Karl about a band he had to reconsider. *In the beginning they were a runty, snotty amalgam of influences having yet to find a true aim other than taking its lead singer's ADD out for a walk*, I said, *but now it's like they understand that their real gifts lay in their ability to—*

Write elegant, said Rose, *but still somehow majestically— spastic?—songs.*

Yes! I said.

I hate that guy's hair, said Karl.

Why? I said. *Because he has a lot of it?*

False prophets, he said. *You two know better than that.*

The problem of male glamour, said Rose, who was now talking to herself.

Are we being patronized? I said. But secretly enjoying it because it felt like protection, which is to say a desire to possess, which meant something like love could be lurking about.

Not if you stay away from that guy.

What do you know? I said, now suspicious. *What does Tracy know?*

Karl looked weary in a way that suggested he wanted to remind us that he didn't have to know something to know something.

If there is no story here about Rose or me getting gloriously mixed up with some lead singer or drummer or bassist, it is because we were deathly afraid of looking like groupies, like hangers-on, like ghouls from the sixties running around in crocheted vests and hot pants looking for a bus, any bus, where's the bus, back to San Francisco. Like women who didn't know how to dissect a song, an album, a moment, a movement. Who didn't know how to properly appreciate or despise or defend or contextualize what they were listening to. Our love for music was pure, even when sex had something to do with it—which wasn't often, given our time and place and personal preferences—and we needed it to remain pure because, we sensed, we were going to need this love for the rest of our lives, and we did not want to risk having this escape route to contemplation and release cut off because we'd gotten too close to the very flawed, possibly psychotic, people who created it. And mortals like Karl were beautiful enough.

Later, at some quarter to two in the morning, after the three of us had realized that we'd all gone to state schools, and we'd all been spanked with a wooden spoon or bare hands or both, and we'd all been told never to talk with food in our mouths or put our elbows on tables, and realized that our friends were our friends because they'd been similarly abused, and yet here we all were, drinking and writing in New York City right alongside all the Ivy Leaguers, Karl said: *We're the kids they never saw coming.*

Give us some nicknames, said Rose. On a Wednesday. March, 9:30 or thereabouts. In London, the staff of the magazine flown over for a festival. The three of us in a pub near Oxford Circus whose floor was covered with Astroturf. She and I on one side of a booth and Karl on the other.

You, he said, pointing his left index finger at Rose, *are Rose of Thorndike Hall.*

And you, he said, pointing his right index finger at me, *are Charlotte of Lavender Lake.*

Rose laughed and I clapped my hands together in delight. *Explicate!* she said.

You want every last thing explained, Rose. But his smile made it clear that there was nowhere he'd rather be, nothing else he'd rather be doing. On a Wednesday. In March. In 1999.

He said he'd remembered the titles of books we'd told him we'd read as girls—because they were the titles of the books his sisters stuffed into the sides of van doors to read on drives out to Nevada campsites. Remembered the titles' many iterations of girl and geographical root. Rose of Thorndike Hall, then, because she was prickly and dramatically forbidding, as a house with that name would be, and the grand staircase that was her soul climbed impossibly, strikingly high; Charlotte of Lavender Lake because, like the Gowanus Canal, you had no idea what on earth was at the bottom of it, and for how long it had been there.

Mysterious depths, you see, he said.

Rose's chagrin blew through the booth like a draft from the street—she thought Karl had bestowed just a bit more poetry on me, I guessed. I struggled to find a joke to make.

Rose, said Karl.

She tucked her head down and said *Okay, okay*, without looking at him, and I knew, I could tell, that they had exchanged these kinds of words before, in even darker, quieter rooms, their clothes no doubt on the floor, and felt my own chagrin start to kick up within me.

Now you, I said to Karl, *are the boy with the thorn in his side*.

He looked surprised. As if he knew I was capable of a joke—but not a true jab, not a true dig. Then he recovered.

Not very original, he said.

Rose laughed. *But she's right*, she said.

Otherwise, she and I were a cyclone of words attempting to destroy all specious nonsense with our withering sarcasm, and Karl was a house on the ground with two steady lights on refusing to be carried away by our hoarse demands. A dog in a yard one county down who kept at his bone while he watched us splintering the world away with our anger.

You two are crazy, he'd say, but not without affection.

When Rose left tables or booths to get second or third rounds, I kept talking out of some nervousness at being left alone with the thing I wanted but should not have— and out of some shame, as my big fat suburban parking lot mouth, crammed on a Saturday with cars, encroached upon Karl's wide-open spaces of Western, self-possessed silence.

Your eyes talk, too, you know, he said, that night in London.

I looked away, into the crowd.

I'd almost forgotten that I'd come to New York to write. I used to joke with Rose that she had Silenced My Voice, and she used to say *Don't joke about that, I was a monster*—but on the other hand I was having too much fun exhausting myself from staying out late, from waitressing, from telling Rose everything that had happened in my life until the day I'd met her, from listening to Rose tell me everything that had happened in her life until the day she'd met me, and I'd forgotten that a piece of mine was finally going to run. On a website that many of us read and had started to think was more important than the *Voice*. It had been written so long ago it meant nothing to me; when I looked at the final version on the screen my eyes glazed over with lack of interest. *Am I stupid?* I asked myself. *These thoughts seem stupid.*

But Rose didn't think so. *Why didn't you tell me?* she said, standing at my desk one Monday morning, holding up a printout.

I don't self-promote. Perhaps I was a little frosty when I said it.

Rose rolled her eyes. *I have some comments. Do you want them?*

Yes! I said. *Please.* And now I could make everything up to her by being in debt to her red pen. Which in Rose's case, and my case, was always purple, because we both thought that red screamed *Idiot!* too loudly.

Tracy, walking by, heard Rose and stopped. *Yeah, I read that thing of yours, too. What are you doing still sitting here? Get a better job.*

Rose, staring at Tracy. Tracy, ignoring Rose.

I feel like your friend is judging me, Tracy said, nodding to the cover of *This Year's Model*, which I had propped up on my desk behind my computer.

He is, I said.

Get a better job, she said, and walked off.

You've given this to Karl? said Rose.

No. I said I don't self-promote. Also—

Yes?

When I interviewed for your job he told me my writing wasn't that strong.

Karl! Rose rolled her eyes again.

Who knows what that was about, but I—

That was twelve months ago, she said. *Do it.*

I dropped that piece in his inbox with a note. Stood at the copier with the magazine after everyone had gone for the day, stapled the two pages together, sat at my desk in lamplight with black Precise V5 in paralyzed hand. I spent thirty minutes attempting seven disastrous notes on hot pink Post-its—

Drink me

A little night music

From the desk of Henrietta Stackpole

From the desk of Don Juan's Reckless Daughter

*From the desk of the frayed edges of Patti Smith's black
satin necktie*

Here's one more from your radio sweetheart

Hello carnage my old friend. Love, Nancy Spungen

—before I settled on four idiotic words: *Hot off the presses.* I dropped it in Karl's inbox and over the next few days watched as a pile of magazines, books, seven-inches, and CDs grew on top of it.

After two weeks went by, I knocked on his office door, entered, and asked if he had read what I'd written.

Why do you need my approval? he said.

I turned red.

You don't need my approval to be what you're going to be, he said. *You need to be the one believing in yourself. You can't ask other people to do it for you.*

Did you not like what I wrote?

That's not it.

Is it because it was mediocre?

No. You know it wasn't mediocre. But I thought it was—sentimental.

The fluorescent light, the stained ceiling tiles, Karl's black button-down shirt, the gray industrial carpet, the very fake and very dark wood grain of his desktop, the poster of Bob Dylan. I can still see that office, even remember what the weather was like outside, even though the office had no windows. Standing in that office I felt shame—a shame I felt often enough on my own—for being a woman mainly interested in the lives of bygone women. I was no better than a collector of shells. Or Beatles paraphernalia. Even worse: I was looking in a mirror for my reflection.

Is there anything you love? I said.

That's dramatic, he said. *What does it matter what I think? Why should it matter, if you liked it?*

I never know if I like it. I can only like it once I hear that someone else does. I only know that I like doing it.

Then that should be enough, he said.

It isn't. I stared at him.

You're going to have a lot of trouble if you can't get that sorted, he said.

You're being difficult and I don't know why, I said, and walked out of his office.

Into the ladies' room, where I locked myself in a stall and cried. Then I went back to my desk, grabbed my things, found Rose, and told her we were going for a drink. It was 3:15, according to Rose's computer screen.

When I told Rose what had happened, in the bleached and ancient Irish bar that sat across the street from the office, she became gloriously indignant for a good half hour—so indignant I felt compelled to play devil's advocate. But she would not listen.

Fuck Karl, she said. *Fuck him.* It was not eloquent or wise, but she drove those words into the ground with such conviction that I let it become a pole I could string a flag up.

I wrote at night and on weekends. I wrote until two, three, four, five in the morning because I wanted to make Karl stand up and applaud. Because I wanted him to stand up and say that he was in love with me but could not admit it. I wrote for Karl the way some girls might have thrown him on a bed. I wrote to make sure I was real.

Soon I was assigned a piece in *The New York Times Book Review*. An essay on the back page. The paper I'd spent high school Sunday nights in summer reading, the paper I'd pick up on my way into my waitressing job and read at the counter when it was slow. The cooks—well, one cook in particular—used to tease me about the book review. Because he had a tattoo crawling across his right knuckles, and I was the only college girl among the waitresses. The only nice girl, as the other waitresses liked to say.

Whaddya got there, Marian Librarian? the cook would say. Or *Whaddya got there, Snow White?* While pouring himself some coffee. He liked it burnt, in a thirty-two-ounce Styrofoam cup, and I made it my job to always keep the pots fresh, just to antagonize him. Kevin. Large and pink and ruddy and ponytailed. Falstaff with a pack-a-day habit.

The Scholastic book order form, I'd say, turning the pages, never looking up.

He'd tear open three packets of sugar, toss them in. *You ever do a three-way?* he'd say. *You ever see a porno? You ever sit too long on a washing machine? You ever do it in a McDonald's bathroom?* I could hear him smiling through the words.

When I do, Kevin, I'd say, *I'll call collect to let you know.* Or: *Here's a fun fact, Kevin: the manager likes me way more than he likes you.* And: *I swear to God, Kevin. Stop being a dick, Kevin.* Still not looking up from the pages. Then he'd get a can of whipped cream out of one of the refrigerators under the counter and shoot it into the cup.

You know I'm just busting your chops, Snow White. Or Marian Librarian. Laura Ingalls. Lady Di. *My endgame here is to see you crack.*

He never screwed up my orders, so I knew he didn't mind me too much.

Go bust someone else's, please.

As you wish, he'd say, and go out back to smoke.

And then I'd wonder if I shouldn't just read the Atlantic City *Press* at the counter just to avoid the hassle.

Or, as my grandmother used to say to my mother and my aunts and my cousins and me whenever we talked back: *Who do you think you are?*

Rose's grandmother used to say the same thing to Rose's mother, and Rose's mother, when the time had come, turned around and said it to Rose.

I gave Rose the piece for the *Times* the morning before I had to turn it in. I had never given her my writing to edit before; it had always been the other way around. She was on deadline herself, and I didn't hear back from her until 10:30 that Sunday night, which made me spend the whole day taking long walks between anxious checks of my answering machine, and, as we paced our bedrooms with our cordless phones and looked out at the Williamsburgh Savings Bank building from different perspectives, that building the center of a clock's face and our apartments at ten and half past, respectively, both of our roommates asleep because they did not have better things to do, she told me

I was dancing around my most important and interesting thoughts.

I can feel you not saying what you need to say because you're afraid to, because you think it's stupid. But just say it. Because nine times out of ten your stupid is someone else's I-wish-I'd-figured-out-how-to-say-that.

Anne Frank? I said, relieved that I didn't have to rewrite the whole damn thing, just elaborate in spots.

Yes. We don't want to be trivial here, but yes, Anne Frank. What would she say if she knew we were wasting our time worrying about what others would think of our thoughts? This is why Karl thought your writing was weak, way back when, she said. *You thought he meant you didn't have style, but it's that you have too much of it. You describe more than you think. These sentences are like, oh, what's the word, right, strongboxes. I can hear the things you want to say rattling around in them, but you have to let them out. Let them out!*

She went on to point out every place I knew I'd stalled and punted. Circumspected and headed for the too-elaborate metaphor.

So all you have to do—and here we both laughed—*is just tell me what you think. Tell me! Rose Pellegrino. Not whatever asshat, as Tracy would say, is paying you.*

I sat down at my computer and finished at three in the morning. From then on, whenever I found myself stalled and squirming, I heard Rose's voice telling me to just write what I meant, and saw that I could. Mostly.

The *Times* editor was impressed, she told me, because I had written to word count exactly and, not only that, turned it in on time, and, not only that, she said, I had written something she didn't want to do a blessed thing to.

That's right, I said to myself but did not say to her, *I am not messing around. This is life or death with me. With me you get all of the Harvard brain at a quarter of the price. With me you get someone with everything to prove and everything to lose. With me you get all of the resentment but consequently all of the fire. And by extension what the hell*, I continued to myself but did not say to her, *is everyone else up to, if you're so impressed by me doing exactly what the job requires? Who is blowing this off and screwing it up as if their life did not depend on it?*

I wrote three more times for that editor until she informed me that they were giving the back page over to the daughter of a famous writer.

My sense here is that I may be the better writer, I said. *Is that correct?*

It's completely unnecessary to say out loud what the both of us already know, said the editor. She had never sounded this impatient.

And why is that? I asked the editor, who then hung up on me.

Let's figure out where this girl lives and set fire to her, Rose said, when I informed her of this development. *Because obviously writing circles around her isn't doing the trick.*

The night before that first essay appeared, walking back to the train so late on a Saturday night it was morning, Rose and I spotted a truck delivering the *Times* to a bodega in the East Village. The radio in the cab of that parked truck had started to play Billy Joel's "New York State of Mind" while its driver unloaded it.

No, I said, watching the papers pile up on their bench as the saxophone and piano swung punches at each other in the night-on-cusp-of-day.

Yes, said Rose, reverentially and giddily, as if life would never again send such a comet of serendipity through our skies.

I wish I had been able to be content with traveling just that distance, with making it just that far: standing in New York City under the stars, staring at your name in print in a publication that you respected, in a font of record, next to a friend who was somehow even more excited and impressed than you were about your achievement, a friend who knew just how much luck, determination, sacrifice, and forbearance of arbitrarily dished-out nonsense perfumed the ink that was staining your hands.

I asked the driver if I could have a copy of the paper, and he tossed one my way.

Nice catch, he said.

I played softball, I said. He needed to know he wasn't talking to some trust-fund princess.

She's in there, Rose said to the driver, as he stacked more papers on the bench. I elbowed and shushed her. *My friend has a piece in there.*

We were ignored, and rightly so. We huddled together under the awning of the bodega, stood in blinding fluorescent light, gloried in the scent of bacon coming from the grill inside, and looked at my words, which took up a whole page. I could not read what I had written. I glanced at the space the words occupied, pleased at the expanse of it, pleased to see my name, my thoughts, in the familiar typeface, and then closed the review. We went in to the store to pay and Rose—I almost wrote *my sister*—said to the man behind the counter, *My friend has a piece in the paper.*

Oh! The man behind the counter smiled. *Take it! For free!*

No! I said.

Yes! he said.

If it happens to one of us, it happens to both of us, said Rose, as we walked out of the bodega.

I used to think that Rose must have uttered a magic spell when she uttered those words, because a month later it was her name that appeared in the paper of record. In the Sunday Arts and Leisure section. She rewrote it eleven times in two weeks, and I drank as much coffee and slept as little as Rose did while she worked on it. She wanted to send me every draft, and she tended to send them at one in the morning.

You'd be a good mother, she said, over the phone at three in the morning, draft five, as I typed, rewriting one of her sentences, cordless to shoulder, and watched the B41, lit from within like a glowworm, float down Flatbush.

Rose always slept late, so I headed out that Sunday morning and bought three copies—two for her and one for her mother. My arms felt heavy with flowers as I walked to meet her at Tom's on Washington Avenue, where we settled in to omelets as large and misshapen as maps of the United States on our plates, Western for me, Mexican for Rose, and we never deviated from this order, even though we always talked about it, and complained to each other about not being brave enough to court disappointment even in this small way, but this was a ritual as steadying as Mass, so why deviate from coffee in thick white mugs; rye toast glistening with butter; scratched tin forks, sometimes missing tines; buttered, crumpled napkins; swipes of butter smeared on the front page; hot sauce on hash browns. The clatter of plenty for $7.95.

Rose in a red-checked housecoat with nearly all of her curls tucked in a green and orange jungle-printed turban she'd started wearing because she'd seen an ancient receptionist at Condé Nast sporting one; me in pigtails, cuffed jeans, my red Pumas, and a gray sweatshirt that falsely identified me as a counselor for Camp Longhorn at Inks Lake in Texas. I called her look Auntie Mame Gone South in More Ways Than One; she called mine Landlocked and Loaded Pippi Longstocking.

You believe in me, she said. *I used to think only my grandmother did.*

Rose, I'll probably believe in you more than I'll ever believe in myself. You and New York! That's probably all I'll ever believe in.

Rose grabbed my hand across the table with a theatrical flourish, lowered her voice to a whisper, and, as the waitress poured us more coffee, and, as if she were parched and had just crossed a desert, croaked out the words *Don't ever leave me.*

6.

Karl's father was dying from pancreatic cancer, he told the staff in a meeting, and he was going back to Utah to be with his family. Nicole burst into tears. *No!* someone shouted.

Let's quit, I wrote on a corner of a notebook page, and slipped it to Rose.

Rose wrote on the back of that scrap and slipped it to me. *I don't know*, it said.

That Sunday, because Rose was still not sure we—or she—should quit and go freelance, I suggested that we take that day to walk around the city, starting at the foot of the Brooklyn Bridge, to talk and come to a final decision. We started at seven in the morning because we wanted the city to ourselves. Wanted the quiet. It was August and the sun was already making us sweat.

We walked through Chinatown, stopping here and there to admire the oranges at all the fruit and vegetable stands.

I never want to eat them, I said. *I just want to hold them and sniff them.*

Me too, she said. *I guess we'll get scurvy one day.*

From there we walked into Little Italy, and on to Mott Street, where Rose's grandmother was born, in a tenement building, Rose said as we walked, whose street number Rose's grandmother always claimed to have forgotten.

My people would kill me if they knew I was quitting a perfectly good job to try to write, Rose said.

So would my people, I said. *My father in particular. Which is why I'm not telling him.*

Rose's look: dubious. And in fact, I had just decided that on the spot, partly to convince Rose, and partly to convince myself.

Who do we think we are, walking away from perfectly good money, I said, *is the question we're asking ourselves, in the voices of our ancestors.*

Is the money that good? she said. *But yes. As your people and mine might say: Who do we think we are?*

The hired help? I said. Because sometimes—often—I felt deluded to want what I wanted.

Rose laughed. *Yeah. When is that going to end? With the daughters we'll never have, or with the daughters they'll never have, or what?*

Who did we think we were?

When we were girls, we thought we were Ella of *All-of-a-Kind Family* and Laura Ingalls of Walnut Grove and Francie Nolan of Williamsburg. Despite being made well aware of the history that had conspired to make us very comfortable as we read in our twin beds, we felt very little distance between our suburban lives and the lives of these girls. We were just as delighted by what delighted them— new dresses, school pageants, music lessons, trees, boys— and had intense curiosity for what we ourselves had not experienced. As we walked, Rose and I talked of the way those scenes, those homes, those streets, still lingered in our minds. Talked, too, of Caddie Woodlawn and Laura

Ingalls and Anne Shirley, and of the romance of making something out of nothing—it was necessity, it was poverty, we knew, that conjured hard candy out of maple syrup poured on cast-iron pans full of snow, but we were fascinated by that magic and those books made us long to live in a dugout by the banks of Plum Creek.

Why had we loved those immigrant and pioneer stories so much? Did we already want to escape cars and supermarkets and malls and highways? Did we already know we wouldn't want much—that is to say, wouldn't want much in the way of material goods? Were we made too happy by the commemoration of small earth-bound pleasures to want to see what might live in outer space and inside dragon-guarded castles? Were our own immigrant ancestors too much with us?

Yes, said Rose.

At noon, the sun high and white in the sky, we drifted toward Washington Square Park and wended our way through guitars, trumpets, keyboards, pigeons, sleepers, readers, lovers, chess-players, cops. Large and tranquil dogs sleeping like lions on the blacktop and toddlers popping like corn all over the grass.

We can live on beans, I said, as we walked through the arch.

How much do you like beans?

Rose told me about a TA she'd had in college whom she once overheard talking about having found a quarter in the couch that day, a Thursday, which meant the TA could get a Snickers from the vending machine, a Snickers, with peanuts, because that was protein, which meant she could tide herself over until Friday at noon when she got paid.

I think about that all the time, she said. *I don't ever want* to claw through a couch looking for money. I don't ever want to be that broke if I can help it. And I can help it. By not quitting.

I didn't want to be broke, either. I lived in fear of being broke, and that story Rose told about the Snickers and the quarter made my blood run cold. But my desire to see how seriously I could take myself without the scaffolding of school in place—how seriously I could take myself before I caved—was stronger.

What's scaring you? I said.

The number of times my mother made us scrambled eggs for dinner. Having to use baking soda to brush my teeth because my mother didn't think we should splurge on toothpaste that week. Shoplifting a dress from J. C. Penney for a seventh grade dance and not getting caught.

You can't argue with someone's childhood. But I tried.

You're forgetting about the money we made from the bar. We each have about three months' rent saved up.

The equivalent of a quarter in the couch, she said.

We could work at the bar again. Or waitress.

I didn't go to college so I could do something you only need a tattoo to qualify for.

Rose. Because I could not say what I felt myself about to say, which was: *You sound like your mother.*

Why aren't you scared? she said.

I am *scared*, I said. *But I'm also tired of watching other people get what I want.*

Me too, said Rose.

The night before Karl left, Tracy threw him a party at a bar located just inside the entrance to the 1/9 at the Fiftieth Street station, in a space that had been formerly occupied by a shoeshine stand. It was less a bar than a cave of an unfinished basement whose concrete floors and walls were painted fire-engine red. It had no name—it did not need one—but we all called it Radio City because the red matched the shade on the walls closing in on the naked light bulb in the William Eggleston photo on the cover of the Big Star record. The jukebox and old wooden bar top had been imported from an Irish hole-in-the-wall a few blocks deeper into Hell's Kitchen that had been try-ing to turn itself into a sports bar and wanted to hide its petticoats. Open bar, said the invitation, from 9:00 p.m. to first light, and that night Rose heard Tracy—who was drunk in a way we'd never seen, which is to say that we could tell she was drunk because she was talking a lot—telling another girl that she'd paid for the open bar with-out actually really *paying* for the open bar, because she and the owner, who used to be a lighting tech for Megadeth, went to high school in Forest Hills together, and the two of them had unfinished business Tracy thought she could trade on, but now Tracy felt guilty because he was so fuck-ing sweet and all she'd wanted was free booze for Karl, which really wasn't much of a gift, free booze, what the fuck did that matter, some fucking open bar, when Karl had—and then some couple started a fight right next to Rose and she couldn't hear the rest of it. Karl's face in the dark, floating and darting about like the aftereffects of a flash gone off, looked happier than I thought I'd ever seen it, younger than I thought I'd ever seen it, so free of worry and reserve that I almost ran up to Tracy to tell her not to worry, it was worth it.

The place got so crowded and loud so quickly that at

midnight the owner shut off all the lights, pulled the plug on the jukebox, and shooed everyone out of the bar with a folding chair. He had to carry at least one person up the stairs and back onto Fiftieth Street, where the sidewalk had filled up with shouting and meandering. Everyone was drunk, sweaty, and borderline belligerent in their joy.

Out on the street Rose lit a cigarette and Nicole asked if she could try one. Rose was in the middle of handing one over to her when Karl appeared beside us. He said nothing, just put one arm around me and one arm around Rose, and held us tight.

What's gotten into you? I said to him.

Yeah. What gives? Rose said. *You're groping us in front of the children.*

I have had a lot to drink, he said. He touched his nose to my cheek, rubbed it up and down, slowly. I became instantly wet.

Take advantage of him, said Rose. *He's a mess.*

He is a mess, I said to Rose. Stalling. I searched her face. I saw no animosity, no anger, no irony. He moved his mouth over to my ear and whispered *Somebody needs to put me in a cab.*

Wow, said Nicole, who had just tuned in to the conversation. She stared at Karl, who now had his head buried into Rose's neck. *This is amazing.*

Are you testing me? I said to Rose. Because I was a little drunk, too. *Is this some kind of loyalty test?*

You're crazy! she said. Her eyes were full of delight at the mess we were all making out on the street, at the mess she was now queen over. *Get out of here! Go! Take him home! If you don't I'll be pissed.*

I wanted him so badly I took her at her word.

There are no Roses in Utah, said Karl.

Just mountains and cactuses, said Rose.

I'm serious, he said, and untangled himself from the two of us.

We don't want you to go either, Karl, said Rose. She kissed him on his cheek.

Do you have a condom? Nicole said to me. *Make sure you have a condom.*

Rose laughed.

In the back seat of the cab I'd hailed he curled up on his side and put his head in my lap.

Will you do something for me? he said.

I would do anything for you, I said, keeping my voice bright and ironic so that even if he remembered the words he would always wonder whether they had been a joke.

Don't be jealous of Rose, he said.

A few minutes later he fell asleep, despite the 1010 WINS playing at top volume, and his head sunk into my thighs. I brushed the tops of his bristles with my fingers, felt his skin under the hair, drew stars with my fingers on his skull the way I used to draw them on fogged-up car windows. He did not stir. When the cab pulled up in front of his building in Cobble Hill, I tapped his elbow with my middle finger three times—pressing E on the keys of a piano, testing the depth of its tones. He sat up, slowly, took a breath, and pushed it out through puffed cheeks. I got out of the cab and handed three twenties to the driver.

You don't have to do that, he said, staring at me across the hood of the car.

Too late, I said.

I think I'm almost sober again but I want to sit here until I know for sure, he said, once we entered the brownstone. He sat down on the heavy wood stairs in the vestibule. A green carpet, tough as Astroturf, stained, its fibers fraying, covered the floor, and the humidity of the night mingled with the years of stale cigarette smoke trapped in the white stucco walls—smoke that might have already been stale the year we were born. I took a seat three steps below him, and turned my body so that I could curl up and rest my head on his lap. All I could see were his knees, his Doc Martens, and the carpet, and because his face was hidden from mine it made me bold.

Tell me what you think of me, I said.

He laughed. *I think you know.*

I could tell you what I think about you, I said, and did.

I think you idealize people, he said, when I finished. But he sounded a little unsure of his own interpretation, and I had felt him listening, absorbing the sound, sitting quietly, as if listening to a fire or waves.

I think you spend too much time trying to protect yourself, I said.

Well, he said. Then: *You don't miss a thing, so I have to believe you.*

I don't want to go home, I said, made even bolder by his compliment.

I don't want to hurt you.

How would you hurt me?

I'll never come back here, and you'll never leave.

Someone on the floor above opened a door. Neither of us moved or spoke. Karl turned his head toward the top of the stairs. The person listened for a second and shut the door, quietly. Now we whispered.

And I don't think you really want to be involved with anyone, he said.

He might have been right—I might have only wanted to be involved with him—but I would not admit it. I said:

Well, now you've hurt me, so you might as well sleep with me.

He laughed again. *I break it, I buy it?*

Something like that.

Don't be hurt, Charlotte. His voice, my name. It turned the word into a kiss. *I didn't mean it as an insult.*

A passing siren forced a pause.

I don't want to go home, I said.

You can come up, but I—

That's fine, I said, and it was, because I would do anything for him.

He led me up the stairs to his apartment—hot, stuffy, unsurprisingly neat, sparsely furnished—and then up to the doorway of his bedroom, which was just big enough for a full-size bed and a sliver of a wooden nightstand. He took off all his clothes. I felt him watching as I took off mine.

You don't get to watch, I said.

It's too bad we'll never get to the part where you boss me around and I like it, he said, still watching.

Yes, especially because we've already gotten to the part where you boss me around and I like it.

Very funny, as usual, he said, and climbed on top of the bed.

I followed. We shifted to face each other. His pale skin, the moon turning his long body longer. Eyes searching and alert. Then he faced the wall, brought my left arm around his waist, and said *Now don't let go.* The last thing

I remember: nestling up close to him, as close as I could get, the front of my knees locked into the back of his, burying my face in his shoulder blades, thinking that his skin smelled like skies heavy with rain.

In the morning, I dressed in the living room then walked around his apartment committing everything to memory. All the scavenged and borrowed furniture seemed to hang together despite having been scavenged and borrowed— even the table in the kitchen, round, pebbled-glass top, white metal rim, white wrought iron legs, that had clearly been designed for a concrete patio. An empty French press sat on top. Of course a French press: an affectation, but one that helped him avoid waste of both materials and electricity. Although that kind of prudence was its own affectation, too. The couch and the pot holders and the dish towels were all navy blue, just like his bedspread and his sheets. As if any departure from that color, anywhere, would make too loud a noise in the forest of his enemy. Examined the pictures of his sisters and his brothers and his mother that sat on the mantel of the marble ghost of a fireplace. Everyone looked like they could take a joke, which made me wonder, for a split second, whether Karl had been adopted. Walked back and forth in front of the bookshelves to see if they would tell me something I didn't already know. They didn't. I pulled a book down from the shelf to see what his marginalia would say.

SMUG PRICK, he'd written in his usual small caps on a page of a volume of Lacan's seminars: *On Feminine Sexuality, the Limits of Love and Knowledge.* Karl. I put it in my bag. I needed a souvenir and I'd been meaning to read it for years. Then I left. To stay would be to beg.

On the walk home I crossed over the Union Street bridge and stopped to look out at the algaed surface of the canal, at the tarped-up boats that appeared to be operational houseboats or might be floating coffins, the low brick buildings, the water towers, the clouds. I could never not stop and look whenever I crossed over that bridge. It was a poisoned body of water, but a body of water all the same, its conversation with the sky forcing stillness on all the speed around us. This view and its bricked-up silences sufficed for beautiful, for me, and if this was how I felt about the city's neglected corners and its wastelands, Karl might be right: I would never leave.

Back in my apartment, just as I opened the door, the phone rang. I picked it up.

So did he propose to you or what? said Rose.

I burst into tears.

You really did love him more than I did, she said, as I cried.

So she had been testing me. So she had loved him, too. Or did she mean something else? Rose kept talking. She told me to meet her at our usual place in an hour so we could, she said, go over every bit of what happened between when I left her and when I picked up the phone, and on the walk over I talked myself out of any suspicion or anger. The person I really could not live without was Rose, I thought, so I would pretend that I had not heard her, as she was pretending she had not hidden true feelings from me. I needed to believe that we were indeed not just anybody, and that one of the ways we were indeed not just anybody was that we wanted to be happy for each other rather than jealous of each other. Men would come and go. They were not the point. They were not the point.

Karl sent an email later that night—three lines that did not require a reply.

> Very unsentimental exit, that. I approve.
> Your fan,
> K

7.

We wrote. Rose assumed the position of freelance journalist
and I was—well, I was something between freelance journalist and critic, and my beat was the long-dead or over-
looked female genius. None of what we wrote mattered,
in the end. What mattered was the fact that we were just
about able to live off our freelancing.

When I wasn't conducting what I called séances in
print, or writing what my editors called critical essays with
a dash of the personal, I interviewed musicians, writers,
filmmakers, and artists for websites that no longer exist.
Rose wrote cover profiles and trend stories for women's
magazines. If women were pole dancing in the name of
empowerment, or taking up any other overtly feminine
art or wile that had previously been disowned or frowned
upon by feminists, but was now being reclaimed by feminists, or the feminist-adjacent, in what the editors wanted
everybody to think were vast hordes, Rose was there. This
being just before and just after the year 2000, there was a
lot of that kind of thing going on—partially, Rose and I
used to think, a return-of-the-repressed situation brought
on by the decades we'd just spent having to prove how
much like men we were, how desireless and rational we
were, in order to be taken seriously.

I couldn't write what Rose wrote—couldn't handle being strong-armed and sworn at by publicists, or being rung up by irate women in Florida and Wisconsin who claimed they'd never said what had been printed when they most certainly had and there was tape to prove it—but Rose could. Actually, as Rose liked to point out, it wasn't that I *couldn't*, it was that I refused, and she was right. I used to tell her that being raised by women who showed their love purely through shouting did more for her career than if she had gone to Yale.

Famous people loved her. Once in L.A. an actress asked her if she could stay over for a few days in her Malibu house because, as the actress said, Rose's eyes didn't ask her to be anything other than the child of God she knew she really was. Another time, in another Malibu house, a queen of rock in the middle of her mudslide toward obsolescence stole Rose's stretched-out, clearance-rack, sad black cardigan from Loehmann's while Rose was in the bathroom and then tried to make up for it by pushing a blood-stained designer slip dress on her in exchange. A legendary pirate of an actor wanted to fly her out for a weekend in Tahoe, told her he'd arranged for one ticket to be left at the United counter at JFK, and she went. Bought expensive underwear, got her blond hair polished to a platinum, got a pedicure, but he spent the whole time talking about the actress who'd just dumped him. *It was like Holden Caulfield with the prostitute*, Rose said, not without amusement, from the hotel room she had evacuated herself to.

I was monologuing to you in my head the whole time, she used to say, whenever she came back from these assignments, and I loved nothing more than to sit with her in her apartment, or my apartment, or some bar, some restaurant, listening to her unpack these absurd souvenirs from Los Angeles, London, or the Lower East Side. The singer in the band who called her whenever he came to town. The actor who wanted to spend all day with her looking at records after his interview ended. The screenwriter who wanted to spend all day with her looking at records after his interview ended. The married director who found himself calling Rose in the town car from the airport to talk about that week's *New York Review of Books*.

None of this stuff is real, Rose would sometimes say of these interactions. While she liked the attention from these men, she was under no illusion that any of her stories meant anything more than diversion, flattery, amusement, or more evidence of the varieties of human experience.

When she started talking like this, I would say, *Well, do you want to be married?*

Oh God no, she'd reply.

Neither did it make me jealous that she could leave a bar at nine o'clock at night, go home to bang out something in three hours, and then sleep like a baby where I might still stay up all night obsessing—I knew that's what it was—over a handful of sentences. It didn't make me jealous that editors called her up to write and my phone never rang. It didn't make me jealous that she appeared on panels and even showed up occasionally on television— getting in fights with famous conservative pundits about breastfeeding in public, or with famous second-wave feminists about the legitimacy of Madonna as an icon of female empowerment. Or that all of this came to her because she cared more about getting the work out there and less about the objective worth of the work.

No, I rooted for Rose like she was the Mets. I rooted

for Rose because it meant our team was winning. No men and no parents with money to help us, and we were winning.

If Rose hadn't been Rose, and we hadn't been friends, this never would have happened: Waking up naked and alone on a Sunday in Palm Springs, in a house that some band had filled with coke and a cast of thousands one weekend, crawling around on my hands and knees in a beige-carpeted, already-sweltering bedroom in the early morning before everyone else was up, looking for my clothes, and when I stopped for a second to try to think where else they might be, Rose hissed my name from underneath the bed, and I screamed, but everyone was still so passed out they didn't hear me, and they didn't hear her either, cackling, as she squirmed her way out from under it, still fully clothed, platforms still on, and told me the story of how she got there, which told me how I'd gotten there: Rose was tired and drunk and wanted to hide from the drummer who had not taken any of her hints, some of which were outright insults, and the singer, who kept telling everyone I reminded him of the girl who copied *Standing on a Beach* for him onto a ninety-minute Maxell tape in 1987, wanted to get away from the drummer, who earlier that night had told him he'd never be as good as Prince, and the singer and I ended up in a room that appeared to be unoccupied, but then I kicked him out into the long desert of a hallway and locked the door behind him because I was naked and drunk and all he wanted to do was talk about how much it killed him that he'd never be as good as Prince. He might have actually started crying; I can no longer actually remember. Rose told me that at one point she heard me tell him *Yeah, well, okay, that's fine, I'll never be Jane Austen either, so why don't we just get down to business?*

Rose used to call that her favorite Charlotte story.

Because I was not yet Jane Austen, I started reporting on what Rose and I used to call female trouble for one of the women's magazines she wrote for—birth control, hormones, depression, anxiety, breast cancer, ovarian cancer, cervical cancer, Pap smears, pregnancy, breastfeeding, in vitro fertilization. It seemed not to matter that I didn't want children or that I wasn't really sure where my clitoris was. I figured out how to read a scientific study and how to get what I needed out of doctors and researchers in one phone call. Although it was technically Margaret Byrne who wrote those pieces. That was the byline I used—my father's mother's maiden name. It was also the byline I told editors to use when I submitted copy to the fancy travel magazine a friend had put me in touch with. The irony: in the last ten years of her life, my grandmother never once left the house. Was it irony, or was it a Mass said in memory of her reclusive soul? I loved being able to call Rose up and say *Pack your bags, we're going to Berlin!* Or Buenos Aires or Glasgow or Miami. Poland, the Czech Republic, Japan. Mexico, the South of France. While I really did love traveling—another form of levitation from real life—there was something dutiful in my march, and Rose used to make fun of my underlined and dog-eared Rough Guides, which I read at night like novels.

I took any assignment anyone gave me because I was haunted by Rose's story about the TA and the Snickers bar. I thought about that Snickers bar a lot. As a consequence I spent more time trying not to be broke than writing the kinds of pieces I believed I was capable of. It worried me until I received a note from an eighty-five-year-old critic whose work I'd grown up admiring. It said:

In lieu of "mentoring" you—patronizing to you and exhausting for me—I enclose the following command. You must do nothing but write.

Somewhere in this period I moved, for the first time, into an apartment by myself. A junior one bedroom between Fourth and Fifth Avenues in Park Slope. To be able to live alone, in such a quiet, light-filled, tree-shaded trio of rooms, for $850 a month—I felt incredibly lucky. I woke up to birds. So many birds, in the spring, it was as if the tree outside my front windows held one hundred nine-year-old girls on a Skittles high. I could hear myself think. Standing in my kitchen, drinking coffee from a percolator that my father's mother had given me when she learned I was moving to the city, I could stare at the tomatoes and roses out back grown by my landlady's mother, whom I lived above, and didn't care that they were not mine to touch. I could stare at the backs of buildings and raise my eyes to miles of blue sky.

When I dropped off one of my first rent checks, Mrs. Rivera, whose husband had moved their family to Park Slope from Puerto Rico in 1959, and who had raised five children in the house where she now sat, due to MS, in a wheelchair, grasped my hand, stared into my eyes, and said *I like you. You're quiet, like me, and you don't smoke.*

I like you, too, I said, surprised. Happy, too, and grateful that she approved of me. *Thank you for letting me live here.*

She closed her eyes and waved the hand that was not holding mine, as if to say *Please, it's nothing.*

And when my mind was not ticking away productively in the quiet, it crackled with anxiety as I lay in bed or rode the subway trying to calculate which checks from which assignment would go toward what bill, what beans, what dentist's appointment.

None of this stuff is real, I would sometimes say of the articles I published. I couldn't pretend that my writing was going to get me where I needed it to. It would not get me the PhD I'd abandoned. It would not get me confused for Elizabeth Hardwick no matter how hard I tried. I had nothing, really, to say—only the compulsion to say something and get paid for it. The furiously highlighted and underlined books sitting out on my desk, books ruffled with brightly colored Post-its, looking like a sky full of birds exploding in midair, were nothing but a symptom.

Whenever I said things like this, Rose would give me a look and pointedly change the subject.

Meanwhile, we tore through men like they were shitty six-packs. As if someone had told us it was our job. We thought we were having it all. We might have been taking revenge against all the young men at the publications of record. Such as the one sitting on the lower rungs of a storied masthead who told me they already had one moderately talented girl writing about her feelings. The one who said he hoped I understood but he had to go with the writer with name recognition who'd pitched the same story. That happened a lot. The one who told Rose the same thing. The other one who told Rose the same thing. The one who told Rose she shouldn't write so much for women's magazines. The one who told Rose she wasn't a journalist, she was a therapist. The one who told Rose she needed to write some stories with statistics before he assigned her anything. The one who said he couldn't see me writing about the fight over a stadium that might go up in my backyard in Brooklyn, but he could see me writing about this porn site he'd heard about that was run by women for women. The one who liked to rewrite my book reviews without telling me and then put his name on it if he estimated that only about a quarter of my original sentences remained. And his cubicle mate, who at yet another party said he could assign us a threesome.

Has that line ever worked for you? I asked him, as Rose walked off, back to us, middle finger thrown up like a punch.

Once, he said. *It's a numbers game.*

It was funny enough, so I slept with him. To prove he didn't bother me. That none of them did.

Rose and I never talked about the actual sex as much as we talked about the people we had it with. The sex, frequently, was not much to talk about, what with everyone drunk and tired and holding their cards close to their chest, and it could pale in comparison to the moment you realized that both your mind and your body had yet again proved irresistible, and you were going to sleep with them—the fires that climbed, the electricity that blazed, in the elevators, in the cabs, in the bars, on the street, in the corner of party after party. That feeling of, as Rose used to say, *Game on, motherfucker.* Of knowing you had closed yet another deal.

Tell me everything, she'd say. *Start at the beginning, and don't skimp on the details. Where did you meet him, what did he smell like, and where did he grow up? What did he order, how much does he hate his father while also knowing that he already is his father, that kind of thing, and all of it.* And I obliged, was happy to oblige, was almost giddy while obliging as I told her about the band managers, booking agents, publicists, adjunct professors, many adjunct professors, and many former graduate students who'd turned their backs on academia before it could turn its back on them.

Sometimes, I said, *it's just like eating a bag of Cheetos. No more, no less.*

Rose laughed. *You're hungry, you're bored, you go out to the kitchen, to a bar, a party, whatever, and think to yourself, what's in the cupboard?*

Exactly! So then sometimes I wonder why even bother. You go out to a party, it's all the same stuff, in the same fridge.

They're Cheetos, she said. *They taste good.*

Sometimes these stories involved married men. I never once worried about their wives. I never once imagined any of them would fall in love with me so hard they'd have to worry about their wives. And I was shocked to find myself so undisturbed by what I might have once called my amorality. Not so shocked that I did anything about it, however.

I don't feel bad, I told Rose. *At all.*

Why should you? said Rose. *You could even be doing their marriage a favor.*

I gave her a look.

You know I'd tell you if I thought you were doing something wrong, she said.

We were twenty-nine. We felt absolutely free. And in this way we felt stupidly rich.

Until Rose received a letter from the children of the owner of the brownstone she lived in. She'd been living above an aging matriarch as well, an Italian woman whose family had owned a coffee-roasting business that had been in the neighborhood since 1946 and was barely hanging on, and in the wake of their mother's recent death, they wrote, they had decided to sell the building, and would put it on the market at the end of the month. She called me in a panic. She had no savings and the grandmother, who loved Rose, and in fact sometimes confused Rose with her daughter, had been waiving her rent.

What? I said. Loudly. As if she'd told me she'd been arrested for embezzlement. *Why didn't you tell me?*

Stop shrieking, said Rose.

Oh really?

Okay, okay. I'm sorry. I'm just—would you have told me if you were in the same position?

No, I said, *I probably wouldn't*. Which was a lie. I definitely would have, but that was beside the point. It wasn't the time to ask her where the money went, either—who knows where the money goes in New York, especially if you have better things to do than to follow every bounce of a quarter down into the gutter? It wasn't the time to ask if the shoes, and the coats, and the handbags were actually bought on sale. It was an opportunity to show Rose—really, to show myself, because on many days I was desperately afraid that my heart was a defective piece of machinery—that I was strong enough, responsible enough, and generous, loyal, and forgiving enough to lean on. That I was a true sister. A mother, even: throwing open the door and asking no questions.

I told her that, pending approval from Mr. Rivera, my landlord, she could stay with me, rent-free, so she could save up some money, if she didn't mind that it was not a huge place. Rose, hyperventilating, said *Thankyouthankyouthankyou.* I hung up on her fourth *Thankyou* and called Mr. Rivera, who said it was fine by him, the two of us was nothing, he'd had a woman living with her two kids up there in the years before I came along, but I needed to ask his mother. Concepción. *She's the boss,* he said.

Las chicas. That's what Mrs. Rivera called us, whenever we went to Key Food to get her groceries because her home health care aide had a migraine, or swept the stoop or shoveled snow off the stoop, or presented her with red tulips just because it was spring and they looked so beautiful blooming in plastic buckets outside the bodega and we felt lucky that she liked us. *Las chicas.*

Rose and I took turns sleeping on a pullout couch I bought from the classified ads in the *Voice,* and while I wrote at my desk, she wrote at the kitchen table—a red-edged Formica number, inherited from Tracy, that stood on spindly chrome legs freckled with rust. Rose typing: a continuous, insistent clatter, the keyboard beaten up like a forty-eight-hole Whac-a-Mole. Charlotte typing: shooting off intermittent gunfire every two minutes, occasionally broken up by a testy punching of the delete key. Typing Monday to Friday, or through Saturday and Sunday if Thursday had been too festive, and drinking too much Café Bustelo with cinnamon, which is how Mrs. Rivera took her coffee, or so I deduced from the bright yellow cans I saw in the recycling bags and the scent that rose up from her basement kitchen every morning since I'd moved in.

After Rose and I married, both our homes smelled frequently, if not primarily, of coffee and cinnamon, and I sometimes wonder if the houses that Rose's daughters preside over will smell the same.

At the time, we were incredibly pleased with ourselves. We thought we were outwitting someone or something and further planting our flag on some battlement in the process. So I ignored the expensive makeup and moisturizers that started showing up in the bathroom cabinet. It made me sad, not angry, to watch these open secrets pop up above and around the sink like a little forest of mushrooms. What my mother's mother used to call the devil must have been lurking around Rose's premises if she thought she needed all this armor now, when we were still a couple of honeydew melons. If she thought so little of her future that she'd rather blow her money than save it. But how could I tell Rose what to do with her money? I was not a parent or a spouse or the IRS. I could not tell Rose what to do with her money, but I could be even more responsible with mine.

A website I wrote for needed someone to fill in for an editor who was on maternity leave. Nine to five, technically, and five days a week, but probably way more than that. Did I want to come help out? asked the man who edited me. The executive editor. Yes, I told him.

Just rewrite them, the executive editor told me as I sat in his office fuming, my first week, over the lazy rambling copy people who sat at home writing in their pajamas routinely turned in. I'd sat at home, too, doing the same thing, but never ever in pajamas and never once with this level of blithe apathy. *They know that's what you're going to do, and they know we'll pay them anyway. That's why they turn in piles of shit.*

I enjoyed the feeling of omnipotence it gave me, translating someone else's incoherence into five thousand or two thousand or five hundred words suitable to print, and I would stay there late, entranced, until I made the text say the thing everyone thought it would say when it was pitched, and in the voice of the writer who'd pitched it. Everyone was happy, and if the writer wasn't, I didn't care because it was their laziness and entitlement, more often than not, that had led us to this place. *Your fault, not mine*, I sang to myself as I wrote them firm and chipper emails.

Rose liked to come by the office at the end of the day, which was sometimes nine o'clock, and go through the advance copies and advance CDs piling up on the free table. The free table being the top of a large gray filing cabinet sitting outside my office where the editors dumped all the unwanted books and records they'd been sent by publicists in the hopes that they would be mentioned on the site. Part landfill, part Portobello Road. *This way to Crap Mountain*, the executive editor's assistant wrote on the back of a piece of letterhead, in black Sharpie, and taped above the pile. Whenever a therapist has tried to convince me that it's an achievement to have published any book at all, I always think about that pile of galleys outside that office, and the flood of advance copies sent to Rose and myself at the apartment, and how dozens, maybe hundreds, of those galleys ended up in blue plastic recycling bags out on my street, Rose swearing when we had to heave those heavy bags out to the curb, and how it all amounted to a copious pile of evidence pointing to the fact that actually, anybody could publish any damn thing at all.

You're a mountain lion, remember, said Rose, as she sat

in a folding chair in my office, waiting for me to finish composing an email to a writer who liked to throw fits over minuscule word changes. *Don't let them turn you into a house cat.*

One of my jobs was editing the book critic, and the first time I called her up with questions and edits we ended up on the phone for an hour talking about *The Virgin Suicides* and Destiny's Child and Christa Wolf and Monica Lewinsky and Britney Spears. *You're fun to talk to*, she said at the end of our first conversation on the phone. *How old are you again?* Lynn. Irish, from Omaha, who escaped to New York in 1970 to be free, and, because she was what she called pretty enough and talented enough, she'd been able to finagle her way into writing for all the places she'd set her sights on, and had been able to end up in bed with most of the men she set her sights on. Men whose bylines still showed up regularly everywhere while Lynn's showed up only on the website. She also taught at NYU. But the articles for the site and the teaching weren't enough money, so she worked for a transcription service on the weekends. She'd been a Kelly Girl in college and could type eighty words a minute.

On a night when the executive editor and I and the vacuum were the only noises left in the office, he stood in my doorway telling me that he and Lynn and the editor-in-chief used to work at *Rolling Stone* together, and that he thought the editor-in-chief felt some need to protect her, that maybe she owed Lynn a favor, or something bigger than that, and so she hired Lynn and the rule here was that no one could mess with Lynn's copy.

No one mentioned that to me. I had definitely been messing with Lynn's copy, and was somewhat mortified.

I knew she'd take you seriously, he said, and walked away. The executive editor, who wore button-down shirts tucked into his jeans to assert and solidify his authority. Graying, tall, impassive, laconic, like a farmer who'd for centuries watched crops wither and watched crops flourish, and knew that if there were gods watching over the harvest, they would certainly not be moved by hysterics. He would sometimes leave a packet of peanut M&M's on my desk in the late afternoon. Unsigned, but I knew they'd come from him. Everyone else in that office was too busy trying to get a job at the *Times*.

Lynn read a piece of mine online and was so impressed by it she mentioned it to the editor-in-chief. *This one's a real writer* is what she said. Over the phone Lynn and I discovered that we both loved a big old wedding cake of a department store, as well as the very particular feeling of calm that could be conjured by standing in a sea of glittering cosmetic counters or gazing out over a field of matronly bras and nude-colored briefs, your anxieties muted through the soothing puzzle offered by limitless choice. So I took her out for lunch every week, at either Saks or Lord & Taylor. We'd order Cobb salads the size of potholes and a bottle of the cheapest white wine on the list, and when I signed the check I felt a competence and omnipotence similar to what I felt when I rewrote a lazy paragraph, even though it was my own debit card I was using to pay the bill. The managing editor told me I couldn't expense these lunches because I wasn't a real editor, so I wrote them off on my taxes instead. Lynn told me I should.

Every time we met she showed up in black sweatpants and a black sweatshirt under a Vivienne Westwood trench coat. Penny loafers, no socks, or cowboy boots. Lynn's signature scent: one cigarette smoked outside in the cold and Annick Goutal's Ce Soir ou Jamais. She was my height, exactly, skinny, with thick auburn hair pulled back in a bun. She wore no makeup on her face but her nails gleamed dark red. An excommunicated mother superior; Madame X incognito in exile was how I described her to Rose. The oracle of Lower Broadway is what Rose, who demanded a dramatic reenactment of every conversation I had with Lynn, called her. Rose thought she was crazy. I worried that myself, but I thought it was my feminist duty to refuse to imagine that inside each highly intelligent unmarried woman of a certain age lived a Bertha Rochester three missed periods away from setting the house on fire.

The first thing Lynn said to me, that first lunch, after we ordered: *If you want to keep on writing you need to marry a lawyer. Don't give me that look! It won't make you any less of a feminist. We've been able to turn stripping into a feminist act, so why can't it be feminist to marry a lawyer to get your own work done?*

I was too pure to marry a lawyer. Don't be too pure for too long.

Never get involved with anyone who never got the love he needed from his mother. Don't even get into bed with them.

Grunge always sounded like whining to me.

Philip Roth? I will go to my grave having never read a word of him, and I suggest you do the same.

Always make sure you have fuck-you money—that's what someone once told me and I'm passing it on to you. I mean a stash of cash that'll let you take off should you ever need to get out of a situation you once thought was Camelot.

I now recognize Lynn's style of conversing—the style

you arrive at when you spend too much time by yourself, so much so that you forget that other people's thoughts don't go about that naked in public.

Lynn lived with her mother in a loft in SoHo. A painter bought the loft for her in the eighties when he learned he'd gotten her pregnant at the precise moment he'd proposed to the daughter of an even more famous painter. Rose and I used to love talking about whether this meant he loved Lynn more. Did Hamlet love Ophelia?

No, you don't get to know who the painter was, Lynn told me, when I asked. *It won't tell you anything about me that you can't learn from my writing.*

After these lunches, I'd stand outside the entrance to whatever store we'd been perched in and, once I saw that she'd been definitively swallowed up by the crowds on Fifth or Madison, write down everything she'd said in the back blank pages of whatever book was currently in my bag, or as much as I could on the insides of my hands, if I had nothing to write on. I might not have been as discreet as I thought.

The last thing Lynn said to me, over the phone: *I'm going to ask the executive editor to handle my copy from now on. No, no arguing. It's nothing personal. Purely archetypical. You can always use my name like a credit card anywhere, if you think they'll accept it. I just can't look at your face anymore. You listen too closely.*

This isn't your fault, the executive editor told me. Lynn had given a daughter up for adoption back in Nebraska, and this wasn't the first time she'd taken a young woman under her wing only to fly off after getting too close. *This is my fault*, he said. *I forgot this could happen.*

The woman I was hired to replace had decided to stay at home with her newborn, and the editor-in-chief called me into her office to offer me the job. A big glass desk; bookshelves loaded and stretching to the ceiling. She paid me several concise and sincere-seeming compliments on my writing. One piece, in particular, she said, had her thinking of David Foster Wallace.

You can't be serious, I thought to myself, and then *Don't mind if I do* and *Is there more where that came from?* I paid her wordy but sincere compliments on the depth and verve of the writing on the site.

I just want to make sure you want to do this. What about time for your writing?

Oh, I said, trying to sound dismissive. Trying to give the impression of someone who could take it or leave it, who knew that things came and they went, who knew that money mattered more than art, who could embody breeziness and detachment when she was actually single-minded and a bit obsessed. And because I felt we were speaking honestly, and because I thought I should experiment further with this breeziness, I got the idea that I should be clear about what I might need from the position, like all the women's magazines said you should.

So I said: *How possible would it be for a person to take a kind of maternity leave if they happened to get a book deal while on staff?*

I don't think you could argue that a book has the same social value as having a child, she said. Impersonally, offhandedly, as if she had not been conversing with someone who wrote. As if we were not sitting in a city that had been sold to us as a crucible for liberation and self-invention.

Then what are you doing with an office full of them? I said. She appeared amused.

You shouldn't take this job, she said. *Let someone with less ambition have it.* She might have been affirming me in my quixotic pursuit; she might have been telling me to get the hell out of her office. I thanked her for her time and rose from my seat.

That night, I spent many hours in a bar in Brooklyn listening to Rose and our friends decrying the editor's words. Our friends, who, like us, had grown up believing that work would allow us to be free, and keep us that way, talked of Susan Sontag and her notion of being freelance—of being an intellectual entity unencumbered by allegiances that could hamper our intellectual production. No one could say that they owned us. Could the editor, shackled to her blowouts and her big glass desk, say that? They talked about William James and his notion of the unbribed soul, because we prided ourselves on being women who owed nothing to no person or entity, to no man or corporation, and they pitied the editor for her laughably retrograde view. *What year are we in?* I heard someone say.

Tell them that insane thing Lynn said about marrying a lawyer, said Rose.

You tell them, I said.

8.

A friend had asked me to speak on a panel organized by a literary magazine I'd written for—the question being whether romance and feminism were mutually exclusive. She'd invited an economist, a philosopher, a poet who had become famous for writing a memoir about her dead sister, and me. I was the cultural critic, she said. My name was not as well-known as theirs, and I had not put myself in front of an audience since graduate school, so I spent hours filling a document with passages from thinkers and writers who could speak to that question, hours reading too much and typing too many words that, as I read back over them, seemed to be mostly about the failures of the sexual revolution. I discovered that on paper I sounded like an ambivalent beneficiary.

You sound unconvinced about the inherent value we ascribe to sexual freedom, said Rose, after reading through the notes, *but less sure about the value of—I guess the clinical term would be monogamy.*

I know, I said. *I am that confused. I don't know what the answer is.*

So which side are you on?

Why do I have to pick a side?

To sell the book you're writing here.

I had not thought of it that way.

And people love to think that any kind of critique of feminism, because that's essentially what this is, is automatically conservatism.

Yes, I know. I know. Would admitting to my confusion solve the problem?

Rose laughed. *Maybe. This is a mess, but you're definitely making me think harder than I usually do about my own bullshit, so thank you for that.*

I spent almost as many hours looking for a new dress to wear. Rose told me to buy the most expensive one, which was of course the only one I wanted: a black shirtdress, button-down, silk, shantung, from the fifties, flared skirt, tiny red roses on tiny green stems, priced at $250. From a vintage clothing store in the East Village that no longer exists—a claustrophobically enchanted forest on East Sixth Street whose Lilly Pulitzer dresses and leather jackets and fur coats and veiled hats and lamé dancing shoes excreted themselves like kudzu from the corners, the floor, and the doubled-up racks along the sea-green walls. The woman who owned it used to be a model in the seventies. Jeannie. She'd grown up in Florida and regularly flew back home for the estate sales that kept her in business. She had the voice of Rosalind Russell doing a Phyllis Diller impression, or the voice of Phyllis Diller doing a Rosalind Russell impression, and Rose and I often went into the store just to listen to her talk people into and out of whatever they were trying on. If I hadn't liked Jeannie so much I would have asked if she could lower the price.

Spend the money, Rose said, as I stared into the mirror at the front of the store. *That dress is definitely going to earn itself out.*

Listen to your friend, said Jeannie, who sat on a red

wooden stool behind a glass case full of charm bracelets, tie clips, scarf pins, and sunglasses. She'd been sifting through carbon copy receipts and typing on a calculator. *Never underestimate the allure of being buttoned up. Men love it. Loooooove it! Makes them feel like it's Christmas and you're the only present their drunk bastard father ever sent them.*

I bought it.

Did you write that down? said Rose, as we left the store.

I showed her the back of my receipt and the rollerballed scrawl. Then we walked to Veselka and drank coffee and picked at the same plate of pierogies for three hours, talking about how terrible I felt about Lynn and about how infuriated Rose was with the guy she wanted to break up with.

I'm starting to hate them all, she said.

The stage lights blinded me so that I could not see the faces of the crowd, could see only that there was a crowd. I didn't say much during the discussion, because the other young women sitting next to me were not talking about love as an emotional state, or sex in any way, shape, or form, but instead about the economic and political inequalities that affected, or afflicted, heterosexual romantic partnership: unequal pay, women's unpaid labor, the ethics of care, abysmal American maternity leave policies, the glorious state-sponsored compassion of European family leave. I knew these statistics, hated this state of things, but could not add, in any productive way, to this conversation. The other panelists were full of numbers and an intimate knowledge of labor law—even the poet, whom I sometimes envied more for her Edwardian mess of curls than her increasing fame. If you had hair like that, I thought, it would all but command you to make yourself seen and heard. I was bored; I was envious. I was also amused: here I sat, the lone doofus who had taken the assignment at face value while they had all, seemingly without planning on it, acted on herd instinct and run in the same direction for safety.

Or, as an agent had said to me earlier that week: *Do you really want to be known as a woman who only writes about sex?*

She'd taken me for a drink to see if I was someone worth representing, and wanted to know whose careers I envied. One of the writers I'd mentioned provoked that reaction.

Are you saying we get to choose? I said. *I think I just want to be known.*

Or, as the economist said, with comic exasperation, but also some bitterness, after reporting the number of hours women spent doing housework and then the number spent by men: *Is this what we get when we win?*

We had not won, I sat there thinking, if it was still much easier for a group of women to talk about numbers and policy than it was to say what they really thought about the energies at play between women and men when they asked too much of each other or asked nothing at all. Much safer. Not even the poet was willing to do it. If we did focus on the romantic and the psychological, they— we—I—could appear to lose sight of the political and economical and expose ourselves as narcissistic, quietist, sentimental, frivolous, adolescent, emotional. Fixated on the narrowest of subjects. They could be accused of getting too personal, and they'd expose their heart of hearts, which people might mock them for, because our heart of hearts might have never caught up to or conformed to our times, and the times, no matter what decade you were talking about, always seemed to demand nihilism and hedonism—or their distant cousin, emotional detachment. Or so it seemed to me, that night in 2003, when I was thirty.

The question and answer period arrived. A young woman, long pale blond hair, glasses, sitting, placidly, next to what was most likely a boyfriend, raised her hand and said, *I came here tonight because I thought we were going to talk about love.*

So did I, I said, and a few people in the audience laughed, and when I heard the laughter I started talking about why I thought we had all stuck to the facts and avoided the topic of feelings. I felt my mouth moving, felt people listening, felt them leaning into my words, felt them waiting for the next ones. I heard laughter once, and then again, and another time, and the stage lights warmed my face, turned me heliotropic. They drew me up tall and pared away fear. This was what it must be like for all those musicians I'd interviewed who went on and on about feeding off the energy of a crowd, I thought. I'd always rolled my eyes at them, but here was the adrenaline rush I'd heard them talk about, and the faces loved me, I could tell, and it felt a little like being tempted by Satan, to watch as you coaxed an audience into the palm of your hand, because if you were this good right now you knew you could get it all the time if you wanted to. And I wanted to, wanted to, wanted to.

But not badly enough. At some point during my monologue the economist laughed, too, but the poet, immediately to my right, had stiffened a bit and kept crossing and uncrossing her legs. I sensed disapproval, or displeasure, maybe even something you could call fuming, and her reaction was the only frequency I could tune in to. I ground to a halt and broke off midsentence.

I should let someone else talk, I said. I sat there listening to my ears ring and watching other people's mouths move.

Aren't you the cutest thing? said the poet to me, as the audience clapped and we stood up from our seats. I thought about the picture of her I'd seen in the *Times*, lying on her side in a green strapless gown on an antique settee, in someone's brownstone parlor floor, her hair swirling above her like a meringue, her rhinestoned cat-eye glasses letting her get away with looking much too much like an odalisque in the paper of record. Why should she have everything? No, what I really meant was: Why the fuck should this bitch like herself way more than I like myself?

Aren't you hostile? I said.

A look of surprise crossed her face. I wasn't so cute, after all.

I never saw the poet again—she became very famous and I did not—but what she said made a deeper cut than Karl's *I thought it was—sentimental*. I could interpret what Karl had said as *Change your sentences*. In that case I had been charged with a problem to solve, and if I knew how to hide my true self but reveal just enough of it, I could solve it. What she'd said sounded like *Who do you think you are?* and in that case my true self—its presumption, its shallowness, and its greed for attention and approval—was the problem, and the only way to solve it was by not writing at all. No reviewer of my books would ever be as forceful or perceptive in their praise as she was in her spite, and even though I didn't respect her, I chose to believe her. I wanted what she had so much of, which meant she must know something I never would, something no one had bothered to teach me, something that had not been spoken of in all the many books I'd read, and for a long time, every time I sat down to write, *Aren't you the cutest thing?* would pop up like one of those mechanical corpses coffined in the darkest corners of a boardwalk haunted house, and on very bad days it could make me stop typing altogether.

Why I chose, over and over, to believe my fears rather than believe in what people had called my talent, when I wanted so badly for people to know my name the way they now know the poet's—I'm still not entirely sure.

The look on that girl's face was priceless, Rose said, arms linked in mine, as we walked with some friends to a bar. *Amazing*, she called out to the cold sky over Twenty-Sixth Street. *It was like watching a woman watch another woman steal her boyfriend right out from under her.*

I stopped walking, unlinked my arm from hers, put my face in my hands, and groaned.

Oh who cares, she said, linking her arm back in mine and dragging me on. *You know that catching some hate from another woman is the only reliable way we have of knowing whether we're winning.*

Six months later, the agent and the $250 dress and I sat at a series of conference tables peopled with smiling faces, resounding with compliments, in a series of publishing houses in Midtown. My book, about a group of women artists who lived in New Mexico in the early twentieth century, didn't sell for much, because of the subject matter, and because the only people who wanted to publish it were other artistic and ambitious young women eating beans for dinner as they hustled to prove to their male bosses how unerring their instincts were. I didn't care about the money. The money was not the point. Making people know my name was the point. Talking with people and being public was the point, and if you wrote about dead people with fascinating lives, it would get you on NPR, so a few years after the first book came out I published a second, another group portrait of women who were, said the jacket copy, cultural revolutionaries. People loved to talk about women who had replaced marriage with a string of lovers, or had a string of lovers while also being married, or refused to play any of those games and went to live in literal or metaphorical deserts where they could be left alone to pursue an ideal or a vision. *We're all bottomless pits when it comes to the topic of sex*, said my agent. But my interest was more practical than prurient. How did these women say no to the world around them? When did they do it? Why did they do it? They couldn't help it—that often seemed to be the answer, and sometimes these women called their inability to get with the program feminism, and sometimes they vehemently refused to claim their victories for that cause. Why do we marry when we could be doing other things? That was the real question driving these books, and, I sometimes thought, the real question at the back of the minds of all the women interviewing me: Why do we still keep marrying?

9.

A few weeks after I sold my first book, Rose got pregnant. By a painter who'd taken an interest in her on a Saturday night, in a rambling, crumbling farmhouse up the Hudson. I sensed there was some slime at the bottom of his glassy pond, but a little bit of slime did not deter Rose. *Like mold on cheese*, she'd say. *If you're hungry enough, or bored enough, you're just going to cut it off and get to the parts you can swallow.*

Several hours later, she came to tell me she was going to spend the night with the painter, who lived in a shed on the property.

Come pick me up in the morning? she said. Her face made radiant by the joy of conquest.

But I didn't leave the party. I fell asleep, after a long conversation that I was hoping would end in sex, along with about fifteen other people, in the parlor, at around three in the morning, wrapped in a Pepto-pink acrylic afghan that did not smell too strongly of basement. Four hours later I woke to a room filled with gray light and the sound of a woman shouting outside the house. I wrapped myself in the afghan, crept over a few bodies, and looked through a window.

Out on the lawn Rose stood naked, arms crossed around her breasts, hunched over just a little, and shivering, because it was the last week of April and spring was still unsure of itself. Behind her, on the narrow strip of blacktop that separated the yard from a cornfield, a red flatbed truck sped by, honking its horn. Twenty feet away from her stood a woman who did not look American: short, tan, very slender, hair in a bun with a fringe of bangs across her forehead, and the white button-down and the jeans she'd tucked the shirt into were crisper and cleaner than most. It looked like Rose had been discovered in a bed she should not have been sleeping in and had been, with great force, routed from it. The woman started shouting again. Her accent was French, and now a chill ran through me: one of our worst nightmares involved being appraised and found wanting by the French, whom we venerated even as we sometimes suspected they were not relentlessly uncompromising but merely insane.

This is what people who are not free do, said the woman. *They take from others because they have no courage.*

I am free! said Rose.

Yes, yes, because you said it out loud in public. The woman threw up her hands and shrugged. *Yes, fine, you're free!*

I tiptoed over two more bodies and out the front door. Rose saw me on the porch and her face fell. The woman turned to see what Rose had seen and then turned back to Rose. The front door opened and I could tell that at least one other person was now out on the porch with me. I walked across the cold wet lawn and handed Rose the pink afghan. She ripped it out of my hands and, as she wrapped it around herself and ferociously tied two corners of it in a knot above her breasts, shouted, *If you were really free you wouldn't care who he fucked!*

No, the woman said, *I'm free because I know what I want*

and I never lose sight of it. Then she walked, calmly, toward the porch. The group of people standing there moved out of her way as she strode toward the door to the house.

If you hadn't seen that, Rose said in the car on the way back to the city, *I don't think I would ever have told you about it.*

I would have told you, I said.

I know, she said. *Because you're so fucking honest. You're so*—and here she stretched that one syllable out to mock me and my high, high horse—*perfect.*

Fuck you, I said. I'd never said that to anyone in my life.

I'm sorry, she said. *I'm not—*

Go find some assholes to be friends with, if you think I'm such a fucking drag.

I didn't say—

Fuck you, I said. *You're lucky I think there's nobody on earth like you.* I sounded just like my mother, and it killed me.

I'm sorry, she said. *I'm sorry.* She began to sob, and hunched over in her seat and cried so loudly my ears started to ring. In the five years we'd been friends, I'd never heard Rose cry. It broke my heart and wiped all my hurt feelings away. I pulled into a Taco Bell parking lot that looked out over a traffic circle that looked out over strip malls slung as low as the rain clouds starting to move in.

I'm a mess, she sobbed. *I'm such a fucking mess. What is wrong with me?* All of it sounded like an argument she had been having with herself since she was small.

Rose! I said. *You are not a mess. You're a poem!*

She cried harder. I sat there with my hand on her back, looking away from her and out at the strip malls so that she could have a little bit of privacy as she cried, filling with rage at all the women who knew their own mind and had no pity for those who had mistaken the insistent voice of desire for a needle on a compass.

When the tears came to a stop she sat up, slowly. After staring through the windshield for a bit, she said:

What if deep down we're really just good girls?

I did not know how to answer that question. It was one of my deepest fears, too.

Say something, said Rose.

When I finally spoke I said: *Why do we think that's the worst thing we could possibly be?*

I could feel Rose thinking beside me. *Kathy Acker,* she said, and I laughed, really loud, almost cackled, and she laughed, too. *Or the patriarchy. Or Kathy Acker was brought to us by the patriarchy.*

We may never know, I said, and started the car.

I'll eat Taco Bell for breakfast if you will, Rose said, and I pulled up to the drive-through window.

And then her period was late. It was not the first time in her life she'd gotten pregnant when she did not intend to, and she was more pissed than anything else—pissed at herself, pissed at the guy, pissed at his wife, pissed that the doctor who'd administered her last abortion was no longer practicing. Pissed at me for asking why they didn't use a condom. What really bothered her, she said, what really made her feel sorry for herself, was that she didn't have the money to pay for it: a few articles killed, too many paychecks tied up in back offices, and not enough pitches accepted to make up for it. That's what she said was making her pissed, and I took her at her word. I immediately offered to pay for the abortion. Rose refused, but it was the obligatory refusal of the proud and cornered, and I signed that check for $650 like I was signing the Declaration of Independence. To this day it remains the most politically useful act of my life. I still believe that, even though Rose later told me that it had cost only $350.

Rose, asleep on the couch in the days after, napping profusely, while I cooked and wrote and worried about her. About the both of us, and maybe I worried a little bit more for myself than I did for Rose. It hadn't just been Rose standing naked on a stranger's lawn as another woman scolded her for reaching too low when Rose thought she had been reaching as high as she could—that was me standing there, too, and the longer Rose slept, the longer I thought about how I'd bailed her out twice now, and how I'd been the one to try for steadier work when she was the one flailing, about how she didn't seem to feel moved, at all, to get steadier work in the wake of her flailing, no, that was me, and some feelings of superiority began to make themselves known, which I did not like, at all. I told myself that I did not have to be Rose if I could help it. And I could help it, by looking for a teaching job: regular pay, summers off. I'd been a TA in graduate school and liked it, had even been told I was good at it, and it no longer seemed wise, if it ever had, to depend on my writing to pay the rent or get me out of a sexually induced jam.

A woman can be stupid, Rose said from the couch, one Saturday afternoon while I typed at my desk, *and a woman can be broke, but she can't be both at the same time.*

Where'd you get that from? I turned to look at her. *Your grandmother?*

Here, she said, tapping her forehead.

I'm writing that down so you don't forget you said it.

The next morning when Rose came into the kitchen for coffee I told her I'd had an idea: she should get a proposal together for a book full of sayings from her grandmother— well, a book that she could *posit* as a collection of sayings from her grandmother, but one that in reality she would fill up with stuff that just *sounded* like it could be utterances from someone who had begun life swaddled in a dresser drawer on the Lower East Side and ended it in a plot in the Locust Valley Cemetery on the North Shore of Long Island. She ran out of the kitchen, brought her laptop back to the table, sat down, flipped it open, and said, *What was that thing I said last night?*

She spent a week drafting a proposal. Sometimes she'd ask me to help and then my own grandmother found her way into the pages. The line Rose had thrown out on the couch became the book's first sentence, and a friend put her in a touch with an agent and she sold it, the book would be paperback only, not hardcover, for enough money to move out into her own apartment—five blocks away—and pay me back for the abortion.

To celebrate I made a reservation for dinner at the Gramercy Tavern. Rose and I had a fondness—a weakness?—for the kind of room that flattered your good taste by never becoming smug or uptight about its own, and we thought this one was the apex of the genre. We'd been taken there for drinks by men in the twilight of their prime and agents at the dawn of their ascent, and whenever we sat at the bar we felt as if we'd been asked to sit for a portrait that would one day prove legendarily bewitching. Cosseted by all that dark wood and warm light, the city flowing like a river past the abundance of glass that lined Twentieth Street, the city at its most becalmed and amiable, a person might be forgiven for thinking all New York really wanted to do was to reach out and bless you, or otherwise caress you. But Rose did not feel like rising to the occasion that night. We'd just been brought the first of what I assumed were going to be several glasses of champagne when she said:

This place is too good for the book I just sold.

Rose. But I knew what she meant. The book had been written not for love but for money.

It's a check, and I needed it, but your book's going to be a real book.

We'll see about that, I said, pretending not to sound as guilty as I felt. I thought of something else to say, something I thought I wouldn't have to work too hard to believe. *I will never tell you that you have to feel grateful for selling it.*

Good, she said. *I don't.*

Her immediate and unrepentant refusal to pay any respect to her good fortune—to even pretend to pay any respect to it—made an immediate and cranky liar out of me.

Okay, I said, *maybe try just a little bit harder to act like you're at least relieved that you're not totally broke anymore.*

So which is it? she said. *Are you going to let me feel how I feel or are you going to lecture me? Would you want your name on this book?*

Come on, I said. But I had already insulted her by not answering the question.

Okay, I'm asking again. Would you want your name on this book?

No, I said. *Fine. But—*

But nothing. So don't lecture me.

Don't get mad at me because you didn't have any better ideas. That's not my fault.

I could tell—the ire in her eyes clouded over—that she knew I was right. But she had to say something.

You know what's incredibly annoying? she said. *The way you spend three days dicking around with one paragraph and wringing your hands over it when you know it's better than anything I could write or anybody else could write. Fuck you. What a fucking waste of time.*

Whatever makes me spend three days on a paragraph, I said, *must be the same thing that keeps me from getting pregnant by assholes.*

I stood up from my chair and walked out. We didn't speak for a week. *Don't ever leave me,* she said, the night she finally called. Instead of *Hello.* Instead of *I'm sorry.* I didn't apologize either.

10.

Peter was a lawyer. A corporate lawyer. Rose was not, she said, deeply in love with him, but she was attracted to him. How could you not be? He was handsome, the kind of textbook tall-and-handsome that Rose had previously never bothered with—black curls that had just started to go appealingly, discreetly gray; dark, intense eyes that came with a set of surprisingly noticeable lashes; and an expensive taste in menswear that elevated his camel coats and gabardine pants a cut above those worn by all of his other brothers in what we called white-collar crime. Peter looked definitively, exotically, like a cartoon of an adult male, professional class edition, and Rose said that this departure from what she called her usual muesli mix of art-damaged ruffians was proving a powerful aphrodisiac. Also fueling the aphrodisiac: Peter had conjured his wealth out of thin air. He'd come from what he called a shitty family from a shitty part of Connecticut and had made all his money because he'd vowed as a boy that he would never be that poor again.

They'd met at a Mets game. He'd asked her for her number because he was particularly impressed by her trash-talking, and Rose had said sure, what the hell, why not? We were thirty-one and it was still possible to treat dates as pure data.

Do you like him? she asked, with an uncharacteristic amount of anxiety.

I did like Peter, quite a bit, and Peter liked me. If you left the two of us alone at a table or in a movie theater lobby we'd find something to laugh about. *Bring Charlotte,* he'd say, if he'd gotten a reservation at some crazily over-booked new restaurant or tickets to a Knicks game or had rented a car to drive out to Montauk. It was Karl and Rose and Charlotte all over again, in some ways, save for the fact that neither of us were pining for Peter. But I could certainly see why Rose wanted him around. He sounded like Jimmy, sometimes—a Jimmy who had a habit of sending the wine back if he didn't like it. A Jimmy who had better things to do—like make piles of money—than drink too much and crash cars into 7-Elevens. A Jimmy who cleaned up nice and stayed cleaned up. Peter also had a habit of calling me Charlie. It was what my mother's father used to call me, and I liked it, a lot. I worried, however, and tried not to worry, that in marrying Peter Rose might have been turning back toward home rather than lighting out for new territory.

After six months Peter proposed and she said yes. She said yes, she told me, because she was sick of all those almost-famous assholes who'd screwed with her head, and being able to go to Mexico in February just because you wanted to was pretty nice, and she'd had all the sex, she said, that would give her memories on her deathbed. Also, Peter had said that as long as he was around her mother would never have to worry about money. It sounded supremely logical, and I could not decide whether that meant it was a terrible idea or a very good one. But I had not been the girl eating scrambled eggs for dinner and brushing my teeth with baking soda, and as the days went on I felt a small surge of relief materializing as I realized that Rose's problem with money would no longer be a problem for me. So I could only imagine how relieved Rose might feel. Even if what she was feeling wasn't pure, blinding, once-in-a-lifetime love.

Still, I'd always imagined Rose marrying—well, sometimes I couldn't imagine Rose marrying but when I did I always thought it would be to someone she found while traveling. Someone from another country, perhaps, or an expat, or—and that was as far as my imagining went. Someone a little more—glamorous. A little more obvious a conductor of human electricity. Rose herself was that kind of conductor, and I was, too, in my own way, and it's what made us dangerous to ourselves and others—that ability to instantly connect with and be delighted by people. The attributes that made us want to write—curiosity, focus, and lability in both the negative and slightly less negative senses of the word—made us forget where we were and who we were, if we wanted to get to the bottom of you, whether you were a book or a movie or a painting or a person. We disappeared as we stared at and queried the other, whether that other took the form of a book or an ocean or a face floating across from ours on the subway—while also sensing that we were most ourselves, or the best version of ourselves, while utterly disembodied in this way.

That kind of person might have brought Rose more misery than she wanted. I look back at my own marriage and think I must have felt the same. Rose and I might have always wanted to be the star of the show, and we might have felt a longing, left over from childhood, for an unflaggingly indulgent, and eternal, audience—a longing that we thought we could quiet with writing but did not. Maybe Rose sensed all these things, too, but could not say them out loud, or even formulate them as words, because to do so would be to admit that the face she showed to the world—defiant, fiery, wisecracking, stonehearted—was nothing but a mask.

But when she told me that Peter had offered to pay back the money she received for the book she'd sold but refused to finish, I found myself a little less willing to let all this pass without comment. I wasn't sure that she should be rescued so completely from her unwillingness to honor that contract, and it made me think, from time to time, about what that musician had said back when Rose and I first met—*Rose, I'm having trouble deciding whether you're actually smart, or just ballsy and hot.* And sometimes I fantasized about quoting Rose to Rose—*A woman can be stupid, and a woman can be broke, but she can't be both at the same time*—and asking her whether marrying Peter meant she wanted to be stupid for the rest of her life. Instead I said:

Do you really love him?

Even if she answered with a lie, I could sleep at night knowing that I'd given her an opportunity to tell the truth.

He loves me, she said. Which was not the same as *I love him*. It was not an outright lie, so I could go on respecting her enough to lie to myself and say her compromise didn't matter, wouldn't matter. If she were anyone else—but she wasn't. She was the person with whom I'd changed my life into something like myth. Someone who I thought needed to remain in my life until death. So I swallowed words and banished thoughts because we still had miles to go.

Rose must have been the only person I've ever truly loved, because she was the only person I've ever made excuses for when she failed to live up to the image I had or wanted to have of her.

I made the veil for her dress, which she decided to buy new, right off some rack. She and I went on a hunt to the garment district, where I bought some Balanchine-worthy tulle, and then fashioned a trim from a tablecloth that had belonged to Rose's great-grandmother, a tablecloth that Rose always thought was too lacy but couldn't bear to discard because of all the Seven Fishes it had seen, and I stood by Rose's side in the Brooklyn Botanic Garden, on a gray day in mid-September, the clouds moving sluggishly above us, in a pale blue brocade party dress from the sixties that had been my mother's, because Rose had decided that I would be her something blue. I stood by Rose's side praying that I would never marry for money.

At the reception—I'd be lying if I said that the reception, which was held in a rented-out restaurant prodigiously full of period detail, replete with twinkling lights twined through branches popping with cherry blossoms, tables and bar tops cascading with unusual flora in shades of pink and green, white tablecloths floating like clouds under tin ceilings like icing, with rivers of hors d'oeuvres winding through the forest of guests, didn't make me consider selling my soul because of the endless supply of safety, cleanliness, and comfort it promised. Hours after I prayed that I would never have to marry for money, standing and drinking wine in the middle of this reception, knowing that the beautiful reception was only the beginning of many beautiful rooms to come, clean, white, spacious, tranquil rooms bedecked with charm and flowers, I revoked that prayer, and wished that someone would come along and sweep me with a huge pile of cash into a house, I didn't care who they were, as long as they left me alone to write whatever I thought I had in me to write.

I gave a speech that I'd worked on for three weeks. When I finished speaking, I looked up and out at the tables. Faces beamed, hands clapped, and two people asked for a copy. One woman, a friend of Ann Marie's, said, *That was an aria, honey, not a speech.* Rose ran over to where I was standing and gave me a big, fierce hug, I gave her a big, fierce hug back, and hoped its ferocity said the things my speech had failed to articulate.

At around nine o'clock that evening, I walked into the ladies' room and found Rose sitting on the tile floor, picking the pearls off the hem of her gown and tossing them on the floor.

What are you doing? I said. I was aware that in my shock I did not sound sympathetic.

Look at this, she said, picking off another pearl and pitching it to the ground. *Why would you charge people thousands of dollars for a dress that'll fall apart ten hours after you put it on?*

I turned around to get her mother. *Do not get my mother*, I heard her say as the door shut behind me.

Ann Marie was sitting at someone else's table, talking away. I placed a hand on her shoulder, apologized for interrupting, and told her I needed to talk with her. She excused herself with a worried look, and hustled us both off to the bar.

I told her that Rose was having—I searched for the words—something of a breakdown.

You mean nerves? she said.

No, it seems like more than that.

Well, it's a big day—

No, I said, firmly, hoping that if I repeated myself with enough emphasis she would hear what I was trying to say to her. *Like a panic attack.* Because I could not say: *Like she shouldn't have done this in the first place.*

Said Ann Marie, becoming impatient: *Take her a drink, tell her it'll be fine.*

We've been drinking all night! I was angry—at Ann Marie, at Rose, and at myself.

Charlotte, Ann Marie said. Snapped. As if I were a ten-year-old neighbor kid who'd forgotten her manners in someone else's house. Finish the performance, she was saying, because if you persist in thinking you are exempt from this or any other performance, it will lead to even greater unhappiness.

I grabbed us two whiskeys at the bar. Back in the ladies' room I sat down next to her, handed her a glass, and we downed the whiskeys in silence. She continued to pick the pearls from her hem and toss them onto the floor.

What were acceptable feelings of deep apprehension, and what was conscience, rising up to remind us that we had put ourselves in the wrong place? How could you tell? Who was there to ask?

I remembered: one of my aunts telling my mother that every minute of her wedding day she thought about bolting, and that every night for the first year of her marriage she slept with a bag packed and waiting for her in the back of her closet. I mentioned this to Rose.

I don't know, I said. *Pack a bag, put it in your closet, and see what happens after a year?*

She said nothing. I tried again.

He's an honest-to-God adult man, I said. *The rest of them are feckless children.*

A few minutes went by. *Make me go back out there*, she said.

I stood up, took her glass, then took her hand. I dropped the tumblers in the sink—they cracked like ice cubes hitting cold water—and we went back out to the reception.

What do we know, anyway? she said, as she followed me out the door.

We were thirty-two.

What did we know, anyway? This was the question Rose and I had been asking ourselves all our lives. What did we know, anyway, not having lived through an economic depression or a world war like our grandparents, and not, like our own parents and uncles and aunts, having grown up in houses besieged by unexpressed sorrow and rage?

After exiting the ladies' room, and handing Rose off to Peter, I went to the bar to get another whiskey because I could not think of anything else to do, and I did not want to think about what might be happening a year from now or three years from now. Jimmy happened to be there, too.

Hello, beautiful, he said.

I'm not in the mood, I said without looking at him, as the bartender handed me my glass.

You're too young to talk like that, he said.

I turned to him. Jimmy, slowly, took the drink out of my hand.

Come talk to me, he said. *I got your drink as hostage. What're you gonna do, wrestle it off me?*

In the velvet dark of the dregs of this party, Jimmy

suddenly appeared as a rakishly suave apparition in a well-cut suit and luminous gray silk tie. What the Hawaiian shirt had forbidden, the suit and tie made possible.

Ten minutes, I said.

And then what? he said.

I go home. But I knew I wasn't going home.

You're not going home. My second heart swooned. He handed me my glass, gave me a single nod, a curt *Salud*, and we drank.

You know the mob used to dump bodies in the river here in this neighborhood? he said, speaking nervously the way I could sometimes speak nervously, and this change in register made me start, because I did not think that people who had been in prison would ever be made nervous by anything outside prison. *I don't know that firsthand, or even second- or thirdhand, I gotta stress, I learned that from a book. Honest to God. And then before that, long before that, in the, uh, I think it was eighteenth century, two brothers, two Revolutionary War vets, bought the land from the Dutch and they were going to turn it into some kind of summer vacation place, and they wanted to call it Olympia.*

I stared at him and tried not to look too surprised.

Give me a two-minute lull in conversation and all kinds of stuff starts coming out of my mouth.

I continued staring at him. I couldn't help it.

What, you think I'm too much of a mook to like history?

No, I said. Which was a lie. *Maybe I'm surprised we might have something to talk about other than Rose.*

Maybe you're a little bit of a snob.

First, I said, *even if that is true, there are much, much worse things to be. Like a child molester. Or Karl Rove.*

That made him laugh.

Second, if you don't watch it you're going to ruin this before it even has a chance to start. His eyebrows reared back. I took a drink with what I admit was a bit of studied, performative coolness.

So where am I going if I'm not going home? I said.

Jesus, he said. *Gimme a second.*

Every night that Rose and Peter were away on their two-week honeymoon, Jimmy came over to my apartment after he got off from work and we would drink from the bottle of whiskey he'd brought until my hesitation had evaporated. His patience made me feel safe enough to become insatiable, and I needed to feel safe in order to become insatiable. He was the first person to fuck me in a way that made me realize all the force that word could imply, and the first person to show me that something like love could reside in that force. Which made it very easy to forget that I was doing exactly what I had promised Rose I wouldn't do. I thought we would stop when she came back but we didn't. By that time I had become addicted to having him inside me. That's what I told myself but I also just liked him. Liked being around him.

It was easy to compartmentalize—like a man! I crowed to myself—because Jimmy and what he gave me had no place in life as I had lived it. There was no taking Jimmy to book parties or readings or to the bars and restaurants Rose and I hung out in—not just because we would be seen, but because Jimmy would be severely out of place. Jimmy could take me to what he called his old man bars in Bay Ridge, and I could talk to the regulars and the bartenders, because the Jersey Shore was Bay Ridge's close cousin, but I did not know where I could take Jimmy without having to explain myself or make excuses for him. He was something to have privately and in snatches. I'd been developing, or might have always had, an appetite for detached engagement—a taste for swimming about in a state of no more, no less—and Jimmy seemed to perfectly answer that need. I was a woman getting my needs met. No more, no less.

Of course, I also could have been trying to hoard something for myself while Rose decorated a brownstone in a neighborhood that in the early twentieth century had belonged to Italian immigrants, a brownstone replete with more-intricate-than-usual moldings and tin ceilings, replete with a quiet, shaded yard and a pine tree standing humbly, shyly, in the middle of it, replete with tall windows that let in so much sun the light almost obliterated the walls, buffed original hardwood with a perimeter patterned like the top of a Japanese puzzle box, a breakfast nook with a bay window, closets in the bathroom that allowed you to buy more than four bath towels and more than one roll of toilet paper at a time, laundry in the basement that allowed you to indulge in actual, and multiple, washcloths for the first time in your life, and to stop buying underwear because you'd run out and were too busy to go to the laundromat, replete with so much space you were practically forced to buy decorative items in order to create a sense of warmth and history.

Rose and I did as much research as we could on the people who'd lived in that house before she arrived, but we would never discover who painted the two Tuscan landscapes that sat on opposite sides of the vestibule and greeted you when you opened the heavy oak door. Whoever had painted it had seen an artistic opportunity created by two rectangles made out of molding and had used a very glossy oil paint, applied with lush but careful strokes, to fill those spaces with cypress trees, terra-cotta rooftops, and a wash of pale and peaceful blue sky shining down on a grayer lagoon below.

Those brushstrokes don't look homesick, I said to Rose, the day she showed me the house and those paintings, which she was particularly excited about.

No, they don't, she said. *They seem—more proud than homesick.*

Those cypress trees did look very proud.

But what do we know? she said.

Enough not to ever paint over these, that's what we know, I said.

Another thing we could not discover through public records: Rose and I were sitting outside on her stoop drinking coffee when the son of the eighty-eight-year-old woman who had apparently won the house across the street in a poker game stopped by to welcome her to the neighborhood.

I used to smoke pot in that upstairs bathroom, he said at one point during the conversation.

You want to see it? said Rose. I rolled my eyes at her nonchalant yet still overeager attempt to ingratiate herself with the lifers.

Nah, he said, smiling. *I live in the now.*

It sounded like something Jimmy would say—although Jimmy might mean it less than this guy actually seemed to. I felt some pain at not being able to share this thought with her, but the fear of what she might do if she knew was stronger.

Is it me or does this feel like playing with a gargantuan Barbie Dream House? I said one Sunday afternoon near Union Square, while we waited for a woman to ring up some drapes at a store I still can't afford to buy anything in.

I could tell by the way Rose concentrated very hard on reviewing and signing the credit card receipt that she did not think this a very good joke.

I don't know, she said. *I never had one.*

Neither did I, I said sharply. Then, softer: *I'm sorry. What I meant to say was that I'm having fun.*

She nodded. An uncomfortable rest of the afternoon followed.

I neglected to tell Rose that I was sleeping with her uncle, and Rose neglected to tell me how much her couches really cost.

At the time I wouldn't have said I was jealous of Rose's money, and I don't think I was. I was still hopeful that I would have a large enough portion of what I had desired while a girl, which had never involved money to begin with, and I was still physically revolted by the thought of a man footing my bills. But that didn't mean I wanted to judge Rose for accepting an offer that had dropped in her lap. I couldn't. It didn't matter. We still spent more hours and more cash than we intended at the WFMU record fair. Still stood too close to the paintings at the Whitney or the Met or MoMA, so close that the security guards were forced to ask us to move away. Still loved to sit next to each other in a middle row at Film Forum, grinning in the dark at the irascibility of the wild-haired lifers, at their black T-shirts and black jeans, their army jackets and wool berets. *Long may it wave*, Rose would say, whenever one of them turned on an unsuspecting audience member with a cry of *Your perfume is burning my eyes!* before the start of *Killer of Sheep* or smacked the snoring face in front of them with a rolled-up *Voice* in the middle of *When a Woman Ascends the Stairs*.

New York was still New York, essentially, even though the people around us had started to marry and have children; to buy houses and cars and make Costco runs. They were quietly but ruthlessly and probably unconsciously seeking ways to import the suburban into the urban. But wasn't it disrespectful to this city, I thought—actually, blasphemous—to wish for it to be as comfortable and steady as the towns we'd spent our lives dreaming, whether idly or feverishly, of leaving? I did not judge these people, either—it was too early in the game for that—but I wondered at what I saw unfolding around me. I kept on wanting what I'd always wanted—to be seen as a writer worth reading and to love someone whose body and mind I could not get enough of—but watching these people, friends, and friends of friends, start shaping their lives to look like the ones I thought we moved here to avoid had started to make me question my own plan. Not theirs. Mine. It could make me a little confused about the validity—the solidity—of my own desires. The teenage girl who congratulated herself loudly for living against peer pressure had become an adult woman who second-guessed departure from the herd—and should she even call it the herd, and risk sounding like a fourteen-year-old boy who's just discovered Nietzsche? It was much easier to stand in defiance of peer pressure when I was sixteen, seventeen, and twenty-one—the pressure back then was to give in to bad sex, bad music, and wine coolers, and the people making the rules were insecure, power-mad children. It was harder to take a principled stand against marriage, because I understood that it had brought many people joy and comfort, and harder to see who the enemy was, because these were fundamentally decent people who still missed their subway stops because of a book.

Rose loved to trash-talk all the people going on Costco runs, and goaded me when I trash-talked all the people panicking about getting their one-year-old into P.S. 321.

You should write about that, she'd say whenever I trash-talked.

What, and sound like a sore loser? I'd say. *No thanks.*

No, just the voice of a generation, she'd say.

I'd sit in Rose's kitchen on a Sunday afternoon, the two of us talking about books we were reading and books we might write, of people we liked and people we didn't, of musicians we liked and musicians we didn't, of movies we might want to see, of snatches of conversation we overheard during the week on the subway or in lines for coffee, tossing jokes old and new back and forth, tossing ideas for things we might find to eat in her kitchen back and forth, for things we might cook for another dinner party in my apartment, talking and feeling buoyed up, and up, and up by our talking, feeling shored up, up, and up, by our talking, and then I'd find myself lying awake on a Sunday night thinking that I was a fool to want more out of heterosexual companionship than a kitchen that gleamed like a fortress made out of stainless steel and vintage ceramics.

And then Jimmy would leave a message on my answering machine, rescuing me from having to spend some sleepless nights sorting true desires from acquired notions.

Jimmy and I didn't talk about books, but we talked about family, which was what nearly all of my favorite novels were about anyway, so it was really just like talking about books.

You love your father a little too much, princess, he said one night.

So what? I said. *How is that making a problem for you?*

I'm not worried about me, he said.

We talked about New York, and what it was like in the late eighties, when I used to cut school on occasional Fridays and take three trains to the city for the privilege of walking in and around and up and down Tower Records on Broadway and Lafayette. Sometimes the trains were just as much the point as the records. In the late eighties, when Jimmy had a job at the Fulton Fish Market. Sometimes Jimmy was in the mood to wax poetic about the concrete floors and the sunrises and the fish guts and the gunshots, and sometimes he wasn't. When he talked of that time and place I thought of Melville and Whitman and Dickens, so: really just like talking about books.

We laughed a lot together. He could tell a story, and so could I. Jimmy loved to hear me talk about the dumb shit, his words, the private school students I taught said and did and thought and fought over.

I like your smart mouth, he said one night. *I've always liked a smart mouth.*

Jimmy could have been a writer, Rose used to say. *If only, if only, if only,* she used to say. Rose and I had the luck of being born to women and men who did not want to repeat the mistakes of their parents. They repeated some of them anyway, but this vigilant awareness of not wanting to perpetuate the worst of it at least prevented them from inflicting physical and emotional abuse. Jimmy was not that lucky. His father used to beat him, and once, Rose said, broke a few ribs.

And another night: *You look like all those girls who come into the bakery, but there's a big fucking difference: they never fucking smile. Never! Is this what books do to people? Cheer up, I always wanna say when they come in there with their little librarian glasses and their little fabric bags. Did your one and only cat die? Did your father forget to foot the bill this month? What the fuck?*

Oooh, I said, laughing. *You're not supposed to tell women to cheer up.*

Why the hell not?

Yes, why not? I paused. *Well*, I began, *it supposes that women exist only to prop up society's psychic economy with their self-effacement.*

What the Jesus fuck, he said.

Just don't ever say it out loud. I don't want to have to visit you in prison.

The look on his face told me that I had been very stupid, and very spoiled by my innocence, if I felt free enough to make that remark. My face burned, and he must have noticed.

It's okay, he said coolly. Which made my face burn even more.

I frequently begged him not to smoke on my stoop, because I didn't want it to bother Mrs. Rivera. He refused.

It's either this or cocaine again, kid, he'd say. And I would sweep up the cigarette butts in the morning after he left.

We hardly ever spoke of Rose, and we never spoke of prison. I asked once and he said, *I don't want to talk about that with you.* Neither did we talk about politics. If I finally knew what I thought there was to know—such as, for instance, he was as racist as all the old and young Italian guys in my neighborhood now or my neighborhood back home, or that he held intricate, poorly informed conspiracy theories about liberals and their agenda, I'd be forced to spend some time weighing the value of personal satisfaction against the value of defending these abstracts by refusing to consort with someone who denigrated them. I made lists of the worst offenses he could possibly commit and examined my heart to see what it could stand if it knew how closed-minded and ignorant he could be. But these mental preparedness exercises were all very abstract, too, and often it seemed to me that getting into a fight with Jimmy about politics, and trying to tell him why he was wrong, could end only with him thinking that I was patronizingly trying to reeducate him like the pinko commie that I was. No battle would be won for the things I believed in, and I would lose Jimmy to boot. The personal: zero. The political: zero. So, I thought, let's go with privileging the personal.

And Jimmy might have been on his best behavior, maybe, because he knew what a college girl talked like and looked like, knew what a Rose talked like and looked like, and perhaps had thought it best to keep his more pungent thoughts to himself if he wanted to keep being let into my apartment.

I was very tempted, several times, to ask him why me of all people, until the night he said, *I like how much you like it*. I was also essentially naked of associations: I didn't know him when. Or we were both bored and looking for shocks, or you could say that we both had serious problems with the world as presented to us—only my way of dealing with that feeling of being shut out of what everyone called real life was to write, and Jimmy's had been to drink and take drugs and erupt into violence. And I hope I am not fooling myself when I say that I think the both of us knew this.

Once he drove me out to Dyker Heights to look at the Christmas lights and then to get pizza in Mill Basin. Because Rose would not be anywhere near there, and because no one I knew would be in either Dyker Heights or Mill Basin, unless they, too, had grown up in the southern end of the Jersey Shore and sometimes craved a very easy night of it around people who reminded her of the people she grew up with.

Is this your latest? said the waiter, when he came to take our order.

I laughed out loud. The waiter looked at me like I was crazy.

On the contrary, said Jimmy, seemingly unfussed. *She's my last. A bottle of your most expensive white wine, please, Sir Asshole.*

That was a joke, he said, when the waiter left, and said it so smoothly I believed him. *You don't deserve to be spoken to that way.*

Should I be your last? I said, batting my eyelashes, so he knew that really, I could care less.

Princess, he said, so that I would know that really, he had it all under control here, every last bit of it, *you and I both know that would be one of the stupidest things we could ever do.*

I picked up the skyscraper-tall menu and hid behind it because there were no fans here in the twenty-first century to screen our flirtations. *And*, I began, but he finished the sentence for me.

And I've done some stupid things, he said, from behind his menu. I could hear him smiling. His foot found mine and pressed it, once, a kiss, under the table, and then disappeared.

That night at the restaurant I gave him a Christmas present—an encyclopedia of New York City history that must have weighed ten pounds. He was visibly moved, and I tried to not be visibly pleased with myself at intuiting so accurately what just might please him.

I don't think anybody's given me a book in my whole goddamned life, he said, as he slowly flipped through the pages. And then stopped abruptly to wipe his hands on his jeans. *Oh shit. Fucking pizza grease. Shit.* And then wiped his fingers on one napkin, then another, closed the book shut, and set it down carefully in his corner of the booth.

Who has it better than us? he said, when he looked up.

Sometimes I think I was the happiest I've ever been, eating pizza and drinking warm white wine in a booth in a packed Mill Basin restaurant of no discernible decorating scheme save marble-topped surfaces, while sitting across from Jimmy and laughing at his running commentary on the room, my heart rushing and lit up like the BQE while he stared straight at me and poured me a third glass. Unless I think about sitting in a booth with

Karl and Rose at O'Connor's, or sitting with just Rose in a booth at O'Connor's, or WXOU, or the In-N-Out Burger off Hollywood Boulevard, everyone's Saturday night beginning or ending or exploding all around us, white paper wrappers unfurling like fireworks on red tray after red tray, like white water lilies on red pond after red pond.

Unless I think about Jimmy driving us into parts of Brooklyn I knew existed only because of the subway map, just driving in the dark and listening to Stevie Wonder or the Bee Gees or Marvin Gaye or Donny Hathaway or the Clash. I would wonder, as the night deepened and grew in tenderness all around us, as the red and white lights of traffic waxed and waned around us like hundreds of morning stars, whether this was all a person had the right to ask from another person: silent affinity as you share an awe of some object, some art.

I feel safe around you, he said one night, to the windshield, as he drove me home.

I feel safe around you, too, I said, and wished I'd never said it. I was afraid to call this safety love.

One night I heard him arguing with someone over a parking space on my street. I went to the windows and there he was, standing outside his car, passenger door open, shouting at someone who had their car just about angled into the last open spot on the block.

You absolute motherfucker! he shouted. *You swooped in right in front of me!*

Jimmy had begun to pace back and forth in the small space between the two cars in some kind of agony, swiftly, his body coiled, his hands to his head in some kind of disbelief.

Calm down, calm down, my friend, said the other man.

Then Jimmy swerved away and out of his agony and planted himself directly in front of the man. *I beat a guy almost to death in prison, man. I don't think you want to tell me to calm down. I think you want to get your fucking car out of this fucking space.*

Yeah, yeah, said the man, and Jimmy lunged at him and took him by the shoulders.

Hey man, hey man, hey man, the other said, each iteration of that phrase getting more and more frightened.

I ran out of the apartment, down into the street in my bare feet, and shouted, *Knock it off!*

The two of them looked up. Jimmy let go of the man's shoulders.

You don't need that parking space, I said. *You're not coming in tonight.*

Well fuck you, too, said Jimmy. *Fuck you, too, princess.*

That particular *Princess* sounded like an envelope containing a letter that read *Bitch* within.

No, I'm sorry, fuck you. Don't make me feel like I'm the problem here because I can't take this kind of opera.

I went back inside. A half hour later I smelled cigarette smoke coming through my open windows. I looked outside. He was sitting on the stoop, facing the street, smoking.

Come up, I said.

He put his cigarette out, sat there for a second, and came up.

I wasn't afraid of him. I was afraid of the work loving him would require—the constant monitoring of whatever he said or did and the constant monitoring of others' reactions to him.

Tell Rose about me, he said. Lying in bed that night, facing each other, his hand between my thighs.

No, I said.

Why not? Yes, why not?

Your father would love me. Trying another window to see if it was open.

I know. My father might also, depending on whether or not Jimmy was wearing a hat, think he was a little bit ridiculous.

So what else do you need to know about me?

Don't you think it—

You think if you take me to some reading I'm going to shit in the corner like nobody taught me where the shit needs to go?

I wanted to laugh so badly—the scene he'd tossed out was so vivid, and so vividly put—I had to bury my face in the pillow to stop it.

What's wrong? Are you laughing? Why the fuck are you laughing?

No, that's not it!

I think that is it.

Okay, yes, so I take you to some reading! You'd be bored, you'd hate it, and you'd start talking shit about everyone, loudly, before we even made it to the exit.

How do you know I'd be bored?

You're right, I don't know that. I removed his hand from between my legs and sat up.

So what is it?

There are—structural problems. Someone in college had used that line on me while trying to explain why he didn't want to keep dating me over the summer. According to that guy, it was too far a drive from Exit 13 on the turnpike all the way down to Exit 20 on the Garden State Parkway. It sounded like a load of bullshit at the time, and here it was floating up to the tip of my tongue from some recess of hurt in my heart, here I was using it on someone I cared about because I did not want to hurt him, and was still young enough to think I could avoid it with strategically placed words.

Structural problems? What the hell does that mean?

I mean that we live in different worlds, and love isn't enough! I did not know where those last four words had come from.

Love isn't enough? He sat up, climbed over me, out of the bed, and disappeared into the living room. He came back and stood in the bedroom doorway with his pants in his hand. *That's all there is, lady!* He pulled the pants on and zipped them up with a force and precision that made me miss him already. *You know what? You're so smart, you're stupid!*

When three weeks went by without a call, I knew it was over.

At Jimmy's funeral later that year, I thought I might die. It was the first time I'd carried alcohol in my purse to get through an event. The first time I stood in a ladies' room stall staring up at the particle board and the not-quite-obliterating-enough fluorescent light, taking long, careful sips until I thought I felt my heart rate slow and my breathing level. Not out of a flask—too much work, too much of an affectation. I'd stopped at a liquor store near Penn Station before getting on the LIRR and bought three in-flight-size bottles of vodka that I zipped into a cosmetics bag. I never drank vodka, but neither had I ever been to a funeral of a man who happened to be both the uncle of my best friend and my—well, in the nineteenth century they would have used the word *lover*, but again, too much of an affectation, too much like jewelry you want to show off, too grand and clean a word to lay on the grave of whatever it was we'd been doing. He was killed while driving home from work one night. He was not drunk, which I was relieved to hear.

Rose and I learned at the same time. Late August, a Saturday, very warm. The two of us sitting in her yard and talking, drinking iced coffee and staring into the branches of the pine tree, talking about how right we'd been to not get on a packed train to Long Beach that morning.

The phone rang, and she headed inside to answer it. A few seconds after she picked up I heard her shout *No!* I ran in and found her on her knees on the kitchen floor, hands on her face, crying.

That night, after leaving Rose's house, I went out and bought a bottle of vodka, because that would be quicker and more potent than wine, and then drank myself to sleep using a quarter-cup measuring cup because I had no shot glasses, kept pouring the vodka to the eighth-cup line of the quarter cup, as if being very methodical would make this more medicinal, and repeated this action until I fell asleep.

At the funeral, I was just numb enough to be able to speak to people without slurring my words but just dead enough to panic to be able to sit in the church without bolting.

Rose approached the lectern, and set three double-spaced typed pages out in front of her. She stood very still and then picked the pages up again, staring at them before beginning.

No one will ever love me the way my uncle did, Rose said. Then she turned to look at Peter. *My apologies to my husband.* Everyone laughed.

My uncle, she said, *loved me in the way my father should have, but never got the chance to.* Her face crumpled into tears and she brought her fist to her nose to plug them up. Everyone waited. Rose took her fist away from her face.

I'm not going to be able to do this, she said, staring down at the pages, *so I am going to ask a friend of mine to read these words for me.*

When I reached the lectern, Rose grabbed my hand in the sloppy, territorial, and ferocious way she did whenever we stood in a dark club and a song we loved announced its imminent arrival. My panic subsided. I read out a eulogy to the man I also feared had loved me in a way I would never experience again.

At the back of the church, as we all filed out, Ann Marie pulled me aside and clasped me to her for a very long time. I did not want to be rewarded for perpetuating a deception, but I was almost deliriously relieved. The kind of relieved you might be if you'd gone away for a week and returned to find that you'd left the door to the house unlocked, but, as you crept, panicked, around the house, you discovered that nothing at all had been damaged or stolen. That no one had taken advantage of your monumental stupidity. That you had been protected from your monumental stupidity, and you'd better figure out how to prove to the gods that you deserved that reprieve.

11.

Because Rose had landed a backyard on Carroll Street while the rest of us still felt lucky to have stoops to sit on, and because she wanted to share what she'd lucked into with people she liked, she'd dedicated herself to throwing parties in which Saturday nights turned into Sunday mornings, parties that attracted so many people that, standing in the backyard, it felt as if you were in the middle of a public pool. People are still married to the people they met for the first time in that backyard. I thought, and still think, that these parties had the same value as books—they made people feel less alone and distracted them from their troubles.

But I would never say that out loud to Rose, who had not yet published one herself. Though not for lack of trying. The two of us would sit in her backyard for hours, Rose riffing, me transcribing, the two of us thinking that if she talked her ideas out with me, to me, they might end up more alive on the page, and might take the form of a something that could be called a book proposal, but whenever she read back over the document I emailed her at the end of these sessions, the words never felt as urgent to her as they did when she spoke them out loud. I wished I didn't see what she meant, and I wished I didn't suspect that while she might be a fearless reporter, she might not be cut out for writing books—but I could never say those words out loud to her, either, and didn't want to. She would have to be the one to say them.

What I did say, one afternoon when she seemed particularly dejected:

Do you think that you might be holding whatever this book could be to some higher standard because the first—

Yes, she said. *That's occurred to me more than once.*

That was the last afternoon we spent trying to make something out of nothing. She told me later that hearing me say what she'd been thinking liberated her to give up and stop forcing herself, for the moment, to write a book. It would come when it would come, she said, and she threw herself into pitching with renewed purpose. If she resented me for publishing a second book that fall while three different editors at places she'd been trying to break into took stories she pitched and gave them to writers with more name recognition, with two out of the three editors claiming to not know what she was talking about when she called them up in a rage, and the third suggesting he might change his mind if she did him a few sexual favors, she was an even better actress than I gave her credit for. Her disappointment and fury, which I felt almost as keenly as she did, and which dimmed her lights for a good few months afterward, made me hide my own joy over getting better reviews and in better places than the first time I'd published, and keep small bits of good news to myself unless she asked, and when she did ask I hated it because I knew she was forcing herself to do it. It was obviously costing her something to fulfill the role of the caring, involved friend, but it did not cost me anything to avoid these topics, or so I thought at the time, and when Rose told me that she was going to look into getting a job as a music publicist at a firm run by someone who used to know us when, I noticed I felt the same kind of relief I'd felt when she told me she was marrying: I would not have to feel the pain that could come from watching someone I loved keep trying and failing, or the burden of carrying a kind of survivor's guilt if I ended up succeeding as she failed.

What I should have noticed, by this point, was that for all Rose's talk, she was the real pragmatist here, and in the long run her decision to give up on what she'd spent her girlhood dreaming of was not going to torture her the way it would torture me.

She and Peter threw a party to celebrate that second book. She gave a speech, one that, it seemed, she made up as she went along. *Charlotte Snowe is a gift to womankind,* she told the yard. *She will bring you cheeseburgers when you are hungover and you are calling her up in pain. She will type breakup emails for you when your fingers are too angry to protect your dignity. She will read your articles ten times in a row, and she will know what the problem is within two minutes, and she'll never block your email when she sees draft number eleven attached. She won't dance much, but she will bring the records, and those records will leave you weeping in a heap, crying for your mother, by the sweaty empty cooler of beer in that scrappy patch of grass where everyone went to smoke. She will buy you ten dresses for ten dollars at the Salvation Army just because. She knows how to make a fantastic bouquet from bodega flowers. She knows more than you do about nearly everything but will never rub your nose in it. She won't march in the street, but she'll be the sniper on the roof. Her book will make you want to kill yourself, it's so good. Read it! Read it, people!*

When she finished, Peter popped a bottle of champagne and the crowd cheered while I cried.

How did you like the free jazz? she said, as we hugged. *Pretty good, right?*

You can't have meant all of it, I said, still crying, holding her tighter. *Some of that must have been for effect.*

Later that night, Peter and I stood together drinking and watching Rose, in the middle of the yard, wearing a red halter dress from the seventies, with a green dragon embroidered along the right side, as she told a story under the branches of the pine tree, which we'd threaded with lights. She was repeatedly tapping her finger on the chest of the friend of the man I'd brought to the party. The friend laughed and shook his head. I wondered if Peter was going to say something about Rose engaging in what could be narrowly interpreted as flirting, but instead he said *Sometimes I think she wants things so badly it's going to hurt her.*

I remembered Karl, years ago, saying the same thing. Thought about Rose, throwing steak knives at her kitchen wall, one by one, as if she'd spent all her life in a traveling sideshow, after she got off the phone with one of those editors. What I wanted to say, and did not say—*If we could turn it off like a faucet, don't you think we would?*—sounded like a weak defense of the fire that had burned inside of us since childhood. What I also wanted to say but did not: *And because you are cool where she is hot, one day you are going to lose her.*

12.

I met the man I married at a wedding held in upstate New York. Late at night, after the bride and groom had gone to bed, the best man gathered the guests in the bar of the inn where most of us were staying and ordered up an hour of Stax and Motown from the jukebox. The floor was full from the first song, and as the room grew hot and close, Mark and I, left behind by our conversation partners, stood next to each other, leaning back against the bar, talking and watching the dancing. Mark: a professor who talked like a farmhand and swore like a racetrack owner because he knew the ladies loved it. Or so I told Rose. Tall and from East Texas, with a thick pile of dark gold hair thatching this way and that. A fine long sturdy face and quiet hazel eyes. Dress shirt untucked, sleeves rolled up. Courtly and direct. At ease with me in a way that suggested he'd be at ease anywhere.

You're funny, he said after we'd been talking for a while. Looking down at me, taking my measure. *Witty, I mean.*

Usually when people say that, it's a sign that they're not that funny themselves.

Oh, I'm not, he said, smiling.

Let's dance, I said, to see if he would thaw.

To "Proud Mary"? he said. *Hell no. I'm not desecrating Ike and Tina like that.*

Oh, so you are funny, I said.

He smiled, and I dragged him out to the floor, where I promptly turned my back to him, and danced away from him, so that he could get going without me watching. When I turned back to face him the song had reached its crescendo and the crowd, exploding into shouts, stomping, singing, crushed us together. The floorboards bounced. Someone's whiskey spilled out of a glass held high. It ran down my neck, over my collarbone, down under my dress. I looked up to see where it had come from, and then back at Mark.

You're beautiful, he said, and kissed me. His kiss: green like a weeded lot grown lush out of hope that someone would find the wildness alluring. Blue-black like a night in January, which, with its chill clarity, was another form of green. *Don't stop*, I told him, when he pulled away. I thought I could marry him.

You should be more famous than you are, he said, coming into my bedroom one morning, holding my second book in his right hand. He'd spent a few hours on the couch drinking coffee and reading it while I slept off a party. I thought I should marry him.

He needed me, and did not try to hide it. *Don't go home*, he'd say on Sunday nights, and then hold me to him so he could fall asleep. I liked the idea of being needed—perhaps because it lessened my responsibility toward him. I didn't have to work very hard to love him. I just had to stay put.

With Mark, doing nothing together was like singing together. Over and over we went to the same restaurants, restaurants that were never more than five blocks away, and walked in their doors every time with the same excited relief to be home. Cooked side by side on Saturday nights, and he'd tell me about the boys he went to high school with, the football goons who tried to hold up a Whataburger and the preacher's kid who was a serial impregnator, doing a perfect impression of each instance of headlong, wobbly manhood, conjured them with his voice out of the halls of Longview High School and into my kitchen. Drove nowhere together with Dylan or Springsteen turned up loud. *The distance between the Jersey Shore and East Texas is shorter than you'd think,* he liked to say, and he was right. Reading on Sunday afternoons under the same maple in Prospect Park, the two of us spread out on an old pale blue sheet, my grandmother's, covered with daisies, at the top of a slope that poured into a pool of lawn. The books he read were often just that much more serious than mine, and I was much more inclined to pick up the books he'd just finished with than he was to pick up the ones I'd just finished, and I tried not to let this bother me, especially because he'd told me that I was the best editor he'd ever had. He himself was often more serious than I was. Moodier than I was. More changeable than I was. My difficult artist.

You should put your legs down, he said, one afternoon as we lay reading in the park.

Nobody's looking, I said. Lying on my back, knees tented, dress making what I thought was enough of a curtain over my shins. *Besides, it's all yours.*

I know you think that's funny, he said. He didn't think it was funny at all.

I took his hand and set it on the place he would never call my cunt. He took it away and put it on the top of my knees, and pressed down, gently, while still reading his book, until I lowered them.

Run, I told myself. But Sundays in Park Slope were full of couples pushing strollers, couples loaded down with grocery bags, couples holding hands and drinking coffees, couples behind their sunglasses sleepy with self-enchantment, couples who seemed to be relieved to have exchanged animal passion for animal contentment, and on the walk home from the park, they formed a chorus that said *Stay*. I'd never once felt an overwhelming need to have a child, but I was beginning to feel an acute and overwhelming need to be paired up. I did not stop to think that perhaps it was a shared abundance of cash, and not shared companionship, that made the faces of these couples appear free of bitterness and impervious to sorrow.

I hadn't met anyone like him in New York. He was purer than I was, than anyone I knew—more frugal, more diligent. Much less bothered by the noise coming from the culture. Although he had a decadent streak that could manifest itself in cashmere winter coats and long dinners at bustling, glittering restaurants—if he didn't, we wouldn't have lasted. He hadn't wasted his twenties and thirties the way Rose and I had wasted them, the way all the people I knew and loved had wasted them: drinking and talking, seeing bands, seeing movies, seeing art, buying clothes, buying shoes, buying music, buying books, traveling, writing things whose importance evaporated within a week even though we were trying hard to engineer posterity. Mark had been busy reading the ageless thoughts of the very dead, studying at Oxford, hiking through Italy like Nietzsche, teaching heavy course loads, turning his dissertation into a book and then beginning another. His purity of soul and purpose amplified his already ample confidence: he did not doubt himself, at all. He liked what he liked, rejected what he found wanting, and didn't need anyone else to affirm these tastes. That might have been why, even though this very fixed compass could create a rigidity that made me fear idly for the us of thirty years from now, I felt safe lying next to him in bed: he knew what he was about. And it was why his students loved him more than mine loved me.

You shouldn't care what those kids think about you, he always said. But mothers always do.

His own mother loved me. Barbara. She'd always longed for a daughter, and neither of Mark's two younger brothers had given her the next best thing, which was a daughter-in-law, because neither of them had stayed romantically involved with the various mothers of their various children, and there I was, asking her to show me how to make biscuits and gravy and listening to the stories that bored her granddaughters and burdened her sons. Did I love her, as I thought I did as we stood next to each other frying links of Jimmy Dean sausage in cast-iron pans, or was I just hanging around for material?

The sixties ranch house in which she raised her sons contained only one bookcase: a glass-paneled Chippendale, a wedding present from Barbara's grandfather, which stood full of Silhouette romances, cookbooks, diet books, and eighties-era guides to living the Christian life. But Barbara drove to the Books-A-Million near the Walmart Supercenter in Longview, Texas, to order my books, and after she read them, called me up in Brooklyn so we could talk about the women I'd written about. *They just didn't give a damn!* she said, laughing in delight as she gossiped with me about their triumphs and tragedies. *Not a one of them!* Agnes, Rebecca, Georgia, Agnes. Ida, Dorothy, Mabel, Louise. Referring to them by their first names, which is how she referred to the hosts of the *Today* show and the judges on *American Idol*. Barbara, who said my mother must be so proud. My mother had never read either of my books, but I did not mention this to Barbara. Some days I think the highest honor those books ever received was the delight they provoked in Barbara Gillespie, née McKinley, and some days I think it's their truest condemnation.

Why, don't you just have the skin of a girl in a Pond's ad! she said, the first time we met. At a carpeted, climate-controlled Cracker Barrel that had all the charm of a mid-size Midwestern airport, Christmas Eve, off I-20, at a long noisy table full of his brothers and their children and his brother's current girlfriends. Reddish-brown hair, dyed redder, I could tell, from the roots framing her forehead, and pulled back in a gold monogram barrette—a gift from the boys, she said, Christmas 1987. Hot-rollered curls spilling out of the barrette and onto the shoulders of her green cable-knit turtleneck sweater. Barbara didn't need makeup either—her face was smooth and shining and laced with freckles at its edges—and when she told me she'd been using Pond's herself every night since she turned sixteen, I began slathering it on every night, too, until Mark said please stop, it was freaking him out. Her hazel eyes merry and her laugh frequent until she started to cry, elbows on the table and face in her hands, when his youngest brother said his girls couldn't spend the night at her place, and everyone at the table ignored her while she cried, went on talking and reordering because if it wasn't one minor disappointment bringing on the waterworks it was another, and they no longer had the energy or will to distinguish which tears merited attention and which did not.

Mark got up out of his chair and looked down at the carpet for a second or two without expression, as if vacating his own premises in order to play the role of the rescuer she'd trained him to be. As if gathering himself before giving a sermon like the preacher he'd thought he should be. He walked over to Barbara, put his hand on her shoulder, and told her they should go outside and get some fresh air. She nodded, wiped her eyes with her right wrist, and did not move.

Come on, Mom, said Mark. His voice shaded with a tenderness I'd never heard. He sounded about ten years younger than the Mark I knew, and I worried while watching him that this tenderness would never be extended to me. She might have taken all of it. But she needed it more than I did, I thought, as I watched her grab the hand on her shoulder and kiss it once, quickly, warmly, with a gust of grateful affection.

She rose to her feet, and once they were through the restaurant doors his youngest brother, Paul, wide and tired with a faint streak of white in his red-gold beard, turned to me and said, with a sardonic smile, *So now you've met Scarlett O'Hara.*

Paul could joke about his mother's wounded heart going off like a too-sensitive smoke alarm because he had not been Mark. Paul had been the four-year-old throwing yet another tantrum in the supermarket, crying in the seat of a shopping cart because he didn't understand why they couldn't have hot dogs, whereas Mark was the thirteen-year-old sitting on the linoleum next to their mother while she cried almost as loudly as her four-year-old son over not being able to afford to feed three boys on her secretary's salary, and their father, who'd left her to marry a younger woman who let him be the hippie he was trying a decade too late to be, couldn't give them any money because he made no money as an itinerant landscaper. Mark was the fifteen-year-old who made dinner when their mother was too depressed to come out of her bedroom to do it; the sixteen-year-old who watched his mother almost lose her job for absenteeism after being broken up with by his middle brother's wrestling coach; the seventeen-year-old whose father put copies of *Playboy* and *Hustler* in the drawers of his nightstand because he thought his son was too studious. The nineteen-year-old who fell so hard for Greek at UT Austin that he went on to get a PhD in classics at Yale.

That boy, I thought, should not be left alone in the world without company. It was a very strong feeling, and I thought it meant I loved him, when in fact I might have just admired him. It never occurred to me that I also might have been looking to mother someone without having to give birth.

Mark had very strong feelings, too. He wrote me emails, left me notes on the backs of brown paper bags, on pages from notepads I'd taken from hotels, subscription cards from *The New Yorker*, wrote more to and about me than any man had ever done.

In the morning I took his notes on the subway and read them on the way to school. They made me forget I was hungrier for his body than he seemed to be for mine.

Said Rose when I brought this up to her: *My aunt once said that you should marry a friend because you could always find a lover.*

I'm not buying that at all. Isn't it much harder to find a lover?

Yeah, so maybe it was the other way around. It's possible I remembered it the wrong way—

Because you needed to?

Yes.

Are you trying to convince me of something?

I hope not, she said. *I see the way he looks at you.*

All those words, and I'm still not sure what he saw when he looked at me and called me beautiful. What it was specifically, about me, Charlotte Snowe, daughter of Frank and Peggy, that he loved.

I married him because he was the smartest man I'd come across in New York, and he wasn't going to leave me to find a woman who wanted to get pregnant, like two other men before him had. Whenever I felt that my efforts to create what I imagined I could create were faltering, I could look over at Mark, on the couch, in bed, or across a table, and affirm myself by remembering that this kid would not get himself romantically involved with an idiot. And Mark didn't care that I didn't want a family, because family to him had been a torture. I might have questioned Rose's supremely logical decision to marry for money, but marrying for psychological security was no better: each was a futile bid for insurance against pain.

You chose wisely, said Rose, as we stood in a ladies' room at City Hall on my wedding day, and she watched me adjust a cream-colored dress from the 1920s that she'd bought for me off the Internet. It was her wedding gift. *Not just the man but the venue*, she said. I laughed. Rose didn't.

I wish I'd had something much simpler, she said. And

then, as I reapplied a coat of lipstick: *You are a beautiful woman, Charlotte Snowe.* As if she were disinterestedly but expertly appraising a horse.

I think I'd rather be a spirited filly, I said. Someone had called Rose that once during our waitressing nights at the cocktail lounge. Now she laughed.

Let's stay in here forever, she said. I did not want to leave the ladies' room either, because a worry was taking hold as the two of us stood there in front of the mirror: *I am going to make him sad.*

13.

Three years later, a piece of paper dropped out of one of my books while Mark and I were purging our shelves. Our landlord had suddenly and apologetically raised the rent to an amount we did not think it wise to pay, and we were moving from Park Slope to Kensington.

Mark picked up the paper and examined it.

Who's Jimmy? he said. Our backs to each other, each facing a bookcase.

No one, I said. I kept pulling down books, trying to decide if it was dread or arousal flushing my face, my arms, my legs.

Did he know that?

It was a very long time ago, I said, and turned around. *Please give me whatever you found.* As if he were a student who had not heard me the first time.

He walked out of the living room and left the apartment with a slam of the door that seemed to echo long after it shut. The note lay on the hardwood floor.

On the back of an envelope that had contained a bill from ConEd, Jimmy had written, with one of the black rollerballs I always had lying around:

To: Charlotte
From: Jimmy
Re: A FORMAL REQUEST

I had never seen his handwriting. It looked, somewhat predictably, like the handwriting of a man not educated past high school, and I felt terrible, a little, for thinking it—boxy, blocklike capital letters that tilted a little toward the right, letters sprinkled with the occasional lowercased *i*.

He'd written a list of things he wanted to do to me. All the usual words, but because Mark and I would never dream of speaking in that way to each other, and because Mark and I never exchanged anything more than sweet and pleasant release with each other, and because I had been too scared to let myself truly love Jimmy, all the usual words undid me.

I burned the envelope over the sink, to prove to myself that I could live without it, and then walked to Prospect Park, where I was fairly sure Mark must have gone. I knew the route he liked to walk inside the park and thought I might have a chance of meeting up with him. I walked those paths and when I emerged from the woods I thought I saw him sitting in our usual spot. As I walked up the slope, careful to look everywhere but at him, I realized that I was glad to be leaving this neighborhood and its insistence on family as the only kind of heaven.

I sat down beside him. He did not look at me.

Why don't you give me what you gave him? he said.

I didn't know you wanted it, I said.

You don't think I have it in me to give you what he gave you.

That's not what I said.

Why did you marry me?

I love you.

Right, he said.

The person who wrote all that is dead.

He thought for a while.

I don't think the person he wrote it to is.

I laid my cheek on his shoulder. He stiffened.

Mark had seen that maybe I didn't fully belong to him, and he didn't know what to do about this wound other than to become jealous of a dead man. Soon he started saying things like *Do you really need another glass of wine?* at home, or if we were out with friends, and that always produced a few moments of awkward silence at whatever table we were sitting at. If he saw me opening a package of something I'd ordered off the Internet: *You already have enough clothes.* My appetite, in any form, was a threat. If he was trying to shame me out of the third glass or the unnecessary dress or the unnecessarily long happy hour with friends who were not his, it worked. For a little while, and then I stopped caring. We fought over how much I drank, how much I spent, what dresses I wore, and where I wore them, and how late I stayed out. Fought over what I wrote, because he said the books I'd written were nothing more than conversations with a bunch of dead women about how to escape monogamy.

He wasn't wrong.

We made the move to Kensington, and shortly after we moved, I was two weeks late for my period when I usually bled like clockwork. I did not believe the pregnancy tests and was too afraid to go to the doctor to get my blood drawn. I was convinced I was pregnant and did not want to know the truth. Why was I sure I was pregnant? Something needed to punish me for marrying someone I shouldn't have married, and for not telling Jimmy I loved him.

For a week I took to sleeping on the bathroom floor with the lights on, because I'd become convinced that if I closed my eyes in a bedroom with the lights off, the blackness of the room would merge with the blackness behind my eyes to create a total darkness that would blind me, but bright white tiles and bright white walls would let me go on seeing. I didn't sleep. I'd lay there, curled on my side, mind racing. There were also panic attacks on the subway home from school, and when my mind's racing reached the pitch of the screeching wheels of the R train, I'd get off at the next possible stop and stand on the platform, my back against the tiles, bludgeoned and blurred into three or five or ten versions of myself, three or five or ten transparencies, none of them interested in cohering, stood there breathing in and out, slowly, and staring at the passing faces, until I felt solid enough to walk home. Walking fast, walking hard to rid myself of the last of the panic, thinking that it was very strange to be sane for most of the day, to do what needed to be done at my job, to laugh when it was required, to give intelligible answers when students asked questions, but then watch my mind unravel as soon as it knew that for the rest of the evening there would be no one but Mark it needed to keep itself together for. It was strange, to lose my mind in bits and pieces, watching clumps of it fall out and into my hand, instead of losing it so completely I'd have to be checked into a hospital. Especially considering that I'd written three papers on "The Yellow Wallpaper" between my junior year of high school and my junior year of college.

Mark begged me to get a prescription for Xanax from my GP. I filled it and we had a long and loud argument because I refused to take it. I was afraid if I took one I'd go ahead and take them all.

Are you sure I shouldn't go to a hospital? I asked Mark. Four in the morning. Our eyes sore and useless from lack of sleep.

You do not want to go to a hospital, he said. His high school girlfriend, he told me, had spent the last few months of their senior year in an inpatient treatment facility. She had not gotten into any of the schools she'd hoped would get her out of Texas and had tried to kill herself.

Neither of us felt like talking, at that moment, about whether Mark might have a type, and how much his mother had to do with it.

My period arrived the next day. I stopped sleeping with Mark because I did not want to ever be pregnant, and abstinence, I knew, was the only foolproof form of birth control. He held me tightly in the middle of the night, and I dreamed of someone fucking me out of my misery.

Why should I exist if Jimmy no longer did?

That Saturday I showed up at Rose's door unannounced.

I need to tell you something, I said. I stood on her stoop and told her everything. If I didn't tell her the truth, I worried that I might really end up in a hospital.

I'm so sorry, I said when I finished. *I'm so sorry he's gone, and I'm sorry I didn't tell you sooner.*

Rose, standing in her doorway in jeans and bare feet. Arms crossed.

So you read that speech at his funeral for me but never thought to tell me?

I said nothing.

You read that speech at his funeral without breaking

down? *What the hell kind of fucking ice queen are you that you can sleep like that with somebody and not be undone at their funeral?*

I went crazy instead. Shouted it. *Or, sorry, almost crazy. Does that count?*

That shut her up for a little while. She sat down on the top step of her stoop. I sat down next to her. Rehearsed, again, as I had on the subway ride over, what my life might look like without her.

I'm not mad that you did it, she said. *I'm mad that you didn't tell me.*

Would you have told me?

You were the only other person in my life who could have known why it mattered that he was gone.

He was your *uncle,* I said, *and I'd known him for what, five minutes? Anything I might have been feeling didn't matter compared to what you might be feeling.*

You were kind of a coward, not to tell me.

I know.

What was it, between you two?

Take a guess, I said.

She laughed, and I felt slightly less terrified that I would lose her.

Well, right, she said. *Other than that. Did you love him?*

Yes, I said. *I think so.*

It never would have worked, she said, once I'd stopped crying. *Love isn't enough.*

That's exactly what I said to him. For a moment I thought I might be saved.

You said that to him? Rose did not sound pleased. *Out loud?*

Yes. Hesitant.

For Jimmy that's all there was.

We sat there for a while.

What was his reaction to that? said Rose.

He said I was so smart I was stupid.

Jesus. She laughed and shook her head. *My mother used to say that to me all the time.*

Mine, too, I said.

We still had not looked at each other. We had spoken all our words into the street.

Okay, you need to get out of here for a while, she said. *I need to get out of here for a while. We're going on a trip. On me. Where should we go?*

I thought for a few seconds. *Barcelona,* I said. Somehow we had never been. July, we decided, once I had finished with school.

As the taxi from the airport sped past farms and Ikeas and auto parts factories, as we got closer and closer to Barcelona, she and I both came to life, like cut flowers given new water. *Oh, look,* Rose would say, pointing at something outside her passenger window. *Oh, look,* I would say, pointing at something outside mine.

After checking into our hotel, Rose decided to sleep, and I decided to take a walk. The sunshine was prodigious, possibly benevolent. I smelled dog urine, strawberries, newsprint, diesel. I heard mopeds, church bells, barking, Lady Gaga. The longer I walked, the lighter I felt.

Wherever we went in Barcelona that week, the Spanish called us *las chicas.* Shoe stores, cafés, markets, bars, churches, pharmacies. Whenever it happened Rose would elbow me. *Las chicas.* That was the band we were in, the band we had always been in: two American girls with boundless delight, curiosity, and respect for your country's long, long history written all over our faces. Just the sight of us, eyes bright and avid, bellying up to your marble-topped tapas bar would make you pour us extra cava. If we were milling about your market stall staring at the olives, you would spoil us like a granddaughter and hand us delicacy after delicacy over the counter. If we were lying, sunglassed, sunscreened, on the rocks north of the beach, you would offer us free cans of the warm Foster's you were selling to tourists.

Fuck New York, said Rose, as we lay on those rocks.

It can hear you, you know, I said.

Barcelona. Medieval leavings and a beach. Like Paris but much better than Paris. Just this side of too much. Just real enough, just human and shit-streaked enough, we said as we walked along the sea, to keep people from dissolving into blubbering tears at its beauty. We did not want to leave. Because of the sight and scent of tiny, jewellike strawberries—a sugared musk hanging over several corners of the Boqueria, a scent that could sometimes travel all the way out to the street. Because of tinto de verano and pulpo a la plancha. And the stone face of the church of Sant Felip Neri, pockmarked during the Civil War by dozens or hundreds of bullet holes. You could put your hand on the side of that crucified church and feel its wounds. The thirteen geese drifting about in the courtyard of the cathedral in the Gothic Quarter—thirteen because the city's patron saint was martyred at that age. Saint Eulalia. Or, said another legend, the white feathers of the geese served as a tribute to the dove that flew out of her heart at her death.

The steep decline of the short tunnellike street that the saint was said to have been rolled down in a barrel full of glass and knives—a torture devised by her Roman rulers. We bought thirteen daisies, white, at a flower stall on Las Ramblas, and laid the flowers below an altar that had been installed in an alcove carved in the street's stone walls. Something we would never do in New York. A señora with her little dog saw us as she made her way slowly down the hill, in her secular habit of square navy skirt and boxy white blouse, and as she passed by she smiled and nodded to us. We smiled and said *Hola*.

Our third night, neither of us slept in the hotel; we'd found men to take us back to their apartments. The next morning, we arrived back to the hotel entrance at the same time.

You're a terrible influence, I said.

I know, said Rose. She linked her arm in mine, kissed me on my left temple, and turned us away from the hotel doors and back out into the cobblestoned street. *So are you. Let's go compare notes over coffee.*

Don't ever leave me, I said.

We were thirty-eight. It was the most we ever loved each other.

The bus to the beach that day was full of white-haired señoras wearing their secular habit of white poly-cotton blouses and navy blue polyester skirts. I was glad to sit among them as the bus rolled across town and the ocean winked at us from between streets. At the next to the last stop, the señoras clucked and groaned as the bus halted to let what one of them called a *puta* cross the road in platform heels and a silver spangled minidress. Their mouths

and bodies set in resignation, diffidence, and judgment—
closed doors sealed up for the winter.

Why don't you leave? she said, as the bus drifted on.

Why don't you *leave?*

What would my grandmother think?

Rose, I said, *your grandmother's dead.*

Come on, she said, in rebuke. She knew that I believed
the dead were always present and to suggest otherwise was
a form of treason. *Why don't you leave?*

I'm afraid.

Me too, she said. *I don't want to sleep alone. I don't want
to eat dinner alone.*

I don't either, I said. *And I don't want to run off and leave
someone to sleep alone or eat alone. The thought of it makes
me sick.*

You're nicer than I am.

*I don't know about that. It also seems incredibly dumb to
leave someone who loves me in order to find a replacement for
a dead man.*

Does *he love you?*

He thinks he does.

*What if I said this: you'll finally write what you have in
you to write if you leave him.*

I've thought about that, but—

Isn't it pretty to think so.

Exactly.

We passed a marble statue of a winged figure raising a
star into the sky and she said: *I hate everyone we know.*

You're just tired and hungry, I said, in a tone of ironic
concern, patting her knee, *and I think what you really need
is eight hours of sleep and a handful of almonds.*

She snorted. *What I really need is to drive something into a plate glass window.*

I laughed, too loudly, and one of the señoras turned to level a look in our direction.

So instead we got on a plane. Do you mean that you hate Peter?

Not all the time. No. I don't know what's wrong with me. I hate him because he's not me, but I need him because he's not me.

That's what it was like, being married. *Do you love him?*

Yes, she said.

I don't think you've ever said that before.

I haven't?

No, I said.

I think if I talked about my marriage it would bore you.

Rose! Jesus Christ. You're out of your mind.

I don't know! Maybe I'm *bored with my own thoughts.*

Never once have I been bored by your thoughts. Have I ever seemed bored by your thoughts?

No, she said. *No.*

I mean, I said, *maybe I should be—*

But it's too late now, she said, and we laughed. Maybe even giggled.

The bus sat facing the beach, and the señoras rose from their seats, seemingly all together, seemingly all at once, as if rising to meet the end of a Mass.

Do you ever think that half of our problem is trying to be something original when maybe we're just not? she said.

All the time, I said. *And to your point: I feel like I've read that somewhere, what you just said. But to quote you circa the year 1998, we're not just anybody.*

At this point in my life I only know I said that because you keep reminding me. Pause. *You know what my grandmother would think? That we should stop sitting around reading Anne Frank for the five thousandth time and go play outside.*

We got off the bus and walked to the beach.

Later that day, while Rose met up with the man she'd met the night before, I went for another long walk, and I stopped in a church we'd passed several times whose architecture puzzled me: at the top of the church floated a pediment consisting of stones crumbling as if we were in Rome, but then a smooth marble classical eighteenth-century facade picked up where the ruins let off. You couldn't tell whether the facade was a postmodern wink or a Civil War casualty. Sant Agustí Nou.

It was a lived-in, cared-for relic. The floors were made of cracked and gritty marble but they were spotless nonetheless. I heard the iron votive stand in the vestibule before I saw it. When I turned to find the source of the noise there stood a chorus of candles, fully aflame, an active volcano of sputtering, popping, hissing, dripping wax, prayers roasting away like a crackling, juicy chicken. I'd never heard lit candles make that ferocious a noise. I stood there for a long time, staring, listening.

A large statue of a female saint hovered up front, ensconced in a gilded alcove: Saint Rita. Saint Rita. What did I know about Saint Rita? Given the sheen of the statue's plaster, the vibrant red of her cheeks, and the unremitting blackness of her robes and whiteness of her wimple, Rita looked like she'd been fabricated in the early twentieth century. Roses—real, plastic, and silk—bloomed from two brass urns in front of the altar. She rated more roses and candles than Thérèse of Lisieux, my father's mother's favorite, who stood directly across from her—Thérèse, deposed in affection but probably counting it all glory. And to the left of the altar sat a Plexiglas box about three feet tall filled with folded scraps of paper.

Prayers for Saint Rita, said a sign in Spanish, Catalan, and English. *The patron saint of impossible dreams and the love unrequited.*

I looked around the church to see if there was anyone else in the sanctuary. There wasn't. I sat down in the pew that faced the shrine. I looked up at the inscriptions running along the tops of the walls. *Qui petit, acciptit. Qui quaerit, invenit.* He who asks, receives. He who seeks, finds.

I pulled a pen and a small notebook from my bag and began to write, a prayer for each page of ruled paper. Prayer after prayer after prayer.

> *I do not want what I haven't got.*
> *I do not want what I haven't got.*
> *I do not want what I haven't got.*
> *I do not want what I haven't got.*

That one went out to the Rose, and the Charlotte, and the Sinéad O'Connor of 1990.

Then I thought harder.

> *Make me abject.*
> *Make me jealous.*
> *Make me faithful.*
> *Make me honest.*

After folding the pages up tightly and glancing over my shoulder, I fed the plastic box as if it were a paper shredder.

14.

What did we want? We no longer knew. None of our friends knew what they wanted either. If you had told us, all of us, when we were thirteen, sixteen, twenty-one, or twenty-five, that we would grow to be what the world called faithless, we would have protested loudly and said you had no idea what or who you were talking about. We did not think that there would be affairs in our adulthoods because all of us were enlightened enough to marry our heart's desire or not marry at all; we did not imagine that a life spent writing required the accessory of adultery anymore. We thought that because we were readers, scholars, students of history, we would be protected against a certain amount of stupidity and stasis. We felt that we owed the books we'd read proof that we were as open and free as they had commanded us to be. We had been hoping to do something new, but found ourselves pulled toward the old.

We were angry and didn't know it, or angry and didn't think we should be, despite having come of age on an unending stream of women who wielded guitars and rage like swords and shields. Why were we angry? Our hard work might come to nothing, and we had been told everything depended on our hard work. We were not as strong as we thought we were; not as smart as we thought we were. The men we loved were not as strong or passionate as we felt ourselves to be, but they were always less hobbled by doubt; they were always less bothered by how long it was taking to get everywhere, which meant that we were going to have to do everything ourselves, which meant we were going to have to keep dreaming alone. We could have become angry, but we panicked instead. Because none of us were geniuses. Or self-actualized. And nobody had the guts to just say screw it, I'm going to live in a lighthouse where I can write my poems uninterrupted and entertain an unending stream of lovers until my tenderest, most secret spring runs dry. Or nobody had the money. If you had the guts you often didn't have the money, and if you had the money you often didn't have the guts. We were dumb dogs. Tireless workers with verbal aptitude. Self-questioning mystics trapped in late-capitalist bodies. Feminists who were unaware that their belief in the eventual rewards of unceasing individual effort made them secret agents for the neoliberal patriarchy. Falsely conscious; filled with bad faith. Bored.

We did not want to admit we were panicked, and it was turning all of us into the worst kind of heartless brute there is: a woman who fears she's unequal to her hopes.

What's the name of Anna Karenina's wife again? I said to Rose one night, and we laughed because of course I meant to say husband. Alexei Alexandrovich Karenin. We never could remember his name. The way we never could identify with Kitty, and felt much more like Levin—questing, restless, electric with dilemma.

I don't want to be Charles Bovary, someone said to Rose. A musician who was in love with her and refused to be satisfied with riding on the passenger side of her speeding car.

Or, as Charlotte Brontë said, anybody may blame me who likes.

All the men seemed to know what they wanted. Nobody got divorced from or broken up with or thrown out of the house. Another phenomenon our women's studies classes failed to warn us about: male passivity in the face of threat. Peter made jokes about the bruises that mysteriously appeared on Rose's forearms and thighs whenever he was out of town, and Mark was either sound asleep or pretending to be when I slid into bed at one in the morning. One in the morning—that was my rule. I had to be back in bed by then. One in the morning: at that hour it was entirely plausible that you'd just lost track of time and had trouble getting a cab. And in the meantime Rose and I pooled the details of our straying out onto many a bar top. As if we were dumping out pillowcases full of Halloween candy in order to dissect and glory in the haul.

What's going on with Rose and that guy? said some man we knew, one night, watching me watch the musician reach out and touch Rose's hair as they sat in a corner of a bar—a corner less hidden than it could have been.

I'm not her press secretary, I told him, eyes still on Rose and that guy, wondering how pissed I should be with her for putting me in this position.

If you're really her friend you should break that up, he said, and walked off.

Rose and I were the only people who could have told each other that we were making mistakes, but we didn't. When everyone is young—and we were young for a long time, the people I knew in New York—it is hard to confront your friends about the mistakes they might be making. You're not even sure if you should call them mistakes. You can't quite see them, either, for the cloud of sociability you're all generating—a cloud of parties and readings and barbecues and park picnics and concerts and dinner parties and movies and Oscar nights and driving up somewhere for the weekend in several cars.

At four in the morning one Sunday, Mark found me curled up on the bathroom floor at the base of the toilet, waiting to vomit and praying he wouldn't come in.

You're disgusting, he said, and pissed in the bathtub.

I slept on the couch. In the morning I crawled in beside him. He faced the wall, still sleeping. I stared at the back of his neck. When he woke up he turned to face me.

I'm hungry, he said. *Are you hungry?*

I tried hard to arrange my expression so that it did not say *Are you out of your mind?*

Should we get pancakes? he said.

On the walk over to the diner I took his hand.

Don't leave me, he said.

I won't, I said, and hoped I was not lying.

It really didn't matter, later that afternoon, back home, as we stood next to each other chopping and stirring, listening to the radio and joking with each other, whether love or fear had rooted our feet to the kitchen floor.

I need to leave, I told Rose.

Do you have the money to leave?

I didn't.

Could you sell a book in order to leave?

I'd tried that. For the last few months I'd been going to a café after school—I was no longer able to write around Mark—to work on a proposal about infidelity that my agent would eventually describe as an intermittently interesting conflagration of anxieties both shrill and muddled. *I stopped reading at page 5*, she'd written in her email. *You're writing like all that stands between you and a new kidney is this proposal. I know I don't need to tell you this, but that's not how we bring meaningful work into the world.* I didn't reply, and I wasn't ready to laugh about the rejection, which meant I couldn't tell Rose about it.

You know I'm not that kind of writer, I said. *I can't Dickens my way out of this.*

What about your father?

No. I'd never asked him for money in my life, and I wasn't about to start by asking him for money to leave my husband. He had not been the kind of father who thought it was his job to stockpile cash in order to make his daughter's adult life easier. He was the kind who thought it was his job to keep her fed and clothed until she was old enough to leave the house. I wasn't sure how much he had to give, either. He had a bad habit of losing money in the stock market.

I'll give you the money.

Absolutely not.

You know you'd do it—well, you have done it for me.

That was a fraction of this.

You always did have a thing about paying your way.

Should I not have? I could not keep the anger out of my voice.

Maybe I should have had a thing about paying my way.

Yes, I said. *Maybe you should have.*

I'm sorry. Pause. *Go be someone's roommate?*

I gave her a look.

Yeah, okay, I couldn't do that either. A sublet?

It's like I get poured full of concrete whenever I think of leaving.

I'm worried that you're going to wait around for something to explode this.

I was afraid of that, too.

Take the money, she said.

I can't.

Instead I let someone who lived far away write to me: the father of a two-year-old girl named Sarah Ann and the husband of a woman named Jaclyn. Ryan wrote and wrote, and I wrote back, because he didn't think I was disgusting, he thought I was passionate. He probably needed to feel passionate, or powerful, too, needed to feel that he was more or other than the boy who married Jaclyn when they were twenty-one, more or other than the professor who had not yet published a book, and sending an email to him was like putting a handful of quarters in a vending machine and waiting for the candy to drop, all of the candy.

Rose asked to see one of them, and when she handed the phone back to me her lack of effusion suggested she might have been a little bit jealous.

Nobody ever left me a ticket at a United counter, so let's call it even, I said.

She laughed. *Oh yeah. I forgot about that.*

Something's happened were the first words of his last letter, and then he went on, single-spaced, for a long time, telling me that the week before he had given a respected author, who had come to visit the university where he taught, a ride to the airport, and while the author did not know exactly what was going on with his driver, he could tell that this kid was about to jump out of his skin, which he was, because earlier that morning Ryan's wife had taken a hammer to his office at home—to his monitor, to his desk, to his chair, to a clock that he'd bought in Vienna during a semester in Milan, the year before he met his wife, who'd never been to New York let alone out of the country. His wife had seen an email to me on his phone, which was now also destroyed like his clock, and all he said when the respected author asked if anything in particular was bothering him was *Family trouble*, and the author, as if he knew exactly, said the email, what kind of family trouble would give rise to the kind of tense and agitated anxiety that can result from people finding out that you are not the perfect person you thought you were, began to speak to him about the importance of a good marriage to good work, of steady habits to great work, said that Flaubert was right even though you didn't want him to be. The respected author had married young, too, and he felt that it saved him from wasting his mind and his energy on trying to win a sexual popularity contest when he was too young to handle it, said that the ritual of taco night reminded him that his ego was always going to be the real child at the table, that his wife knew how to cut his ego down to size with her tongue and the respected author did not think he could live without this woman in his life because of it, said he needed a love that lacerated him and made him see that the fame he had meant nothing because his wife knew his real dumb heart and was not fooled for one second by the adulation he received, and that was real life, nothing else was real but the refining fire of her wisdom and the continual disparagement issued forth by his children.

I had been reading all this out loud to Rose but here I stopped. I could not imagine a woman saying things like this—or at least, none of the women I knew. None of us had ever been so secure in our success, if we'd had any, that we felt free enough to denigrate it, or to worship love for making us see how hollow the realization of our success really was. Women might say of family life that it had helped them become better multitaskers. That was what I had heard women say when they wanted to talk about the magical powers of children—children were gifts who had given them a proper relationship to time. Not to themselves.

This respected writer's work had always seemed a little too pleased with its own cleverness, and the Byzantine, breakneck nature of the cleverness seemed to be an expression of some fundamental innocence. I'd never liked it. But what did I know? I could be accused of harboring some serious innocence myself. If I was not so innocent I would never have squandered my husband's love and trust the way I was currently doing, would never have seen it or seen time as an unlimited resource.

Keep going, said Rose. *I want to know if this letter ends exactly as I think it will or whether people are surprising, like everyone always says they are.*

After hearing all this, he wrote, he felt much better able to be reconciled again to his real life, the life that he'd been perfectly fine with until he met me, and I wasn't real, no offense, but he couldn't help but think the author was the Jesus worshipped by his wife and his mother at work, trying to show him some sign, some way out and back to the good man he needed to be, even if he hated being it sometimes, in order to remember who he was and that it was definitely not his father, who had run out on him and his mother when he was thirteen.

You know how to pick 'em, said Rose, reading over my shoulder as I sat at my laptop.

His last line, a line he said he did not want to be his last, but he was in a hurry, he was writing this on his mother-in-law's iPad because his wife had whisked them all back to her childhood home for the summer, and his phone was no longer alive: *I keep thinking that you should have children and I should get back to trying to publish a book, and that if we'd had these things in our lives none of this would have happened.*

Rose put a hand on my shoulder. I tried to make a joke. *I might have just destroyed the clock*, I said.

You know what, yeah. If that's all that she'd gone to town on, if she'd limited her rage to one significant object, made, you know, one discriminating choice, then you would have known that she was some kind of artist, too, and not just a fucking wife.

Just wives. The phrase was an insult, the way we used it, the way our friends used it. The way *my wife*, whenever I heard it, seemed demeaning, distancing, an erasure, a complaint. The way *my husband* never did. Was it the long *i*, the one syllable, the way it rhymed with *gripe* and *strife*, its unfortunate similarity to *whine*? The way it rung with the sourness of a Catskills punch line and centuries of grievance? Both words, *husband* or *wife*: a suitcase you packed all your real feelings into so you could carry your life into public. The woman who had wreaked jealous destruction on objects was just a wife, but she had shown more love for her husband than we had ever shown ours. You could even argue that she had shown more might in the face of betrayal than our husbands had. It was not clear why Rose and I should consider ourselves elevated creatures in comparison.

So we believed that possessiveness was the lowest form of female affection. So we lived in New York and dressed the part and argued about books with our friends in expensive restaurants. So what. Rose was just a publicist and I was just a teacher.

I would not ask my father for money, but I found myself telling him about Jaclyn's husband, because if anyone had the power to shame me into right action the way this man had been shamed by his wife and this author, it would have to be my father, if it could not be my husband.

Did it make you feel alive? said my father. We sat next to each other on the beach in folding chairs, keeping watch on a fishing pole he'd planted in the sand.

Yes, I said.

It turned out my father had served, when he was barely out of his teens, as the other man for an older woman who was the receptionist in the front office of a frozen-fish company where he loaded trucks. Unintentional hilarity: the husband worked for the FBI, found my father loading the trucks one morning, and successfully intimidated my father out of fooling around with his very pretty wife, who, said my father, was probably having an affair with the boss as well.

She was crazy, my father had said of the woman he'd had an affair with. That, I did wince at, because of the misogyny that might have been lurking behind that statement, and at the truth that might have been lurking behind that statement. I'd started to get the feeling that I really was probably truly crazy, as was Rose, as were all of us who were running around the city in the middle of the night, lost and hungry, shooting our excess flame up into the stars like gas flares over the prairies.

15.

I was shocked, but not too shocked, when Rose told me she was pregnant.

Please don't judge me, she said.

You'd know if I were judging you.

You don't have to say anything to judge me, you know— it's when you get really quiet that I know something's up.

I'm not judging you. I'm just—

She waited for me to finish.

How much of you is doing this because you think you should and not because you want to?

Like you've never done that before, she said.

Yes, I said, *and I'm unhappily married.*

Where has wanting what I've wanted gotten me?

I'd thought the same thing, many times.

Is Peter asking you for this?

She said: *Did those books make you feel like you deserved to be alive?*

No, but I know how I'd feel if I'd never published them.

Does teaching make you feel like you deserve to be alive?

Yes, I said. *But not always. And it never makes me* thrilled *to be alive.*

She laughed.

Well, no, sometimes it does, I said.

If I had it in me to sit down and write a book from start to finish, she said, *I don't think I'd be doing this.*

Why do you think you can't?

I really don't know, she said. *I must be afraid to.*

That's what I'd suspected, and had not wanted to admit, even to myself.

What if I wrote only for the attention? she said.

Please. That's all anyone writes for. What are you going to tell your daughter when she asks you why you stopped writing?

I don't know. I'll tell her I'd done all I'd wanted to do, which I think is mostly true.

When we were—

Kids? she said, and laughed. I laughed, too, and said:

When we were kids, you got the kind of attention I'm still waiting for.

She shrugged. *But here we are. No one knows my name for the reasons I wanted them to—*

And nobody knows mine at all.

You could change that, if you wanted to.

That might be true, I said. *But we're talking about you here. What else? What else will you tell her?*

She thought. *I'll tell her that I wanted to try something else, and that she should never be afraid to try something else when the time is right.*

That doesn't sound like total bullshit. So much so it made me wonder whether it was time for me to try something else. Like finally accepting the dean's position I'd been repeatedly offered by the head of the upper school. Or becoming a florist.

I don't know if I would have pushed myself to write half of what I did if you hadn't shown up, she said.

Hearing that made me feel like I deserved to be alive, and I told her. Rose raised her glass and I raised mine to meet it.

Just make sure you have a girl, I said, *so we can make this party last longer.*

She smiled, and was about to speak again when a woman stopped at our table, a woman who looked like every other woman in the restaurant we were sitting in, like every other woman in Rose's neighborhood: tense and expensively maintained. Beatifically harried, her face framed by blond tendrils escaping a hastily arranged ponytail, her intricately and brightly patterned wool coat falling away to reveal a second or third child on the way.

I'm sorry, this woman said. *I was sitting at the bar and I couldn't help but overhear you saying you were pregnant, and I just want to know how you can do something that irresponsible.* She pointed at Rose's glass of wine.

She's four weeks along and French, I said. *Leave her alone.*

As the woman walked away, Rose poured what was left of her glass into mine.

16.

I hope you're alone for the rest of your life, said my mother-in-law, in a letter she sent me when she learned I was leaving Mark. I believed that I would be, because her son had done nothing but fail to put a stop to my wanting. Her letter put a stop to my writing. I couldn't work for months. Every sentence was stained with the selfishness, her word, she'd seen and deplored.

Let me get this straight, said my mother. *There's nobody else. You're leaving for some idea you've cooked up.*

She's unhappy and she doesn't like the guy anymore, said my father. *Leave her alone.*

Other people said things like *Well, at least there aren't children involved* or *Well, at least you didn't own a house together*, and I was offended by the assumption that divorcing without having to divide up these assets meant that the trauma was less of a trauma, and the ordeal was less of an ordeal. I couldn't tell whether these people thought that it really was lucky that I did not possess children or property, or whether it was suspicious, my lack of these anchors, and my unwillingness to stay.

They're jealous, said Rose. *End of story.*

No, I think they're glad they're not me, I said. *Jealousy can't always be the motivating force behind people telling you things you wish they'd kept to themselves.*

Details I would be keeping to myself: the muscle twitching in the middle of Mark's cheek when I told him I no longer wanted to be married. The two of us, in those last weeks before I moved out, sitting like blocks of marble in restaurants filled with other people's almost raucous affinity for the friends and lovers they'd met up with. Mark sitting next to me on the edge of the bed the morning I left, wiping soundless tears from his cheeks. Crying so hard in the car on the way over to my apartment in Ditmas Park, so hard the car-service driver pulled over on the BQE, thundering with traffic on a windy, white-hot summer morning, to ask me if I was okay. The undeserved kindness made me cry harder. Over the friends I would lose and the gossip I would become.

Before I left, Mark made me promise that I would still go with him to a wedding we'd been invited to in Texas— the second marriage of one of his best friends. Of course, I told him.

It'll be hellish with you, he said, *but it would be even more hellish without you, and I don't want to have to spend any time explaining where you are. Something like sorry, she's dead in a ditch somewhere.*

Which is where you'd like me to be, I said.

That's not funny.

I wasn't trying to be funny.

But yes, I wish you were dead in a ditch.

Would you believe me if I told you I wished I were, too?

Oh yes, he said. *And I wish it made me able to forgive you.*

On the plane I popped the Dramamine I'd bought at Hudson News and washed it down with a tiny bottle of Sutter Home chardonnay—a cocktail for air travel self-erasure passed down to me by Rose. Mark, reading a very long book beside me, gave off a chill when I ordered a second.

The wedding took place outside Austin, in a green field, with mountains in the distance. Bright riots of wildflowers stood like heralds in mason jars. All of the bridesmaids wearing pale blush gowns the very color of tenderness; all of their faces framed by long loping blond curling-iron curls, all of their crowns showing roots. All blond, all self-tanned, all big of eye and heavily mascaraed. They blurred into one girl and I tried to imagine what it was like to be their kind of compliant. Their kind of dumb, I would have said at a different time. Life must certainly be easier if all you wanted from it was a handsome man who thought you were beautiful and who could bankroll a bunch of renovations, vacations, and educations. As the bride made her way down the aisle, the sunset bled through the leaves of colossal trees whose branches ran like brooks, like elephant trunks, out to the side and down to the ground—live oaks, which I would never have known if I hadn't met Mark, whose childhood home sat in the shade of two. I spent much of the ceremony staring at those trees, because it was difficult to watch another woman—a woman ten years younger than her husband, ten years younger than me—float serenely, joyfully, and blamelessly toward happiness.

After the ceremony and before dinner, some guests sat on a porch that looked out at a lawn full of people laughing, the grass glinting with what seemed to be hundreds of gold wedding bands. I drank primly but steadily, nodding and smiling at whatever was said to me. I left when I heard someone say *I think people who divorce just don't try hard enough*.

At dinner, no one would have ever guessed that I'd thrown my suitcase against the wall while we were getting dressed in the hotel room, or that Mark had called me, as I threw it, a spineless ass. Or that the night before, in the restaurant at the hotel, the bartender, who'd been watching us try not to have an argument over dinner, served us with a check whose dot matrices identified us as *Seats #3 and 4: Couple Doloroso*.

Just before the cake arrived, Mark had taken someone's small boy on his knee, and a silver-haired woman who had been sitting next to me watching leaned over and from within her cloud of gray linens and flaxes said, *Honey, where did you find him?*

I stole him from another woman, I said, and headed toward the bar.

You're going to dance with me, Mark said, standing over me and my fifth glass of wine, after fireflies had started to spark their way through the bushes and the hired band was a few songs in. We did not dance so much as sway in place with my face buried in his chest and his lips pressed into my hair. *You are so stupid*, he whispered.

I hear those words nearly every day.

17.

Two days after she gave birth to twin girls, Rose began to imagine that Peter wanted to take them away and sell them. She was diagnosed with postpartum psychosis, and doctors put her on an antipsychotic.

Back in the hospital, Rose threw a remote control at Peter and a hard plastic cup full of water. A bottle of pills. A plate. A tray and then a book. The book split his right temple open. She was admitted to a mother-and-child unit at the hospital where she'd delivered, and stayed there for two weeks. It was going to be three but Rose drew the line, Peter told me. It was the most cheerful hospital floor I'd ever been on, and its tireless commitment to transcending the dingy was yet another powerful argument for making sure you had a shit ton of money. It was also a powerful argument for getting pregnant and going crazy, if getting pregnant and going crazy meant you'd be quarantined in a very clean room outfitted with room service, the endless and sincere solicitation of your psychic and bodily temperature, and a picture window that allowed you to be sedated by the sight of the Fifty-Ninth Street Bridge and the regular comings and goings of the Roosevelt Island tram.

Rose sat in the hospital bed wearing a bright pink chenille bathrobe that used to belong to her mother over a black Bikini Kill T-shirt—two pieces of clothing I'd seen so many times I'd started to think my mother had owned the same bathrobe and that I'd bought that T-shirt in 1994, too, when in reality the one I'd bought in 1994 said the Spinanes. I knew Rose was wearing that T-shirt for the same reason she'd worn it in 1994: as a big fuck-you. Three books lay face down, splayed open, like a handful of jacks tossed and spilled, next to her, for that was how she binge-read, in a round, diving back into one book when she got tired of the other. Her hair looked as energetic as usual but her face seemed as stripped of light as the trees outside were stripped of leaves.

Do I look as gray as I feel? she said.

You won't be this gray forever.

How do you know that?

Because I know you.

She thought about that, and said *You would make a very good mother.*

Rose, I said. *So will you. I know you will.*

How do you know that?

Because you are such a good friend.

Don't cry, she said as I wiped some tears away with the heel of my hand.

Where are the girls? I said.

Down the hall, she said, *having tea at the Ritz.*

Maria and Josephine. Rose had named them after her grandmothers. Rose held Maria and I held Josephine and I stared into her face on a hunt for the places where Rose left off and Peter began, scouring the curves that shaped her nose, the divot at the center of her top lip, the swirls of blond hair that would surely grow into curls.

Let's meet Maria, I said, and we switched. Maria's lashes were that much longer than Josephine's, and she fidgeted a little bit more. Her hair was much darker. Peter's hair. Their eyes were the eyes of deer who could tell the future, I thought, and said it out loud.

And now you've christened them, she said.

Peter decided that once Rose was discharged from the hospital, Ann Marie would stay in the house and he would move into a nearby Holiday Inn Express. Rather, it was Rose who had decided that, because she thought he needed to stay away for a while in order for her to be absolutely sure she could stop wanting to throw things at him. He asked if I could come over after school a few nights during the week and however much I could give them of my weekend to help, and to have someone in the house who wasn't Ann Marie. I said I would stay in the house and would go to and from work from there, if everyone thought that was a good idea, and he looked very relieved.

Once home, Rose slept as if she were hiding. She slept and she cried, and her daughters cried, too. It was more painful to listen to Rose's tears than the crying of her daughters, for her daughters were still strangers to me.

I did the laundry, folded the laundry, made dinner, cleaned up after dinner, fed the girls and changed their diapers—the girls, that's what Rose's mother called them. That's what she called us, too.

Girls, she'd say, *dinner's ready. Girls, have you seen my phone? Girls, someone's at the door.*

When I washed the dishes or changed diapers, Rose would often stand next to me and rest her chin or her head on my shoulder. One night: Rose's chin on my right shoulder, her right hand on Maria's head. *All I can see is the sadness she will feel*, she said.

On another: I came downstairs to find Rose standing in the kitchen smashing the pills she was supposed to be taking with the bottom of a drinking glass. She stopped when she realized there was someone else in the kitchen and it was me.

I don't believe in them either, I said, *but you should probably take those.*

I will if you will, she said.

I walked over to the counter, picked one up, and popped it in my mouth. She popped one in hers, and I poured us two glasses of water. As we drank and Rose swallowed I spit mine out in the glass and rinsed it down the sink quickly. She did not notice.

Rose was convinced the drugs would leave traces in her breast milk, so she and I sat in her bed or on the couch, each holding a baby, each holding a bottle filled with formula, watching television, or pretending to.

She'd started to make jokes again. One afternoon she said *Let's just watch* The Bachelor, and I said *Our mothers breastfed us while watching Watergate hearings, we can't tell these kids we watched* The Bachelor, and she said *Please I'm an invalid* and then, after ten minutes: *I think my college degree was just eradicated.*

Maria and Josephine. I would put my nose to their cheeks and whisper *Hello, hello, hello, tiny bird.* I sang to them, sang them many Beatles songs. Sang "Rocket Man" and "Daniel," which my aunts had sung to me, and "Kid" and "Alison" and "Fox in the Snow" and "Waterloo Sunset" and "Little Green." I sang to them because I wanted to say *I love you* but did not think it was my place yet.

Once I gave Maria my breast. At the kitchen table. Just

to see. Lifted up my sweater and laid a cloth like a tent over my shoulder to shade her head crowned with its bird's nest of black hair. While I was moved by her helplessness and her hunger, it felt no different than being moved by the helplessness of all the tiny dogs tied to fire hydrants and shaking in the cold outside all the bodegas and dry cleaners of Brooklyn. As far as the physical sensation, I preferred having a man take one in his mouth. Much preferred.

Ann Marie, on her way into the kitchen, caught me doing it. I was almost as mortified as if I'd been caught masturbating. She didn't care, though.

Are you kidding me? she said. *Honey, it's what we're made for. And look at you, you're a regular Madonna.* Like Rose, her compliments, though effusive, never rang false because of the anger that raged like a sea on the other side of that gesture. *You Irish*, she said, by way of offering condolences for my genetically induced prudery, and walked off to Clorox the bathroom or give Rose's bed hospital corners.

Ann Marie never said the words *postpartum psychosis* or *postpartum depression.* She said that Rose had been through a lot, and just needed some rest.

On weekends I'd drag Rose out of the house for walks. We'd head up to the promenade in Brooklyn Heights and back, and she'd say things. Make pronouncements.

I've got two babies and you've got two books.

Do you want one of them? I made too many.

If I ever ask you whether I've made a mistake, please don't answer me.

I gave up, but you didn't.

No. I gave up, and you didn't.

My mother is kinder to me when you're around. Have you ever noticed that? Your mother is kinder when I'm around, too.

What is wrong with us?

Life's hard enough. Why am I making all these complications for myself? He loves me.

Whenever we approached her stoop she would say what we'd always said to each other: *Don't ever leave me.*

I wrote a letter to Rose that consisted of two columns—on the left-hand side of the page, a list of all the things she had achieved, on the right, a list of all the things I admired her for—and slipped it into one of the books she'd stacked on her bedside table.

If you give up, I give up, it began. I tried to do better than that but I couldn't. It worried me that I couldn't do better than that.

I'm proud of you girls, Rose's mother said one night, watching us feed Maria and Josephine.

For what? I said.

You love each other like you're blood when you don't have to.

My mother drove up and stayed three nights. She brought three pans of macaroni and cheese and six logs of chocolate chip cookie dough to put in the freezer because she knew Rose loved both. She also brought a deck of cards, and the four of us played hearts while Maria and Josephine slept. My mother taught Rose solitaire during that visit. Somehow Rose had never learned the game— the way my mother had never learned how to make a negroni, which Ann Marie showed her that night, the way Rose had, once upon a time, showed me.

It's the Sophia Loren of cocktails, Ann Marie said.

I'll drink to that, said my mother, and had two.

I love you all so much, said Rose, and soon fell asleep with her head on the table, in the middle of a hand, because half a negroni had undone her.

You raised this one right, said Ann Marie to my mother, nodding in my direction, as she shuffled the cards one more time, after Rose had gone to bed.

Thank you, she told Ann Marie. *My sisters and mother were a big help. It takes a village, like they say.*

I could have never raised Rose without my mother. Sometimes I wanted to kill her, sure, but that's the price I had to pay. My husband really hated her. Ann Marie took a drink of her negroni, put it back down on the table. *My mother, I mean. Used to say he wished he could poison her instant coffee.*

That sounded a lot like Rose.

Mine used to lock me out of the house if I came home too late, said my mother, scrutinizing her hand. *I'd sleep on the porch on a chaise longue she had out there. A few times in winter. In a wool coat she thought I spent too much money on.*

Ann Marie laughed. *I bet that showed her!*

Then my mother laughed. *The plan was to wear her down, but it wore me down!*

I don't know if I could have ever forgiven my mother if I hadn't had Rose, said Ann Marie.

Yes, said my mother, startled, as if Ann Marie had described a feeling she had known but not been able to put into words.

Everything was different back then, said Ann Marie.

Tell me about it, said my mother, scrutinizing her hand.

That woman can talk, said my mother, as we settled down in the bed in the guest room, *but I've always liked her.*

And then, as I turned out the light: *Just for the record, I don't want you ever thinking I needed you to give me a grandchild.*

Part of me felt that I had been given a blank check, and

part of me wanted to know where the money was coming from.

Why do you say that? I asked her.

Let's go to sleep, she said.

Did you—

No, she said. Later she would say that she did not think her *No* was a lie, because what she had gone through after giving birth to me was nowhere near as bad as what Rose had gone through.

My mother fell asleep right away but I could not. I went downstairs to the living room, sat on the couch, turned on a light, took a book from the shelves, but couldn't read. I watched light from the streetlamp make green stained glass out of the leaves of the plane trees. Rose, my mother, her mother, Josephine, Maria, all asleep upstairs, so many people I loved above me, but I could not rest in that peace. Near midnight in a sleeping house didn't seem like peace, just then. It felt a little haunted. It might have actually been. When Rose and Peter first moved in, Rose told me she'd seen what she swore was a little girl with long blond curly hair in a blue plaid dress run up the stairs one Saturday morning. She'd never seen her again and I'd always wondered if Rose *wanted* to see something like that— a specter so benign and full of life, an apparition so like a mirror, it could have served as a blessing on what she was afraid was a huge mistake.

Rose and I had been described as strong but maybe that had just been the blind stubbornness of youth. Our minds had the capacity to instantly synthesize and distill, but this meant they also had the capacity to instantly offer rebuttals to our most deeply held desires. The quickness with which we could imagine what other people thought—what our families might think, what the people we did not respect but feared would think, what the people we liked would think, what people long dead but still alive in our hearts would think—and how willing we were to let other voices have the last word, might partly explain why our minds, to use Rose's words, had cracked open. Too much noise.

I am so anxious, a student of mine, my favorite, had told me that week. *I am so afraid of people making fun of me, I am so afraid of failure, and I know I will live with this fear forever.*

At some point Maria or Josephine started to cry, and I got up and crept into Rose's bedroom, where Ann Marie, sleeping next to Rose, was sitting up and preparing to get out of bed.

I'll take her, I said.

Bless you, said Ann Marie, and rolled back under the covers.

The tears were Josephine's. I grabbed a blanket, reached into the crib, wrapped her inside it, and on the way downstairs decided to take her outside. I wanted the air. It was almost spring, the day had been unusually warm, and had she met the moon? Rose's pink bejeweled flip-flops, which she'd accidentally worn home from a nail salon one afternoon, sat where they usually sat, which was just inside the front doorway. I slipped them on. We stepped outside.

Out on the stoop, Josephine and I bounced up and down. *Look, Josephine*, I said, though I knew she would not. The moon was full, and as round as her head, which smelled of milk and then sugar, yeast and then snow. Still she cried into my chest, still we bounced. I stared at the moon, which I could never get enough of, because in New York, depending on where the windows in your apartment were situated, how high they were set in the walls, and depending on what time of night you found yourself walking home from the subway, the moon might be hidden from your view for days, even weeks, but here it was, directly above us, purer and more perfect than anything on earth. *Even your little head*, I whispered to Josephine. Purer and more perfect—and rising like clockwork, besides. The moon did not present as friendly as the sun, and for good reason: those of us who walked beneath it did not know what it took to hang in there, up there, night after night, keeping your circle intact, inviolate, distinct from the darkness.

18.

On the night I fell in love with the man I thought I really could spend the rest of my life with, I learned that he and I both spent our childhoods swimming in the blue holes of the Pine Barrens—pools of water sprung to life in the abandoned mines hidden in the sand and trees, their surfaces magnetizing the blue of the sky like a mirror. After about a foot or two of silted bank, there were drops of forty, sixty, or one hundred feet, creating temperatures that could cramp and paralyze and drown you. But you couldn't see the depth because of the mirror, and you wouldn't guess there was such a plunge because of the smallness of the pool.

He liked to say that my sadnesses were like those blue holes: the depths arrived without warning, the surface said nothing of what troubled it. I worried they might drive him away from me. But that wasn't why he ended it. He ended it when I finally told him I'd done to my husband what his wife had done to him, and a great deal more of it.

I'm sorry, he said. *It would be like drinking a bottle clearly marked poison.*

I told him I understood and then begged him to fuck me one last time so that I could tell myself that despite what he'd said, I remained, above all, irresistible. He did me that favor. But I let his decision hurt for longer than I should have or intended to, and let it keep me alone for longer than I should have been or intended to be. I knew I was not supposed to feel shame over my past, or to use the unnecessarily melodramatic phrase *my past* when describing a series of mistakes that I had not been the first woman to make, but I did; I knew I wasn't supposed to feel like a failure because this one man had declared me unfit for partnership, but I did.

Did you have to tell him the truth? said Rose. Sitting next to me on a bench on the pier at Coney Island, watching the old men and old women slip raw chicken thigh onto fishing wire and cast the pieces out into the muddy Atlantic, which always seemed to be wheezing down here as it lapped at the gray-faced sand.

Then what was the point of leaving? I said. *To start lying all over again?*

I hate to say this, she said, *but you may be putting too high a value on honesty.*

That was the day I stopped telling her everything.

19.

If you read to Maria and Josephine at night, they wanted you to get into the bed, get right down under the covers with them, so they could, while you turned the pages, hold on to your hair with their left hand while sucking the thumb of their right. They wanted nothing less than complete and total fusion with the person next to them, but they'd take being nestled as close to you as possible and holding on tightly so you couldn't get away. When they grabbed at my hair I couldn't help thinking of the Rose of 1999 and 2004 and 2010 leaning across a table, arms crossed, eyes bright, focus piercing, ready to hear it all, ready to spill it all, saying *So!* to whoever sat across from her. Rose demanding and receiving connection. Every time Maria or Josephine demanded and received the closeness they deemed satisfying enough to fall asleep to, I would pray for God, or something like God, to send them someone, as early in their life as possible, who was delighted by this need and lived to indulge it.

Whenever I came through Rose's front door they flung themselves at my knees the way I'd seen dancers throw themselves at their partners onstage—as if they were lashing themselves to their dearest mast—and it shocked me into gladness every time. They might have been doing it out of a half-remembered sense that I'd carried them out of cars and up staircases, too, like their mother. Or their desire for another sister, and their seeing that I was not like their mother, because I did not have a husband, caused them to mistake me for someone who could make them a trio. Maria and Josephine at two. They asked for me when I was not there, and when I was there they did not like it when Rose and I got involved in a conversation that did not concern them. We always let them interrupt us, and might have even welcomed their interruption. We no longer needed or wanted to analyze our lives for hours the way we did when we were younger.

Rose's house was now, like my aunts' houses, a place to laugh and eat and make cracks about how much wine we were drinking. Was it often a relief, at the end of a week, to take my place in the Impressionist painting Rose had made of her life, to feel the rustling of tutus and curls against my legs as the girls ran in between and around us, and nod as Rose held a bottle of expensive wine in the air as if to say *Shall we?* and Peter turned up the volume on the stereo? Yes. I belonged there in that house, but I was restless there, and tried to convince myself it didn't matter. At a certain point, I decided, friendship was just like marriage. The idea of the two of you mattered more than the reality, and the form of the thing, not the thing itself, was what you counted on. You could stare at it and ask whether it was worth pressing hard on what filled the form, but I did not want to do that here. I could not bear ruining another relationship by demanding it be more than what it was, when what it was was perfectly fine.

What is going to happen to us? I wanted to ask her. All

the time. But that would mean I was the little sister, forced by habit and proximity to mistake her for the only person I could trust to give me that answer.

We were forty-one.

If you move to New York to be motherless, you may feel a pain as you watch the city, over time, fill up with mothers, hundreds of them, strollers everywhere, so many of them you start to wonder if you are in fact not in New York but in Salt Lake City—an infinitesimally small pain, in the scheme of things, but one that I had a hard time chasing away. Nearly all of my friends in New York, and Rose's friends, were married or partnered, a number of them with children, all of them living in apartments or houses they owned, and it narrowed my vision to the point of depression and made me forget that there were different ways to live a life. I hadn't made good use of the freedom I'd insisted on, it seemed to me, and I'd started to wish I'd saved my money, stayed married, and bought an apartment. I'd started to wish I'd wanted children, too, but it wasn't out of some yearning to be and know another animal. I thought being a mother would exempt me from having to be and know myself.

The mothers outnumbered the reasons I had for living. Said the depression. I knew I should force myself to meet someone or publish something that mattered to me, but I felt unsure of who to be next, and it left me unwilling to make my body or mind that flagrantly public. I'd lost faith that I could be trusted to discover what would make me feel as at home in the world as Rose seemed to be with those girls, and I was suffering—could I use the word?—from feeling the disparity between her apparent contentment and my confusion. From struggling to pretend, to Rose and to myself, that my love for her was not becoming shaded with envy and resentment.

She never mentioned what had happened in those weeks and months after giving birth. Never mentioned the post-partum depression, never mentioned the running around in the night that, I always suspected, had led her to decide to become pregnant. She acted as if none of it had ever happened. Never told me if she had grown to love Peter more, so much more that it made her stop asking other men to give her what she'd thought she needed, or was there someone other than Peter. Or whether what had happened after she gave birth chastened her and made her worry that she could kick that storm up again if she wasn't careful, or whether she was just, you know, too fucking tired to bother. If she felt guilty, or remorseful, or ashamed, or what, for having cheated, a word we did not like to use but that's what it was, and did she know why we did those things, looking back. Never told me if she got jealous when she stood in the Strand looking at the table of new releases, or became furious when she paged through *The New York Times Magazine* and saw a piece she could have written in her sleep.

I told myself I understood this strategy for self-preservation, when I really kind of hated her, and did not want to hate her, for having the balls and the guts to control the story like the publicist she was—for making it look like she was all better now, like she'd buried all her bodies way down in the ground, in a place where nobody would ever find them, and for appearing to have so much going on in her new life that she didn't have time to remember where she'd dumped the people and things that had stopped mattering to her, and didn't care that she couldn't remember. Rose had also developed a habit of changing the subject if we got too near a topic she'd rather not engage with—and because she had been the one to officially lose her mind, I let her. While making note of every time she did. Which made me the older sister: suspicious and keeping too careful a score.

Instead of telling each other what we really thought, she and I spent a lot of time talking about other people. Rose loved, like Jimmy had loved, to hear me talk about the endless parade of absurdities that could befall a person when they taught at a private school in Manhattan, and I didn't mind. Telling her these stories allowed me to laugh about them instead of being tortured by them, and I had been teaching for long enough that there was much more torture in being around the young than there was endless amusement—the boys could tell I was more their mother than a slightly older classmate, and it made dealing with them very difficult, because they already had one overbearing bitch with deepening laugh lines in their life, and did not appreciate having to come to school and deal with another, and it was also becoming harder to laugh as I watched the girls flaunt their bodies, and harder to listen to them demand dress codes that let them flaunt them, and harder to feel sympathy for them when they blamed misogynist double standards for keeping them from this very important right to wear uncomfortable scraps of clothing to school. Watching the dawdling streams of essentially preverbal five-year-olds pass through the lower school in the morning filled me with an intense longing to teach kindergarten. If you taught kindergarten, you would always know for sure that you were the adult in the room and that you were inarguably the person in charge.

Mostly Rose and I talked about what she and the girls were up to, and the fights she and Ann Marie would get into over the girls, and about the mothers Rose knew. I could never hear enough about these women. Whenever Rose sat next to them on playground benches as they bitched about their sexless marriages or the pass-agg comments, Rose's words, some other mother had slung at them in the lobby of a yoga studio, she kept her mouth shut the way she did back when she had to report a story, which led to these women mistaking Rose's silence for compassion and telling her things they didn't tell the other mothers because Rose didn't judge them out loud. They told Rose everything, like who they were making out with in cars driven for secrecy to Bay Ridge Costco parking lots, or the accidental-seeming third pregnancies that were actually last-ditch bids to keep an ATM of a husband chained to the premises. Some of them had taken to calling her in tears from childhood backyards or cabins in Vermont about texts unanswered and overtures denied, and very accidental, and very unwanted, second or third pregnancies, and Rose would tell me that she wondered if listening to these women, sitting next to them waiting for them to give up the goods, and they always did, scratched the same itch that reporting did—laying the traps, collecting the bodies, feeling the energizing heat that came from standing close enough to someone else's sticky situation and then the cool breeze of relief that came from knowing you could always get back into your rental car and drive away. Whether being in the middle of the commotion and chaos generated by Maria and Josephine satisfied, at least for the time being, the need she'd always had to be in the middle of some action.

Do you miss it? I asked.

What I don't miss is having to convince a bunch of assholes that I'm good enough to print.

I took the hint and changed the subject.

When her satisfaction became too painful to sit next to, I would turn down plans with her and the girls to work on a novel that, by that point, four years after I'd started it, she must have assumed was nothing but a fabricated excuse. And I would write, in fact wrote a lot, partly just to ensure it was not a fabricated excuse, but the sentences were dead on the page. They were too elegant and said nothing. I kept at it, thinking something living would have to erupt, but I was too intent on making sure no one could tell the person writing them was angry or lonely. No one ever saw those pages, but they were a forest I liked to go walking in. The paths were well-worn and kept me out of harm's way. Typing and erasing, typing and erasing: it lulled me. Drugged me.

When I could not write I scrolled through men as if they were boots or hotel rooms or duvets on sale. It made me sick but I did it for hours, sometimes, falling asleep with my face on my phone, because I thought it was my responsibility as a single woman to be that dedicated in my search for happiness. I'd run into Mark once while I searched. He'd run into me, too, and sent a message.

You did this to us, it said.

That put me off scrolling for a while.

A few weeks later I saw him at the Strand, wearing the same short-sleeved navy T-shirt, same gray jeans, same sneakers: three notes in a chord I didn't mind hearing again. Saw his face, in profile, from yards away, talking to another man also wearing a T-shirt, jeans, and sneakers. A green canvas knapsack on the floor by his feet, looking new but already marred by a black ink stain at one of the corners. Yards away, and four years later, staring at his cheeks and remembering how the bit of skin just next to his ears could taste of warm salted butter. I turned around and left the store.

Another woman might have been inspired by her students' refusal to live under a bullshit regime and would have written Mark to say no, the patriarchy did this to us, but even if I marched in the street shouting against that regime with hundreds of other women, I didn't think I'd ever be convinced that forces other than my own heart and mind had left me this stranded.

But when Rose and I laughed together over those women I could believe again that we weren't just anybody, and it could make me feel better about still having to jockey for dryers at the laundromat on sweltering Saturdays in August, and could, sometimes, make me feel smug and heroic about sleeping alone—that is, at least for as long as we sat in Rose's kitchen or backyard calling these women amateurs for having meltdowns over unanswered texts or for getting caught making out with the bartender they were having it on with, drinking and rolling our eyes at the way they wrung their hands over potential and omnipresent toxins, or rolling our eyes at their husbands and their Sun Records T-shirts and the way these guys overexplained everything to their children as they walked into bodegas and out of the subway, as if they thought being a parent meant being a docent at the museum called Life. I knew a lot about the lives of people I experienced mainly as faces floating over wine glasses, a lot more than those people might have suspected, and I enjoyed believing, as I nodded while one of these women went on about her *Twilight* addiction, or went on about how she fired her nanny when she discovered the nanny was letting her children eat Doritos, that Rose and I were still on the same team: spies in the house of unexamined privilege.

In the end, Rose and I were just anybody: two women whose friendship ended because one had a family and the other did not. Because one had money and the other did not. Because one had been determined to make peace with her decisions and the other was not.

Just before Christmas that year, my landlady informed me that she needed to sell the big old Victorian that she owned and I lived on the top floor of. Divorce proceedings, she'd said. She would put the house on the market in the spring, it would sell soon after, and we would probably all—she, her two twentysomething daughters, and myself—have to move out by June. I did not, again, have enough money saved up to afford what it would cost to find a new apartment and move into one. I had very little savings, not only because I'd been paying Rose back for the loan that let me leave Mark, but for the same reason she'd bought all those face creams and shoes back when we lived together: I could not imagine a future worth putting away cash for. I'd been trying not to think about the things I'd been buying, and how large the balance on my credit card was growing. It would have been slightly cheaper to drink heavily, but new coats and Pilates classes and expensive candles from France made me feel that I had my act together when it might have been falling apart, and alcohol could leave me with my wounds throbbing and floodlit.

On New Year's Eve, at a party thrown by a writer we knew, across the street and half a dozen houses down from the apartment Rose and I had shared, wearing a dress I'd put on the credit card because I wanted to look as expensive as everything in the brownstone I'd be standing in, Rose told me that Peter had bought her and the girls a house in the Catskills. As she showed me pictures on her phone that I did not inspect too closely, I smiled and said *Oh how wonderful!* We talked for a good hour about her plans for the kitchen, and I realized once again that I could have been an actress, given how easily I heaved all my true feelings aside to take on other, more expedient ones, when the demand arose. Soon we got involved in a conversation with the women standing next to us, one of whom was another writer who'd also just sold a book, a memoir. The writer was saying that she was going to take some of the money and buy a dilapidated Victorian in Cape May. As the group of women crowded around the writer's phone to look at a slideshow of the house, I slipped away to get my coat. It was well before midnight. On my way out, in a front room so packed I was pretty sure no one would notice, I took a bottle of Veuve Clicquot off a sideboard crowded with crudités and cheeses and fruits and slid it into in my bag.

In the cab home my mind grew *dark*, as my students liked to say of sentences that did not uphold the consensus. It was never a compliment, always an apology. They liked to reassure their classmates that despite the *dark* or *depressing* or *emo* thing they'd just read out loud, they were fine, it was fine, they were just having a bad day, they didn't know what had gotten into them, they were just playing around with an idea that was kind of dumb, forget it, and my heart would break for them, for us, because they lived in a world that made them feel they had to hide behind trees after standing in an open field singing a song that told a truth. But sometimes they sounded secretly proud of themselves while disowning themselves, and then I was glad, because often what they were shrugging off were true, searing, potent sentences. I believed in their sentences, loved their sentences, even when it was very hard to love the students who wrote them, but as the cab sped down Ocean Avenue I decided I hated every single one of mine, hated myself for thinking any of them were worth the tortured hours. Two books had not brought me the psychological or financial safety that two houses could. They had not changed me or changed my life. I should not have asked that of them, should not have demanded that they bring me what only spouses and houses and children could bring you, but I had not known any better. I must not have wanted to.

In the apartment I sat down at the desk in my bedroom—a plank of unfinished pine set in an alcove window by my landlady when she learned I wrote—and poured myself a glass of champagne. A few more glasses of champagne, almost the whole bottle.

I drank and stared at the moon. My landlady's cat, which liked to nose itself into my apartment if I forgot to shut my door all the way, crept into the room and leapt onto the desk. It stared at me, tail ticking, then crawled into my lap. I tried to feel grateful for my landlady and er kindness; for this cat who found me solid and warm nough to fall asleep to. For my limbs, my teeth, my hair, a paying job, with health insurance, that did not require me to show up from June 16 to August 20. For breasts and ovaries free of cancer. For never seeing one of my books in a box of free junk on a Brooklyn sidewalk. For the student who just before break sent me an email saying that I had single-handedly restored his faith in literature. But my mind did not want to be bullied. I drank and sank deeper into this old thought: *Why should she have everything?*

I never wanted any of what she had and yet I called it everything. For in New York it did matter what things looked like from the outside, more than I ever imagined it would, and I had not quite been prepared for the part in the story of your life, around forty or so, where you really start feeling, not as a hunch but in your bones, that all your maniacal work might have been worthless and you really are failing yourself now, and because you can't bear to think about your own failings you start looking around at what other people are doing and having because maybe flagellating yourself through comparison will launch you into some burst of actual, redemptive motivation. No one would ask Rose what she was doing with her life: those girls made the answer obvious. I was the only person who would ask her that question, and if I asked her I wasn't sure I would get the truth. Or ever had.

What was I doing with my life? Persisting in fits and starts in some weird quiet version of rebellion against domesticity that, because it was not a bravura performance that could inspire a cause, a cult, a movement, or a movie, was illegitimate.

Why don't you just live upstate with us for the summer

and save some money? Rose said, when I told her what was going on.

That would not be a good idea, I said.

If refusing her help hurt her feelings, and I think it did, she did not make that clear to me.

Are you okay? she said.

I told her I was fine.

20.

I hated his wife more than I loved him: David. A history professor. I gave him, over and over, the sex that his twenty-five years of marriage had failed to provide him with. He thought he loved me and I let him think it. Mark had gotten engaged, and I needed someone to remind me that marriage was a bankrupt construct, needed to remember that men thought I was worth the trouble. I no longer trusted myself to keep a roof over my head, so I wanted protection, competence, and command. He was ten years older than me, and his hands looked indeed as if they had taken chain saws to trees, built bookcases, built treehouses, laid floors, and rewired crumbling houses. They had cradled four infant daughters and turned the pages, four times over, of *Anne of Green Gables*.

His girls: Elinor, Anne, Elizabeth, and Victoria. Also known as Ellie, Annie, Beth, and Vixie. Or Ells-bells, Anners, Queen E, and Vicks. Elizabeth would not be called Liz, and Victoria would not be called Victoria.

Elinor and Anne had been champion gymnasts, Elinor's specialty being the balance beam and Anne's being the vault, before they decided to start a band with two girls from the neighborhood. Elinor on guitar and vocals, Anne on drums and harmony. They called their band Get Off the Couch, Dude! which their father thought was brilliant. I thought it was pretty funny for a couple of teenage girls stranded in Cleveland, Ohio, too. Elinor and Anne thought about calling the band Ugh, Hipsters! but he told them it was a better song title than band name, and Elinor said that as much as she hated to admit it he was probably right. Elizabeth loved soccer, and she and her mother tried to outbake the Cake Boss on weekends. He was a little worried about Victoria, because her closest friends seemed to be Elinor and the two cats and the one dog who roamed the house. He was very worried about the way she and Elizabeth picked fights with each other, mostly having to do with getting proximity to, and attention from, Elinor. Anne, meanwhile, didn't care that she wasn't the one being fought over. Anne had a boyfriend. And this, said her father, made Elinor a little crazy. As the eldest, Elinor thought she should have been the first to do everything and in this way set precedents and examples for the other three—Elinor liked to say that she should serve as a constitution that could be appealed to in the event of legal debate. Anne, being the second in line to the throne, felt no compunction to do anything she didn't want to do, let alone be perfect, so she could slip out of the house and find herself another pocket to stay warm in without feeling the guilt or betrayal Elinor would. Elinor, according to her father, had somehow developed a talent for guilt in addition to all her other talents, because her premature birth had resulted in lung damage that put her on a ventilator for the first six weeks of her life. He and his wife spent five of those weeks thinking they'd lose her, and living with this knowledge, he thought, had made Elinor perhaps too aware of disappointing them. For Elinor, disappointing her parents might be another version of almost disappearing for good again.

Their father called me his eucatastrophe. A word coined by Tolkien, he told me, that referred to the point in a fairy tale when, near the end, all hope seems lost, but then there arises, out of nowhere, what Tolkien called a sudden joyous turn.

His wife: I saw a picture of her once, taken in what appeared to be their early twenties. In his office on campus, on a weekend when she and the girls were away, in the evening, with the lights off so no one would see me, waiting for him to pick up some mail. I pulled out a book and a picture fell out. Of the two of them, standing on a promontory in what looked to be the Grand Canyon, ridged rocks and chipped clouds undulating for miles and miles out behind them. She was beautiful, in a stark and shadowed way. Her very large eyes—they looked brown—glowed intently, and with humor. They made me think very seriously about packing my bags and getting on a plane back to New York. He needed to stare hard at that picture and figure out where that girl was hiding today in his wife, and what role he might have played in making her disappear.

Mostly when I thought of her I couldn't stand the idea of her. She'd been happy not to work; never, in the waning years of the twentieth century, did she ever want to be more or other than she was. I could not forgive her for being a woman who had no other ambition than mothering—for never even having been an elementary school teacher or an administrative drone. For being a willing receptacle, for being filled with nothing but love, for being nothing more than an embodied heart. For taking his name, for taking his money. For being so certain at age twenty-one that she had found the man she wanted to die with. For never being deviled by a horizon. For having a mind so free of intellectual prejudices that it was satisfied by books written by pastor's wives. I could not forgive her for having an undivided heart. For having a pure one.

The women have such hard faces here, said David, the first time he came to visit me.

The women here are beautiful, he said the last time he came to visit.

You've made them up, I would say of his daughters. Thinking of Laura and Mary, and of Betsy and Julia and Margaret. And of Ella and Henny and Sarah and Charlotte and Gertie. And Maria and Josephine. Of Josephine's obsession with *The Nutcracker*, and Maria's obsession with Michael Jackson. Of Rose's own childhood obsession with Elvis and his jungle room, which had come to pass because her grandmother also had a little bit of an obsession with Elvis. Of my own grandmother, whom I once overheard saying—of Johnny Mathis—that he could put his shoes under her bed anytime. *Mom!* said my aunt Carolyn. *Charlotte is* right here! Of Nicole from long ago telling me that she once glued a series of shoeboxes together in order to make her own dollhouse version of Anne Frank's secret annex. And not, she used to stress, for school. Of my crush, and Rose's crush, on Peter van Daan. Of Tracy from long ago telling me that she insisted on being Amelia Earhart for Halloween three years in a row. Of my childhood habit of reading stories about illustrious women of history, any kind of illustrious woman from history, taking books out of our town's dinky, damp-from-the-sea, fluorescent-light-flickering library the size of a postage stamp, sitting on the olive green carpet in my red snow parka with my hood up for what I told my mother when she came to take me home was extra mind insulation—books on Maria Tallchief, Cleopatra, Althea Gibson, Wilma Rudolph, Harriet Tubman, Sojourner Truth, Dolley Madison, Rosa Parks, Clara Barton, Marian Anderson, Louisa May Alcott, Pocahontas, Marie Curie, Ida B. Wells, Anna Pavlova. The three sisters all under five, flanking their father on the bench seat in the very back of the B63 bus one Sunday, legs dangling, faces roving and rapt, while they listened to their father read to them from *The Wizard of Oz*. Of a friend's daughter, Helen, asking me why wasn't I married and then telling me that when I found another husband she was going to be the maid of honor and she was going to wear a dress that had a rainbow skirt, and the cake would be rainbow, too, made of white icing with rainbow sprinkles on top and layers of red, yellow, green, purple, orange, and blue cake inside. Of Ivy, another friend's daughter, on another morning, telling me that she never, ever wanted me to get married again but that she did want me to get a dog. And Moira, a former student of mine, who, one day in class, and I sadly forget why, said *Don't get me started on my obsession with Mary, Queen of Scots.*

Are you in love with him or his daughters? said Rose, when I told her about him. I didn't mention him again.

When Elinor, his oldest, was thirteen, he picked her up from a dance and asked if she'd danced with anyone. *I'm not falling in love until I meet someone who makes me want to break a slate over his head*, she said. She was referring, he

knew, to Anne Shirley and Gilbert Blythe. Her idealism—
or, rather, her ability to turn a piece of text into an arti-
cle of faith—made him proud. As did her total dismissal
of the boys at this event as *cretinous*. *Cretinous!* he'd said
in the car, laughing, delighted, pleased at his daughter's
choice of words, at her definite sense of where the pitiful
world ended and she began. Then he asked her what book
she'd gotten that word from. *The one I'm writing right now*,
she told him, and when he realized she was serious, that it
wasn't ironic, he knew she would be safe no matter what
happened, because he could see that she had become a discriminating, imaginative, opinionated, and strong-willed
human, and those qualities meant that she would never be
hurt by the world, or for very long. Or so he hoped.

You never know what life will bring, he said.

Elinor, who typed this sentence at nine on the electric
typewriter that got him through college, a sentence she
knew he would find because he still wrote first drafts with
it: *It is quite unbearable to hear one's parents fighting when all
one wants to do is listen to the rain.*

She sent a letter to me at school. It arrived in a pale blue
envelope. No return address. A former student, I thought,
and saved it to read later that night.

Ms. Snowe, it began. Matching blue paper. The handwriting neat and balancing itself on evenly spaced invisible
lines, a large baroque embossed capital letter *E*, colored navy
blue, unfurling quite splendidly at the top. *E*, for Elinor.

I'm sorry to intrude, but—

I stopped reading and called Rose, against my better
judgment. She did not waste any time pretending to
sympathize.

I've never thought this one was a great idea, she said. The girls screaming and laughing in the background.

Now you tell me, I said.

You're an adult, she said. *What am I going to do, rain on your parade?* The older we got, the more we sounded like our mothers. Or no: we sounded most like our mothers when we were angry. *Those girls need him more than you do.*

Tell me what to do, I said. Helpless, frustrated, hating myself.

Tell you what to do? she said. Impatient, frustrated. The girls now crying in the background. *You're an adult*, she said, and hung up.

I left the apartment to walk away the shame and rage. When I came home I wrote David and told him I could no longer see him. He called ten minutes after I sent the email, twenty minutes after that, then an hour, and two hours after that, but I didn't pick up or listen to the messages. His calls told me what I wanted to hear. *Don't go*, they said. *Don't go.*

Because you never knew what life would bring, I went online to see who was available, and slept with anyone who'd sleep with me, until one morning, Easter morning, I thought, when I'd gotten up to use somebody's bathroom before sneaking out, and I stood staring in the mirror of the bathroom of an East Village apartment that was not substantially different than all the other East Village apartments I'd spent nights in when I was twenty-four, twenty-six, twenty-eight, thirty-three, thirty-five. Al Green on an iPhone instead of the Magnetic Fields on vinyl, but it was all the same, my breasts the same, because I had not given birth, my face dented and creased a little around the mouth and eyes, but really, mostly the same, still getting me called *Miss* at forty-two, my bag still full of dog-eared, scrawled-up books, several lipsticks, although in Hollywood starlet reds rather than the burgundies of the nineties, the front page of the *Times* still wadded in between my wallet and a day book, my dresses still black, my shoes still black, my tights still black, my head still given hassles by free champagne. The bodegas of the East Village nicer, but still cold at six in the morning and smelling of years of dust and Mistolin pressed into linoleum the color of pigeon breasts. But the ability to hold on to the pleasures of the night before lessening, and the value of holding on to those pleasures lessening, the desire for those pleasures the same, even greater, but daughters of mothers who never knew more than one man may order a coffee as they have done many mornings before and feel that their young self and their old self, being so unchanged, cancel each other out and make a ghost. Make her something as flickering and liminal as the cats who watched her fumble for her wallet to pay for her coffee.

That morning put an end to those nights. In May the house sold. For $1.6 million, the Internet told me when I finally mustered the courage to look. The resentment I felt against the two couples who bought the house, and for their matching brand-new Jeep Cherokees, one gleaming in slate gray, one gleaming in midnight blue, and for their architects, who repeatedly stood in my doorway with matching clipboards and matching linen dresses the color of cloud, and their politeness that smelled a little officious, asking if they could measure the bathroom, the kitchen, the bedroom—I had the usual fantasies of defacing the walls with lipstick and defecating in unexpected places, of dumping chicken carcasses and eggshells all over the hardwood floors.

I don't understand why they wouldn't want to keep a tenant as lovely as you, said my landlady.

Oh I do, I wanted to say, but didn't. When my landlady and her husband bought the house in 1984, they filled the three floors with painters, activists, professors, and psychoanalysts who on the weekends sat around her dining room table for potlucks. After she and her husband had children, they began renting the top floor to artists, and artists only—my landlady's rule. Before me there had been actors, poets, and pianists—one of whom left her piano on the windowed porch and occasionally still came by to play it. I thought of all this and then of the couples who came to the open houses, all of them wearing crisp polo shirts and thin-lipped smiles. People like that wanted privacy—I did!—and could afford to not have to collect rent from the crazy girl-slash-lady moldering away upstairs.

The broker came to my door the day after the house sold to give me two bouquets, one made of peonies and one made of goldenrod, to thank me for keeping the place so clean and bright, so bright, said the broker, that everyone who came through the house always remarked on how cute, her word, the rooms looked, and then at the end of our conversation said that the only way to have any real security in this world is to buy a place.

Come upstate! said Rose. *When are you going to come upstate?* As if I had never begged for her help and she had never hung up on me.

Memorial Day weekend. Everyone at the house that

weekend attractive and coupled, everyone gracious and good-humored. Their children, even when shrieking and crying, delightful. Everything in the house an expression of discriminating taste and the limitless budget required to express it across two floors and ten rooms. I'd brought a huge bouquet of blue hydrangeas for Rose only to find that they were all over the place—in the kitchen, in the bathrooms, on both sides of the couch, blooming purple, blue, and white—but Rose was still delighted.

As you can see, she said, putting the ones I'd brought into a glass pitcher, *once is definitely not enough.*

Before dinner that night I had a conversation on the porch with a twelve-year-old boy about World War II and whether there could ever again be armed conflict that inspired idealism and not rank cynicism. Rank cynicism: his words. Owen. Bangs, as lanky as his limbs, that he flipped into his face while talking, with a frequency increasing proportionate to his enthusiasm, which reached a peak as he described, in great detail, Churchill's bunker at the Imperial War Museum in London. When his mother came to shepherd him to dinner, she apologized, as if her big hairy dog had been too friendly. I told her I hadn't minded in the least, which was true.

I'm convinced he'd talk like that even if he had no audience, she said.

Boys tend to do that, I said.

She rolled her eyes in commiseration and said, *Do you have any?*

No, I've just fucked a lot of them.

Luckily she laughed. She thought I was being funny but I knew I was being—hostile? Passive aggressive? Defensive? Inappropriate? At dinner I made sure to drink enough to slow my tongue's reflexes. Enough turned into too much and on the porch after dinner, as the women surrounding me laughed harder and harder and I grew quieter and quieter, I noticed Rose looking over at me from time to time as she refilled her own glass and the glasses of others.

That night I heard: About a guy who'd bankrolled the graduate degree of his wife—East Asian studies—to the tune of $80,000 but at the end of it she told him what she'd learned after those two years was that she wanted to teach yoga. A woman who'd become obsessed with having a child even though when she'd married she'd assured her husband it was the last thing on her mind, and borrowed money from her parents and his parents to fund several rounds of IVF, and then, seven years after her son was born, told her husband she didn't know she could hate a thing the way she hated her child, and in the middle of the night one night got on a plane to Alaska, where her sister lived, and never came home again. The woman who threw a bunch of her own money at IVF and then on every Mother's Day after the divorce dumped her daughter with her husband to go day drink with a bunch of other mothers who'd dumped their kids with their husbands. Another woman—no, three other women—who started cheating on their husbands once the husbands suggested, and suggested gently, hesitantly, even anxiously, according to the hearsay transmitted on that porch, that maybe they could go back to work now that the kids were a little older because it would be good to have the additional money. The women, who had all gotten used to doing fuck all, according to this hearsay, and liking it, took offense and balked and the cheating turned into divorces that made one guy attempt suicide in a hotel in Midtown after paying for sex.

After a while I didn't feel like sitting there listening to stories about women without jobs who blew through their husbands' money and women who insisted on children and then abandoned them. And even though I knew the women telling these stories were not the enemy—that they had been reporting on the enemy, and even knew that I had been the enemy myself, when I took not the money of a man for granted but his love, or robbed a woman of her husband not for his money but his lust—I felt more alienated from the world and everything in it than when I was sixteen and had the Smiths on an IV drip. But I'd never really been that alienated back then—you can't be when you're absolutely sure the people you love hate what you hate and want what you want.

I stood up to leave the porch, half out of protest, half out of boredom, thinking I couldn't just keep walking out of places whenever they bored me or bothered me and was going to have to figure out what to do about that, but not tonight, when the woman to my left, who must have assumed I was headed toward the kitchen or the bathroom, asked if I could bring a pitcher of water and glasses back out with me.

Sure, I said, perhaps too brightly.

If it's not a problem, said the woman to my left.

Don't worry. Charlotte never does anything she doesn't want to do, said Rose, as she poured wine into someone's glass. It was the kind of thing a mother, amused and not quite having reached annoyance, might say out of long intimacy—out of a desire to assert that long intimacy. Or she'd had it with me and couldn't be bothered to tell me to my face. The way she'd hurt me, just now, and I would probably not be bothered to tell her to her face.

That's right, I said, as I stepped over sandals. Playing along seemed the best defense.

Could she teach me that trick? another woman said as the door shut behind me and the porch filled with laughter.

I want to go home, I thought, while the faucet ran and the night stood still outside the kitchen window, but the thought made no sense because I did not mean I wanted to see my parents or to sleep that night in my apartment. The next morning I got up early and left without saying goodbye.

Was it Rose who had disappointed me, or New York?

Back in the city she asked if we could meet for a drink, and I wondered if she was finally calling me into the principal's office, and cursed myself for not being the one to air my grievances first. When I showed up at the bar and saw Rose, wearing leggings, a massive gray sweatshirt, and the pink bejeweled flip-flops she'd accidentally walked out of a nail salon with but had never worn out of the house, Rose, who put on lipstick to get milk, her face drained from what I knew must have been frequent crying, an already empty wine glass sitting next to the full one waiting for me, it became clear that I was not the one in trouble. But I felt nothing as I took an inventory of the signs of her distress, and that worried me more than her being in distress did. I did not know what kind of help I could give her—or wanted to give her. She had not been much help to me lately.

The trouble had a name—one I thought I recognized. I'd heard its voice on NPR. Younger than us, seven years younger, and the brother of one of the mothers she knew. Born and raised in East L.A. and graduated from Harvard. Nominated for some Pulitzers, plus he went down on her like a deep-sea diver who—but I stopped her. *Okay*, I said. *I get it.* She pulled out her phone and showed me a picture of a man standing in front of a mosque while a crowd moved around him in hazy sun. He was beautiful—the way all foreign correspondents are beautiful, given that constant exposure to death keeps the dullness out of a person's eyes. His skin tanned, but lightly, hair thick and black, as black as Peter's had been, but not a trace of gray, not a trace of fat on his body, not one extraneous object weighing down his person, not a watch or sunglasses or a wedding ring sitting on his left hand like a big fat blinking frog that would not budge. Just jeans and a T-shirt and an expression on his face that said *Hello!* but also *Don't fuck with me!* and I could see wanting to hang around watching that expression change from receptivity to ferocity and back again, hang around wanting to see if my hand could ever be the one to flip that switch, and how often. He'd told her he didn't care that she was married, she said as I looked at the photo and stared at the tilework blazing up and down the mosque. He'd told her he'd wait forever, she said, or take as much of her as it was possible for her to give.

Forever? I said, struggling not to give in to the jealousy those clichés had kicked up in me.

She took the phone out of my hand and kept talking. He'd just met someone who wanted to give him every-thing, and although this person was free, she wasn't Rose, and now he did mind that Rose was married, because he wanted Rose, not this other woman, and he was making demands, he was making promises he couldn't keep, but Rose wanted him to keep making them, and her jealousy of this other woman was so intense it was making her sick, she couldn't see straight, it was like a fucking migraine, and she couldn't sleep, and the girls were constantly crying because she was constantly crying, and Peter had checked into a hotel because he was fed up with watching her grieve someone in front of him, and though he didn't say that's why he was clearing out, she knew he knew what was going on.

I hope he leaves you, I said.

It was clear by the look on her face that she had not expected me to say a thing like that. I didn't think I'd ever say a thing like that to her, and couldn't believe I'd said it. The words that had flown out of my mouth—so quickly, and from some wound that didn't think it needed to seek my consent before making itself known—were stinging me as much as they seemed to be stinging her. She stared at me. When she spoke, she said:

You always did think you were better than me.

Yes, I said. *I probably did.*

She took her wallet out of her bag, opened it, set two twenties down on the table, and left, no hurry, no hurt, her composure revealing my insult for the tantrum it was.

21.

During the last week of school a student showed up wearing a dress I'd bought in college at a Limited Express. The kind of thing the nineties churned out in large batches—long and floral, demure but dramatic. For that girl it was just another piece of vintage clothing, one that she might have paid a laughably high amount for, considering that it had been mass-produced and essentially spun out of plastic. Several women my age, I'd discovered over the years, had owned it too, including Rose, and they all spoke of it with the bewildered, fervid fondness you might reserve for that one dress you gamble your limited summer funds on in the hopes that it'll lead you by the hand into your most cherished visions of the future. Rose had bought hers with money she'd earned working as a cashier at a Waldbaum's, and we'd purchased it the same summer—1993. Hers from the Smith Haven Mall, mine from the one in Cherry Hill, Rose's beige and flowered, mine navy and flowered. By the time we met, Rose didn't have hers anymore. Hungover and bored one morning her junior year, she cut off the bottom half of the skirt to show off a tan, and then accidentally left the dress on a Greek island that August. I still had mine. The dresses in my closet were the closest thing I had to a photo album, and this one had moved with me over twenty-two years and four Brooklyn apartments.

I could have taken this as a sign to call Rose, but I didn't. I was not yet truly sorry for saying what I'd said, and I was leaving in August to take a last-minute job that had opened up at a girls' school in San Francisco. Each day that passed without my writing or Rose calling confirmed that neither of us was willing to say what needed to be said in order to see our friendship through the next few decades, and to choose not to contact the other person despite need or regret meant that we were making a decision to become strangers. When I noticed I felt more excitement at the prospect of leaving rather than guilt over not calling her, I knew that the bones had set and I could start moving about.

Sibling rivalry, said my mother, when I told her about Rose. I'd left out the parts about the married men and made it all about real estate. *That was bound to happen.*

You're kidding me, said my father, genuinely surprised, and genuinely troubled, when I told him.

I nursed a small but powerful fear that my father would die from a heart attack while I was out there. Something needed to punish me for trying to run away from my problems. Mostly I was thrilled not to have to panic anymore about where I was going to live. The school owned an apartment that they rented out to faculty coming from far away, and I could stay there for one year. An alumni endowment subsidized a part of the rent so that it would not be much more than what I was paying in New York, with a dishwasher and laundry in the unit besides, and lucking into that scenario might have really been what I thought I needed punishing for. Why should I have everything?

My mother took me to lunch several times that summer—I think it was her way of acknowledging that she

235

wanted to get a good look at my face before she lost regular access to it—and in various diners, she told me stories I'd never heard before. My mother, with her split pea soup and saltines and iced tea. *I always used to think it was old people's food*, she said, every time she ordered the soup. *Depression food.* It was strange to eat with my mother in a restaurant. We went to the movies together, the supermarket together, Target, Home Depot, but we never ate out together, the two of us alone, had never really faced each other as people with thoughts and opinions to exchange over two plates and two glasses in a restaurant. So maybe she told those stories because she felt she was on unfamiliar territory, too, and wanted a shield. Maybe she felt free to say some things now that I would be three thousand miles away.

Stories like the one where my grandmother left my mother alone in the car whenever she went to visit her oldest sister in Ancora—the state-run mental hospital whose name everyone used as a punch line when I was a kid—and one time, said my mother, a woman in a blue chenille bathrobe, periwinkle, my mother said she later realized the color was, while going through a brand-new box of Crayolas, a patient, unsupervised, out wandering about, came up to the car window, wearing a platinum wig and too much makeup, my mother could not stop staring at the pink circles of blush, she looked like a doll, you think I'm making this up, said my mother, look at your face, knocked at the car window, and when my mother curled herself into a ball in the floor of the back seat to have someplace to hide, the woman started singing, my mother couldn't remember what song, but it was a song that was popular at the time, and the woman sang to my mother with her face pressed up against the window until an attendant ran up to the car and pulled her away.

Everyone used to say Aunt Leola had a heart problem, said my mother, who was too young, maybe about four, to know what kind of hospital she was being left in the parking lot of. *A heart problem*, my mother said, shaking her head and reaching for another packet of sugar. As if to say *Can you believe the bullshit people perpetrate and accept?* It wasn't until years later, when she overheard one of her aunts say to her mother that she'd be damned if the change was going to put her in Ancora the way it did Leola that she understood what had really happened, but still my mother was too young to feel that Leola in Ancora had anything to do with Peggy in Audubon, the quote unquote change being so far off in the future, said my mother, that it was like they were talking about polio in the past. They had an ice cream parlor at Ancora, and my grandmother always brought my mother a sundae in a paper cup as a reward for waiting in the car. They had cows there, a little dairy farm for the residents to help with, as a kind of therapy, said my mother, who didn't know where she'd heard that, maybe in the paper.

Did she ever tell my grandmother about what happened with the woman in the parking lot?

You didn't tell my mother stuff like that, she said. *She'd think you were making it up.*

Stories about my father's mother, who hated my mother because she made my father happy in a way my grandmother never could, because my grandmother had been too busy favoring my schizophrenic uncle who had been smart enough to try to be a priest but ended up in Ancora, too, after he punched the bathroom mirror because he thought he saw an enemy in it. My grandmother had jealousy like rabies, my other grandmother used to say. She was jealous of her sister-in-law, jealous of my mother, of my mother's mother. She fought with my grandfather if he talked too long to another woman at a company picnic, if he smiled too wide at a neighbor after Mass, if he complimented another neighbor on her roses. Fought so loud the neighbors once came over to make sure my father and his brother were okay, my father, six, answering the door, the neighbor woman picking him up and standing in the living room holding him and shouting that she was going to call the cops if they didn't stop. My mother wasn't sure, but she thought the fighting started after my grandfather came home from the war, from Japan, because my grandmother couldn't bear to lose him and the thought of being left alone with two kids again made her go crazy.

She was very proud of you, my mother said. *On that we could agree.*

When exactly did my grandmother become an alcoholic?

During menopause, said my mother. After my grandfather passed away. My father once caught her sitting out on their back porch drinking Listerine out of a shot glass. Caught his brother doing it, too, once, straight out of the bottle, when they lived together for a little while after high school, and tried it himself but it made him feel like an idiot to do a thing like that alone by himself in the house if he didn't really have a death wish.

You should be writing this down, said my mother, as she ripped open a packet of sugar. *Some of this pain needs to be made useful.*

It doesn't work like that, I said. A phrase I hated, but there it was, slipping out of my mouth, and my mother, who loved to say *It is what it is*, another phrase I hated, wouldn't judge. I took a pen from my bag and slid the place mat out from under my plate. I'd almost gotten that pen out earlier, but didn't want to look like a vulture swooping down on the steaming pile of bodies that lay in the middle of the road. I wrote and thought about Rose, running back to rental cars and locking herself in bathrooms to capture scenes and conversations that never would have transpired in front of her if her notebook and pen had been visible. *Or at least, it doesn't always work like that.*

Then what's the point?

I laughed. *There may be none at all! I'm still trying to figure that out.*

You still don't know?

I've been told it's a marathon, not a sprint, I said, and started to write.

My mother shook her head. *Well God bless you*, she said. *You're forty-two. I hope you find out what the point is soon.*

What was the point of having me? I said, still writing.

Oh, stop it, she said. *You and your smart mouth.*

Another diner, another afternoon: *And then I thought I really was going to end up like Leola in Ancora. After I had you.* My mother's—well, she said, they didn't call it postpartum depression back then, they called it the baby blues, and it was the reason we lived with my grandparents for the first few years of my life. It was why there was only one of me, my mother said, and why she didn't drive alone for years, because in the months after she had me she used to fantasize about driving off the side of the road and crashing herself into a tree or a house or another car—but, she reasoned, if there was someone in her car, of course she wouldn't do it. They put her on a drug, my mother wasn't sure which one, and when I threw out the names of the ones I thought might have been prescribed in the early seventies, she asked how I knew all that, and didn't sound pleased, whether because it meant her daughter was smarter than she was or morbidly intimate with instruments of pharmacological torture, or both, I couldn't tell.

All I remember, said my mother, *was that it made me feel like crap. But I took it. Your grandfather made me. I told myself that I would never let myself feel that way again.*

Did you? I asked her.

Yes, but it was nowhere near as bad. I kept myself busy. Too busy, sometimes, your father thought.

In the car home, my mother asked me if I'd ever felt that way.

No, I said.

You better not be lying, she said, as I pulled into the driveway and she unbuckled her seat belt.

I'm not, I said. *I'm not that proud.*

My mother laughed. *Is that so*, she said, and climbed out of the passenger seat.

22.

The week before I moved, while I was going through books
and records, my landlady called up the stairs to tell me
that there was someone standing in the driveway wanting
to see me.

It was David's oldest daughter, looking almost exactly
like the picture taken of her mother in the canyon: expec-
tant eyes, checked radiance. Long brown, nearly black hair,
long white arms downy with dark hair. Long legs. Her
mother's coloring. She wore a peasant dress, from the early
eighties it seemed, purple and beige, faded and flowered. A
tote bag on her shoulder.

Elinor, I said. She stood in my driveway, arms crossed,
her right index finger scratching, perhaps absentmindedly,
perhaps anxiously, her left forearm.

Yes. She appeared to be startled that I knew her name.

I noticed my neighbor peeking over into the driveway
from where he stood on his porch, holding his toddler son
and craning his neck to watch. *Mind your own business,
please*, I shouted over to him. He turned and went back
into his house, making sure to shut the door behind him
quietly.

Your father and I aren't seeing each other anymore, I said.

Her eyes widened for a second. Then she looked relieved. *I came here to tell you to leave him alone*, she said.

We looked at each other.

May I come in? she said.

Why?

Please. I need someone to treat me like a fucking adult.

We can have a conversation out here, I said. *It's going to be short.*

To be brutally honest, she said, *I don't know why, exactly, I'm here.*

We looked at each other again.

How old are you? she said.

Younger than your mother but older than you.

How much older?

If you really don't think you're here to start a fight, you can come up, I said, and opened the door wider.

She walked in and we headed up the stairs. As we entered my apartment I told her that she could have a seat at the table, but she asked to use the bathroom first. When I came out of the kitchen with two glasses of iced tea, she was standing in front of my bookcases scanning the shelves.

Where does your mother think you are? I said, as we sat down.

On a trip to New York with a summer course I'm taking.

Is there actually a trip to New York with a summer course?

Yes, she said, offended.

Where do your professors think you are?

I told them I wasn't feeling well.

They believed you? I said, before realizing that I probably would have believed her, too.

I'm a very good girl, she said. Archly. As if she was very aware of both the value and the cost of that identity.

How do you know about me?

Because he thinks he's invincible, she said, *my father can be careless.*

Yes, I said, and laughed. She gave me a look. She might not have known exactly why she was here but she didn't want to collude, either.

She was looking for a financial aid form on his desk, she said. Her father kept all his active correspondence in a paper-clipped, staggered-in-order-of-importance pile to the right of his monitor. Flipping through this stack of emails two words caught her eye: *My wife.*

Jesus, I said, then recovered. *This was in his office at home?*

Yes, she said. In a tone that meant: *Aren't you lucky that so far I'm the one only one who's read it?*

She said she didn't know what made her keep reading, but she very carefully pulled this email out and saw this sentence: *My wife refused to make love to me.* She scanned the page to find out who her father was writing this to. Some woman. She wrote the woman's name and email down on a Post-it and carefully arranged the stack of papers to look the way they had before she touched them. She knew then, she told me, that her mother was not blameless for what was happening to them, and wondered if she might even be entirely to blame for it.

Well, I began, about to suggest she might think twice about using the word *entirely*—but then stopped.

She said she didn't know what she wanted to do with the name and the email. She knew only that she was tired of not being told the truth.

Soon after, when her father was in Starbucks getting them drinks after picking her up from the library and she was sitting waiting in the car, she opened the glove compartment to look for some tissues and found an envelope with the woman's name—my name—and a return address on it. She skimmed it, she said, because she could not watch as, line after line, a woman turned her father into an object of lust—the bronze statue Elinor had turned her father into had already broken apart but to read these words would be to pulverize it. When she came to the end she saw the woman calling him single-minded, saw the woman saying that his single-mindedness could make him simple-minded, was telling him that his single-mindedness, coupled with his largeness and tendency toward loudness, could create in him a heedless ball of rambunction that made the woman feel that she was dealing with a boy in his teens rather than a man in his fifties who had raised four girls. It made Elinor laugh. That was exactly what he was like, she said. And there was a kindness toward him and a forbearance toward him in those last few lines, she thought, that softened her heart. When her father came back into the car she could not speak. Her father, who had busied himself with complaining about the incompetence of teenage baristas, did not notice.

It was very strange, she said. *The letter showed me—does this make any sense?—that he was the same person even though he'd done this terrible thing. If you saw what we'd all seen, all his faults, and knew he could be infuriating but still loved him anyway, then he was still our father, and we hadn't lost him.*

I'd thought I was a master compartmentalizer, but I didn't think I could have pulled off that sweeping an act of interpretive reclamation, especially if we were talking about my father.

My mother would never write a letter like that, she said. *But why do I want to blame her for it, and not my father?* She looked up at my shelves. *My mother would never read books like this.* Then back at me. *You bought him those jeans, didn't you? The really dark ones.*

He bought them, I said. *But they were my idea.*

My sister thought so. I mean she thought some woman did. Elizabeth?

Yes. Elinor looked at me. *How much do you know about us?*

I don't mean to alarm you, but quite a bit.

I think you do want to alarm me, she said.

And why would that be?

She looked away.

Does your mother know about me? I said.

I don't think so.

You can talk if you need to, I said. Because of every student whose eyes were full of pain they could not find a confessor for, or so blank because they had learned to not confess it, and because my mother would never read books like that either.

The two of us sat in silence. A lawn mower started up across the street.

I sometimes wish that she would die, said Elinor, *because then I would never have to spend the rest of my life in this war with myself and with her. She won't let me go. But it's not like that with fathers. They're like lighthouses, and you circle around them in your little leaky boat, they're something you look over your shoulder at as you paddle, always there, not minding you and your confused whirling around, not even noticing all the splashing you're doing, although maybe they should be, but it's fine, because they're looking out beyond all the whirling, scanning for the real trouble.*

Yes, that's exactly what they are, I said. What I wanted to say was that her father was right about her—he had nothing to worry about, if she could keep herself afloat with words in this way.

She told me that she knew she was a feminist when, at the age of ten, she saw her mother spanking her youngest sister too hard after a routine spurt of mouthiness. She knew the violence had an origin older than that moment of rebellion, and she couldn't think of a time her father had snapped like that or would snap like that. She was aware, too, that her father did not ever have to snap like that because her mother made his life run smoothly, and because she knew how hard her mother worked while her father reaped so much glory, she knew that she should take her mother's side, but really what she wanted was to never be in that position—a position in which she could not see clearly because of resentment, while anyone watching could see very clearly that she had given too much of herself away. Her mother wanted her close to home, so she went to Ohio State. Before she gave in, she tried to bargain with her mother, reminding her that she'd still have her three sisters at home and would be too busy with their schedules to miss her, but her mother said, *It's not the same. When one of you is gone, there's a hole*, but she knew that her mother really meant that when *Elinor* was gone she felt the hole, and what she really felt wasn't a hole but fear of losing her for good, because she'd almost lost her for good at birth.

I told her this story about my mother: When the boy I'd asked to the senior prom stood me up, left me waiting for him in a black strapless dress I bought with money I'd earned from working at the Ocean City boardwalk, I went out to our back steps and sobbed so hard the German shepherd next door ran up to the chain-link fence and started barking at me. My mother came out back, pulled me up off the steps by one arm, and with one slap to my face chased the hysteria out of me.

God! she said. *What is the point of perpetuating this cycle of female-on-female violence?*

I laughed.

I mean it! she said.

I know you do. I laughed because those are my thoughts exactly.

She stared again at my books. An impulse arose and I did not fight it. I got out of my chair and took one off the shelf. *The Dialectic of Sex*—the copy I'd bought to replace the one I'd thrown into a trash can on Fourteenth Street, years ago, to prove something to Tracy, who never was watching.

Nearly every line is true, but I couldn't live up to it, I said, and set it down in front of her.

Like the words of Jesus, she said, picking it up, examining the back, examining the cover. *Chapter six might change my life, this says.*

I'd forgotten about that line of red text running across the top of the cover. Bantam paperback, revised edition, 1971, with a puzzling portrait, by Degas, of a somberly dressed young woman on the front, and I always wondered how angry or wounded Shulamith Firestone might have become at the sight of her work being so grossly, almost punitively, misunderstood. Forgotten: Rose and I intoning that line to each other whenever we wanted to crack ourselves up. *Chapter six might change your life!*

She looked up. *I came prepared to feel sorry for you,* she said.

You should get back to the city, I said, tired of having to play the gracious and indulgent host.

She did not get up. I did, and picked up the glasses we'd been drinking from off the table, hoping she would take the hint.

She said she would take her leave—take her leave!—and we walked downstairs and to the bottom of the driveway. I asked her if she remembered which direction the subway was in, and she said yes, but she didn't make a move. Cars floated past us on my street, one, two, three, four, broadcasting the sounds of salsa, gospel, merengue, and the Koran.

We are both very intense women, she said. Tote bag held in front of her in both hands, looking out across the street.

Yes, I said. I stood there loving her as much as I wished her gone.

23

The apartment had a bay window that looked out on a very small backyard where two hummingbirds liked to spend time. A Meyer lemon tree stood in the corner, which I had real trouble comprehending. Even more incomprehensible: I'd find minuscule strawberries sprouting in the grass come summer.

There were so many things to be stunned by. Pleased by. Students who were less volatile, hostile, and sullen than the ones in New York. Foghorns at night instead of truck horns coming from the BQE; seagulls everywhere instead of pigeons. The smell of eucalyptus in Golden Gate Park, where I could bike without worrying about getting picked off by a truck or rage-fueled cyclists. I hadn't been on a bike since college. The smell of jasmine coming through my windows. Avocados and figs at the farmer's market, driven there not flown there, lying there in unassuming piles, as unremarkable in their number as apples in the fall back East. The red rocks of Corona Heights Park, so high above the city you might have been Jesus looking down on Rio, and the coyote I saw there early one morning, sitting on a patch of red dirt while the wind ruffled the hair on its very straight back, its ears at attention, gazing out at all the buildings.

The unmarked tech buses that floated down Divisadero

in the morning, their cargo shrouded, offensively, behind black smoked glass, were a sinister reminder of the forces that ran the town. Had ruined the town? Pockets of it appeared to have resisted a certain amount of change. On weekend afternoons, on more than a few blocks, the sunlight slashing across the buildings seemed to be making the only sound, and neon signs that had been floating in the night for decades watched over more corners than they might have in New York. The money had not leveled the mountains in the middle of the city, or filled in the canyon, or dried up Ocean Beach. But it wasn't my place to mourn what I'd never met, and I wanted to enjoy what the money had not yet erased. It felt good to move to a city that might have lost much of what people liked to call its character well before I arrived; felt good, almost blissful, to not have intimately known what had been replaced by a Starbucks or a T-Mobile or a quasi-luxury high-rise. To live in the middle of a convergence of several neighborhoods, which arranged it so that technically I belonged to none and could not be held responsible for ruining any of them. It had been weighing on me more than I thought I could acknowledge, having watched New York welcome more and more overt and closet suburbanites, more and more well-adjusted, cheerful young people moving there to drink and have sex and make money before they woke up and suddenly realized they needed a driveway and babies after all, in Montclair, or wherever else their money could take them, like Asheville, if they thought that taking photos with an expensive camera for their food blog meant they were creative. I knew it made you some kind of jerk to complain about watching the city betray you unless you were willing to sit in a community board meeting shouting at your neighbors, but I had never been able to show my love for New York that way. For better or for worse.

New York, where the rusted trails of water running down the subway tiles on the D platform of the Atlantic Avenue stop had become as familiar and as reassuring to me as the wrinkles on my mother's hands had been in childhood.

New York? said the woman who'd sat down next to me on the first morning of faculty orientation, in the middle of the din caused by adults who were out-of-their-minds excited to see each other after months apart. The two of us, seated in folding chairs, introducing ourselves as we waited for the head of school to give her morning remarks.

Well, you definitely look it, she said.

Is it the black?

Yes, but also there's something that says Outta my way, bitches.

I laughed. *Should I throw a zip-up fleece over this? Would that help?*

She laughed. *Please don't.*

So what are these girls like? I said.

She shrugged. *Their mothers are always looking at your ring finger.*

I looked at hers. No rings. I held up my hand to show her—empty, too!—and she smiled. Lina. An upper-school Spanish teacher four years younger than me. Her parents had been born in the Philippines; she'd been born in Arizona. She, too, had fled New York—a divorce—and had lived in San Francisco for ten years. She used to be a copywriter who quit making money to make a difference teaching and then quit teaching public school so she could work in buildings that had heat. She loved her parents and her sisters, and I became her friend for the way she loved them: exuberant complaint and anecdote.

If I hadn't met Lina, I would have never set foot in the bars, one in my neighborhood and one in hers, that looked like the ones we'd spent our twenties in—dark recesses, paneled in wood, booths upholstered in weathered red vinyl, Replacements on the jukebox, Red Stripe for six dollars a bottle. If someone showed you a photograph of the corners we drank on, you might say *Was this taken twenty years ago?* They tended to be occupied by men not too much older than we were, but grayer than we were, men still fixated on this band or that band, this director or that director. A cliché women could never inhabit, I sometimes imagined, because estrogen was protective against a certain amount of waxing pedantic and obsessive past everyone's point of caring—the culture's, your companion's. A date that she and I both ended up on, however, more than a few times, courtesy of the algorithms being hammered out in a Mordor blocks away.

If I were still talking to Rose I might have sent her a postcard saying *Greetings from 1994.* I was still talking to Rose, though. In my head. *I'm sorry,* I said. And *I'm sorry.* Those two words a place to hide until I knew whether I really meant them. Birds in search of branches.

In one of those bars Lina told me about her habit of collecting what she called alternative narratives. Meaning: in her twenties, when she started working, she kept a mental scrapbook where she filed away all the real-life examples she came across of women who didn't have children and took notes on the cast of their faces. The data resisted her attempts to glean a definitive conclusion—some faces looked brighter, she said, some looked bitter, but it was hard to say which side was winning. *I think I drifted into my alternative narrative, to be honest*, she said, *but I'm totally happy to sit here drinking my shit white wine at the crossroads of defiance and ambivalence.*

She invited me to join a book club—another thing I would never have done in New York—and I was welcomed into a group of women who, she said, had experienced a similar drift. I threw us dinner parties and they brought their husbands and girlfriends and often stayed until one in the morning talking.

And now I think having a best friend is something you only need when you're a teenager, I heard one of the women say, as I made the rounds with a bottle of wine.

Most days I could agree with this statement. Most days I was glad to be free of all attachments. I wasn't lonely, but I could grow a little bored. I didn't care—that was the price I was willing to pay for not being responsible for anyone's happiness but my own, and for not burdening another person with my own demands for the same. For living this near an ocean that shone bluer and brighter than the gray-green one I'd been raised in. For the city's quiet, and a solitude that let my psyche grow so still I could look all the way down to the bottom of that dark well, further than I'd ever been able to in New York, and see, not with dread but with a clear, cold sadness, just how much fear had been the spring feeding all my mistakes. I might have needed to be this alone, I told myself, to decide who I wanted to be next.

On other days the quiet that descended so abruptly at dark was unsettling, and all that solitude left me feeling exposed and a little wild of mind. There was no one to tell the smallest, stupidest things to, or the biggest, most haunting things to, no husband, no Rose, no mirror, no amp, no way to tell what I looked like or sounded like or what shape I really took, and when I opened my mouth to talk to all the strangers I now had the pleasure of meeting, I sometimes spoke louder than usual in order to have the pleasure of feeling myself substantiated. The strangers didn't notice, and if they did think something seemed off, and I sometimes thought they did, what could they say? We were strangers.

On those days I took the bus down to Ocean Beach to walk around the ruins of the Sutro Baths and stare out at the water, trying not to feel too bad about needing that much of the sublime that regularly, or too guilty for being able to access it that regularly. The second-guessing of my needs and desires had started to bore me, too.

At the baths one afternoon a woman and I struck up a conversation because I'd wanted to talk to her Siberian husky, and she told me that one of the sea walls at Ocean Beach consisted of headstones that had been swept out of a cemetery when the city decided to develop the land the bodies slept in. She said the cemetery had fallen into disrepair because San Francisco was made up of people who'd cut ties in order to come out West, and those bodies had no one to keep their graves presentable, or send up a hue and cry, her words, when the city scooped up all those bones and stones and dumped them by the water.

Although, said the woman, as her dog barked and seagulls circled, *I've never thought it was such a bad idea, being that unsentimental about your dead.*

24.

My youngest sister is now sleeping next to the dog in the living
room every night, right on the carpet, no pillow, no blanket, and
it drives my mother crazy, because the dog is huge, and sheds,
and my sister's going to school covered in dog hair, but I think
just let her fucking sleep on the floor if it's helping her deal with
the divorce. My second-youngest sister will now only eat bread
with one of these three things on it: butter, mayonnaise, or cream
cheese. Because eating bread with white or close-to-white materials
spread on it allows her to control one aspect of her life while it
totally falls apart. Mediocre family therapy has at least produced
that one enlightenment. The second oldest is having sex with
her dumbass boyfriend, and I'm pretty sure she's too sad to get
organized enough to use protection. I know he's too fucking dumb
to be organized. I can't believe she's dating him. She's so much
smarter than he is, and she tries to pretend she's dumb and doesn't
care about anything just to fit in. To feel loved? I get it. But then
I don't. Do I think more of my brain than she does of hers? Why
should I? Why? It's not fair. I'd tell her she's making a mistake,
but I've done that too many times and it doesn't work. It would
work on me, though. Why doesn't it work on her? Because I'm the
oldest? Because teachers loved me? Did teachers love me because I
was the oldest? Does that mean I'm not intelligent, just obedient?
In my father's new apartment there's never any food, only Cheerios

and beer. My mother drives too fast all the time now, so fast my youngest sister now spends car rides bent over in airplane crash landing mode. The other day my mother hit a deer, and while we all sat staring at the blood on the windshield my second-youngest sister said, "Why aren't we all dead with that deer?" I'm waking up in the morning and hearing voices. Female voices. I don't remember what they say, I just know that people are talking to me. Very boring. I am not Joan of Arc. I haven't told anyone because I went on the Internet for a few hours and cleared it all up. It doesn't mean I need to be treated for anything, it's just anxiety, it doesn't mean I'm headed for an official breakdown. I found a case study about some girl my age whose parents were divorcing and she was freaking out about moving in with her mother and the anxiety caused her to hear the voices of her friends and her family talking to her just before she fell asleep, and the voices would get louder the more anxious she was, and more normal the less anxious she was. Her mind turned the volume up and down. She controlled <u>them</u> they didn't control <u>her</u>. The authors said that the patient "denied" a history of mood disorder and "denied" a history of troubled sleep, and I got so angry at "denied" because blah blah blah men, and what they really should have said was that the patient <u>said</u> she had no histories of those things, but then you know I would deny being imperfect, too.

Every few weeks I received a letter like this from Elinor. No greeting, no closing line, each one a shout from the middle of her life. The first had been sent to Brooklyn and then forwarded to California. I sent her a book for each one I received instead of a reply, and when she mentioned the anxiety I slipped a postcard in the package that said *You need to talk to that family therapist, no matter how mediocre they are, about those voices.*

25.

I'd gone to a show alone only once before. In New York, in
my twenties. At Brownies, in August, Rose out of town, a
singer she wasn't into because she thought the songs were
too sweet, a singer who was just as good a songwriter as Elliott Smith, whom we loved, and was almost as sad as Elliott
Smith, but who in his sadness could flash a bit of deep dry
wit where Elliott Smith did not—could not? That singer
and I are still alive but Elliott Smith is not. At the show I
stood up close to the stool, closer than I usually did, thinking that if I got right up next to that voice and his guitar, to his hands, to his face, so close I could see the dirty
fraying Band-Aid wrapped around his thumb and the acne
scars on his cheeks, I would forget that I had only my own
thoughts for company. But love was not enough. I could
walk cities alone, see movies alone, see art alone, become
ravenous at the prospect of having those experiences alone,
but I could not see music alone. Shows had been too tied
up from the beginning with the need to belong to a tribe,
and with the need for collective acts of tribal witness.

This is what we *do*, Rose once said as we stood in a
long sweaty line for the ladies' room, on another Thursday night, around 10:00 p.m., at the end of July, in an old
roller rink in Philadelphia waiting for a band to take the
stage. On the lam from routine and obligation, while all

the other women back in New York were mothering, sleeping, or emailing their bosses in a panic. We drove home to Brooklyn drinking fountain Cokes and eating Shorti hoagies from Wawa. Laughing and singing. We were thirty-four. We were seventeen.

Now I was forty-two, waiting outside the Fillmore in a line I'd been standing in for twenty-seven years. A bouncer in a windbreaker sat on a stool at the back entrance taking our IDs and stamping our hands. Inside the auditorium, hundreds of us stood beneath the chandeliers, colored light rushing over and around us, our faces, older than the hearts they shielded, raised toward the stage, where, for two short hours, the singer and his piano issued a thunder so total and radiant it made the world outside shrivel up and blow away. Back out on the street, I looked around at the crowd spilling from the exits to remember what we all looked like, who we were, the people who had all been spoken to by the same sound at the same time—class picture, group portrait. We might be irrelevant but we were handsome.

When I turned to walk down Geary I noticed a man, about twenty feet away, standing a little apart from the crowd, almost at the curb. Bent over a phone, wearing a black wool shirt jacket, black jeans, black work boots. I thought I recognized his profile and his coloring and his posture. The man felt the stare and looked up and in my direction. I hadn't been wrong.

You really do look exactly the same, said Karl, the next Thursday, after he ordered the first of what would be three rounds at a bar near a meeting he had on Fourth Street. His drink: Macallan, on the rocks. It made me smile to see that he had come up in the world and grown past those hard-boiled eggs into a little epicureanism. My dress: the one I'd paid $250 for in the East Village.

So do you. In fact he looked healthier. Tan where he had been pale; heavier, rooted, where he had been bony. Eyes warm where they could be cold. His jawline looked as sharp and clean as I remembered it. He had all of his hair and had not jowled.

You laugh more, I said. *It's nice to hear.*

Parenthood lightened me up. Some other things did, too, but mainly that. Should we get something to eat or are you fine?

I'm fine, I said, *but thank you.*

What does Rose think of you being out here?

Rose doesn't know.

Oh, he said. His eyes and voice surprised.

I think at this point the fault may all be mine. There had been no one, until then, to say it out loud to.

I'm sorry, he said.

Me too, I said.

I used to think she needed you more than you needed her.

I sat there thinking about that for a little while. He must have sensed that comment had gone too deep too quickly, or had sent me too far back into the past, or was not his to make, so he changed the subject.

What did you think of the show? he said.

By the end of the evening, I'd learned that: after he moved back to Utah he got a job at the *Salt Lake City Weekly* but New York had spoiled him for the minor leagues, and he didn't want to be writing music reviews or editing them when he was forty-five, didn't want to have to pretend to have to get it up for every next big thing pretending it was timeless genius when it was just that year's version of the zeitgeist in a bottle, in that year's version of a bottle, and he tried writing a novel at night but it was crap, it was like realizing you couldn't draw hands for shit, even though you could draw everything else, noses, feet, lips, but not hands, and he knew he wasn't the kind of journalist you wanted stepping under the police tape, knew he wasn't any kind of journalist at all, but he knew his mind needed to calculate and create and get lost in a problem in order to feel useful and powerful, otherwise it would turn brooding and black. And he didn't need to make his thoughts about music, or anything else, public for them to seem real, in fact he thought they would remain more real, more potent, if he kept those thoughts to himself. So he taught himself web design, bought books, took classes, and the paper hired him to help design and program the website. And now he ran a UX department for a big evil tech company. So that's how that started. Through friends he met a girl, a woman, he'd known her in high school. Ex-Mormon, too. Jenny. A graphic designer who used to have her own radio show at Utah State. So I couldn't hate her too much.

They had three children, two boys and a girl. He didn't want a third child, but she did, and he had no real reason to object to her desire other than ten years in he found himself not wanting to tell her everything the way he used to and he thought she might be turning into the kind of woman his sisters always said his mother was—a better mother than a wife. The children and the life the children plunged them into—soccer games, homework, bake sales, barbecues with neighbors, vacations with neighbors, scrapbooks—

Your wife scrapbooks?

Yes, he said. The Karl I remembered: warning me off the property with a word and a look. Defending his wife's embrace of the homespun and his embrace of such a wife. He should not have been telling me any of this, probably.

—scrapbooks, school projects, Halloween costumes, two dogs and a cat, piano lessons, violin lessons, elaborate birthday parties in backyards—absorbed her the way she needed to be absorbed and it made her very happy. And this was a good thing, her happiness, and Karl loved his children. He showed me pictures of three shy and happy and serious faces. James and John and Suzanne. Suzanne, after Leonard Cohen's song. The result of a deal he'd struck with his wife: she could have the third and he could name her. *How beautiful*, I said, as I looked at them. Because they really were. It was a good thing, he said, to have created a happy family. Neither he nor his wife had known that pleasure growing up. They moved to San Francisco five years ago, when he landed a job at one of the big evil tech companies, and they'd always been planning to move to a blue state for their children's sake and their own once her mother died, and now, because last year Karl got a big deal job at another big evil tech company, she was a self-described pig in shit because she could be a stay-at-home mother, and was now thinking of becoming an event planner, with a friend of hers, an equally maniacal organizer, who was going through a divorce and needed something to distract her, they'd start out pro bono and see what happened.

I could have spent some time judging him for being yet another man content enough to remain married to a wife who, while she might have been his intellectual equal, preferred to exercise her mind's powers through the frighteningly competent running of a household, could have spent some time examining what it was about me that had led me to attract and be attracted to these men, but I didn't feel like it. If that was all I got out of this meeting— the realization that I no longer wanted to waste time intensely envying other women for having loved themselves enough to love their lives and everything in it, for loving their lives so much they'd helplessly lavish even the smallest of tasks with a care that turned anything they put their minds or hands to into works of art—that would be enough. But of course I could tell myself this only because I sensed he needed something from me, and it was going to be my decision whether he received it or not.

I've talked a lot, he said.

It didn't feel like it to me. If I had not known him then, would I have listened this long now? Yes, I thought. Yes.

By the end of the evening, he'd learned that: I'd been married and divorced, I'd published two books, and I loved San Francisco more than I ever thought I would. He asked me why and I told him, and I talked about the city we were sitting in longer than I'd talked about anything else that night.

You always did really love what you loved, he said.

I said nothing.

Only two books? he said.

Only three children? I said.

He looked down at his glass. I might have chastened him but he also seemed to be trying not to laugh. When he looked back up, he said:

Are you happy?

That's one of life's more impolite questions, I said, and took a drink.

Well put, he said.

I'm happy right now, talking to you.

The bartender slid us the check on a brass tray. I pulled it in my direction and Karl pulled it away from me, gently.

This neighborhood makes me spiritually sick, he said, after we'd stepped outside, and I laughed. A true, loud, delighted laugh. It was nice to hear someone call bullshit on bullshit. He sounded aggrieved; he sounded amused by his own grandiose crank. It sounded like New York talking and not San Francisco. Or, rather, an old version of New York. An old person.

He looked at me and smiled. *I was waiting to hear that sound*, he said.

I'm not doing this if I can't have you inside me, I told him, the first time he kissed me, the first few seconds into his kiss. I cried every time I came. The way you do when you discover that your body was right all along, and then remember how useless that information will prove to be once everyone's clothes are back on. We never said *I love you*. He would call from a street corner or some free minute to say *I want you again*, and I would make him repeat it. It sounded like his strength speaking to my stubbornness, his grief speaking to my grief. Three months later I was pregnant.

Your heart and my heart, he said, when I told him, and set his hand on the skin below my navel. As if to say: they live in there. We lay on my bed, naked, looking up at the ceiling. The sun in the bedroom turned from bright to hot and I could feel my skin start to burn. He said: *I wish you hadn't told me.*

26.

My breasts grew fat and my body grew slow and I mono-
logued to Rose in my head. As she used to say. Thought
all the time about calling her and leaving a voice mail that
went something like *Hello it's me congratulations are in
order I have not been looking both ways before crossing the
street and I got hit by a truck, the same truck that hit you
five thousand years ago at least I think it's the same one if I
took down the number on the license plate correctly, the number I wrote down as you lay in the street, yes so I got hit by
this truck which means I have finally caught up to your old
carelessness the one I thought you outgrew the one I thought I
could avoid and here I am trying it on a hand-me-down just
like Karl you had him first, didn't you, and it fits perfectly
he fits perfectly one day I'll fall in love with someone I won't
have to hide from you I always thought you were going to
steal something from me one day when I wasn't looking or
win something one day without really trying not very feminist
of me not very generous of me given that you had nothing
growing up compared to my something anyway I just thought
you'd like to know so you could have the pleasure of judging
me the way I judged you and maybe even be jealous of me the
way I was jealous of you I know the smack you can talk about
other women so I know you will get an immense amount of*

pleasure out of judging me for the hypocrite I have become plus remember the other five thousand years ago when you said catching hate from another woman was the only reliable way we have of knowing whether we're winning well the hate I had for you that night when you were trying to tell me that you still wanted what I wanted which is to say everything and I didn't want to listen I didn't want to forgive you for not being me I couldn't forgive you for never thinking you might have something to be sorry about too anyway that hate was just a compliment you should have known that or maybe you did please don't call back I don't think I miss you as much as I miss the people we were in lieu of flowers please tell Maria and Josephine they should always write more than they read they should always sing more than they listen they should always paint more than they look they should in fact never pick up a book you should tell them to go outside and play and stay out-side and roam and never need or want a home because home only makes you sick for it the way I am homesick for you sorry not you just for the girls we were for how happy we were and it was the most fun I'll ever have just standing next to you on a street corner on the way into some show some reading some party and one day if I ever get over myself which is looking unlikely maybe I'll write this all out and send it to you as an application for your forgiveness but I don't want to work that hard for anything anymore do you but I will if you do no I will if you do please I will if you do

27.

Just go ahead and have it, said the physician's assistant who stuck me with the needle when I went to get a blood test to confirm what the stick had shown. *So many women are dying to have one and can't. You should listen to luck like that.*

The next morning, a Saturday, I woke up with panic pressing down on me. Out of nowhere, I might have said, but that was technically not correct. I wanted to call Karl but I knew I shouldn't, and then did, four times, but he didn't pick up. Ocean Beach was too worn and cluttered to solve this problem, so I called around for a rental car to drive north to Point Reyes. I hoped I did not feel moved to run it off the road. I knew I wouldn't. I wished I could.

On the rocks where the lighthouse stood, I watched the Pacific stretch so far out into the distance it turned into a second sky. The sun shone white across it like a cracked sheet of ice, but none of it could keep me from staring at my phone and hoping for Karl's name to materialize at the top of the screen. In search of a beach to sit on, I drove back through the cattle farms, bumping slowly along the road, watching the cows watch me, hills on the right and sea cliffs on the left, imagining that the Kia was a lunar roving vehicle and we were on the moon.

I settled myself down among some dunes and tried to listen. I tried. And tried! The life inside me wasn't luck. She was more like the line of wrack lying down below me on the sand. Long cables of kelp coughed up by the tide, running parallel to the water, studded with trash from the sea and actual trash—tampons and clam shells, seagull feathers and straws. A trail of broken pieces left behind by all my winds and waves. The residue of really loving what I loved. Of getting exactly what I wanted. She wasn't luck, but I was lucky, because she was the daughter of a man who liked to kiss the freckles on her mother's shoulders and quote that line from Hopkins: *Glory be to God for dappled things.* It might have been all she'd ever need to know about him: he was that tender, that imaginative, that whimsical, that earnest, that alive to the music of words. Kissing her mother like that and not his wife: that reckless and selfish. Just like her mother. But if he liked a song he would play it ten times in a row and still not be tired of it, whether it was a song he'd known since 1989, or a song he'd met the other day, which meant he wasn't just reckless and selfish, he was also loyal and true. Unlike her mother, who had turned her back, many times, and without remorse, on musicians whose songs had ceased to bring her news. Or maybe the only thing to tell her was that he still carried his eight-year-old daughter into the house at night after long car drives, even though his wife said his daughter was too old for that kind of thing, even though he knew that half the time his daughter was only pretending to sleep. He was the miracle. This child was not.

The ocean: wrestling with itself and always coming to the same decision.

Driving back into the city the temptation to call Rose and then Karl again and Rose and then Karl grew so strong I pulled into an overlook just before the beginning of the bridge, got out of the car, walked to the edge of the blacktop, and threw my phone into the ocean. I did not want to need anyone or to need their help so badly. I wanted to get rid of the risk of being disappointed by the people I needed; did not want to risk being humiliated by my need. As the phone sailed through the sky two women standing next to me clapped. *Oh, c'est fantastique!* said one while the other said *Bravo!* and on the way home their approval consoled me the way that futile and deeply unoriginal gesture did not. The phone was gone but the losses—all the losses, any losses I'd ever known—remained. They were heavier and more real than the life inside me.

On the table, in the clinic, as the anesthesiologist inserted the tubes into my nose, I started to cry and told myself not to. There was no reason to cry. Why the fuck was I crying? I must have said these things out loud.

Are you okay, sweetheart? said one of the nurses standing next to me.

Sweetheart? I heard myself say. *I'm forty-three.*

It was harder than I thought it would be to walk out to the waiting room. My abdomen was sore, as if I'd done a hundred sit-ups. I felt sore, too, between my legs, and along my upper thighs, the way I could after long hours of sex. There were cramps. The literature had neglected to mention that my body would howl like a dog trying to tell me someone had gone missing.

Karl drove me home. In the car I felt his worry and called it love. Lina came to stay that night. We sat in my bed talking and she told me her first abortion left her feeling like she'd been hit by a truck, but she bounced right back after the second, and she thought it might have had everything to do with the fact that she loved the first guy and hated the second. The sound of our hair dryers doing a duet over top-volume NPR in the morning brought me more comfort than I would have imagined.

The day after: sitting in an utterly silent classroom as my students wrote, the girls so absorbed by the act of thinking, so unselfconsciously committed to the act of thinking, it was as if I sat in a garden watching flowers in the act of being flowers. Watching them flourish as they would, without objection or interference—that was all the mothering I owed anyone.

The day after that: crying in the bathroom of a Starbucks after school because those flowers were not mine to keep. Because Karl was not mine to keep, and I was so smart I was stupid. Crying for my mother wanting to drive herself off the road in 1973 and for my grandmother drinking to erase herself in 1969.

It took a few weeks before I could walk up or down stairs without halting or effort. By that time it was summer and school had ended. Afraid of what would happen to my mind without work to distract it, I wrote. Every day, furiously, to atone for having let so many things convince me they were more important. Then Karl showed up at my door. I'd told him I didn't want to talk to him, but his wife had taken off for Tahoe for a month with the children, and he said he was afraid of being alone with his thoughts. I let him stay that night. He came back and stayed another, and then arrived the next with a beat-up blue canvas duffel bag.

I didn't have the strength or will to send him packing. I needed him to show me that he was stupid, too.

You're not sleeping in my bed, I told him. *We can't play house.*

Your belated faith in boundaries is touching, he said. But he slept out on the couch as requested and in the mornings slipped into my bed.

We spent our evenings sitting next to each other on the wooden deck in my yard, drinking and talking and watching June turn into July. Listening to the foghorns on the bridge call to one another across the bay—noises he said his children had given names to and created, their words, origin stories for. Sometimes we talked about his childhood in relation to his children. *You don't mind?* he said. I didn't. *We can talk about so many other things.* But I didn't want to. When he talked about his children it made it easier to hang on to the belief that the world contained just as much light as it did darkness. We went back over everything we said and didn't say to each other in New York. *I had a real talent for being a smug prick*, he said. *You weren't the only one who noticed.* He said: *Rose was the instigator and you were the transcriber.* He said: *Neither role is better than the other.* He said: *Rose told me that if she and I fucked it wouldn't change a thing, and it pissed her off how right she turned out to be.* And: *Nobody did, or has, made me laugh the way you two did.* I said: *That's because you left New York.* He told me I was the only person who'd ever been able to make him see what the big deal was about Mary Gaitskill. I told him that I hated to break it to him, but he'd never be able to convince me that I needed to give Tom Waits a second chance.

Sometimes those conversations were really just me handing a draft of my life so far over to him, hoping he'd mark *Stet!* in the margins wherever I'd written *Better?* I could feel ashamed to be so desperate for his reassurance, all these years later, but I'd just aborted a child he helped make, and it seemed the least he could do.

You can be just as miserable married as you can be alone, he said.

You've got to do better than that, I said. *Please.*

Okay, he said. He laughed. *You're right.* He thought. He said: *If you'd wanted what everybody else wanted, or convinces themselves that they want, I wouldn't be sitting here next to you, waiting to hear what you'll say next.*

I took his hand.

Hold on, something else might be coming through. I think it's Kierkeguard. Do you mind?

Never, I said.

Okay. Here you go: It is in fact through error that the individual is given access to the highest if he courageously desires it.

I said his name. Because I could not say *Don't ever leave me.*

What did you want, back then? I said, on another night. In the middle of June. The air, hot and tired from climbing to a high of 103 degrees that day, hung on us like a second set of clothes.

For a long time, it was to leave home and stay gone. That was as far as I was thinking. And then when I got to New York I saw that I really wasn't ambitious. I was serious, and took things seriously, but I didn't have a target for that seriousness. I envied you and Rose because you did. Although I could tell that meant you wouldn't be a very good girlfriend.

You were right about that.

Or, you know, it was a story I was telling myself. Anyway, there came a point where I sensed I was going to have to go back home, and so I was never as wholehearted about New York and anything in it as I should have been.

And then you went back home.

It wasn't a tragedy.

I didn't make a very good wife, either.

That's also not a tragedy. Maybe your ghosts needed you to write an entirely new story.

That's too easy.

I don't know. Walk around with it on for a couple of days and see if it keeps feeling flimsy. What would you lose in believing it? Or why don't you let me believe it for you?

For whatever reason—exhaustion, cumulative and recent—I thought I actually could let him believe it for me, and go on feeling comforted by it even if we never talked again. I knew I should tell him it was time for him to go sleep in his own bed, but I didn't.

You're a good friend, I said.

You're a good friend to me, too. I feel free around you.

Don't you think that's just because I'm not your wife?

No, he said. *I always felt that way.*

What do you want now? I said.

I want to make sure my children are happy enough for as long as possible. Other than that I'm not sure.

He could have said he wanted me, I thought, forgetting completely that I had just decided to let him return to his life. I let the omission hurt, and when I took my hand away from his he must have felt it.

It's funny. You think I have all the power here.

272

I'm sorry. Don't you?

If you want a fight, Charlotte, just say so.

Part of me wanted to push him toward a more definite show of anger, and part of me wanted to play the exemplary mistress who knew her place. The exemplary mistress and her love for her martyrdom won out. Or I really loved him, and that's what shut me up.

I don't want that, I said.

Neither do I. You saw my face when I showed up here. Thinking you might never talk to me again did that to me. You did that to me. You think this isn't costing me anything, but it's just that I don't want to waste the hours we have together by torturing you with an account of the debilitating guilt I feel when I'm not with you. I just want to enjoy you.

Is that all you want from me? I couldn't help it.

No, he said. He started to speak and then stopped. I waited.

I fantasize about going to a supermarket with you, he said, and waited, too. He might have been a little embarrassed. He laughed a little, too. *Fully inhabiting the mundane with you.*

Well, this must be real, then, I said, and hated myself for going for a joke, when I'd also been longing to idle beside him in some frozen section having nowhere to go but home, together. But I couldn't trust his confession, because words like that were the first things everybody regretted once the affair was over and they'd beaten a retreat back to their less disruptive selves—and sometimes I didn't trust him, fearing that if I'd confessed how profligate my own heart was, how greedy for crumbs, it might provoke another *I wish you hadn't told me.*

How could you think it was anything else? he said, sounding truly puzzled.

But I did not want a fight. And we were as good as married, in my mind, because he wanted to talk with me and he wanted to fuck me; he wanted to fuck me and he wanted to sleep next to me. Sometimes he wanted to fuck me because of things I said while talking, because of the music in a turn of phrase or the force of an idea, and then I didn't care what anybody thought, not even myself. All that sweat on our skin and in my sheets must be consecrating something.

Then he'd leave for work and I'd sit down to write and wonder when I'd stop making him larger than life. So what if that's what I was doing? I typed faster than I had in years, and deleted much less of it than I ever had when I read it back over.

I love you, he said, on the last morning of July. I did not answer but held him tighter.

He was on his way out to his office an hour later when the doorbell rang. I opened it and there stood Elinor, one hand resting on the handle of a scuffed gray plastic rolling suitcase. Hair in a chaotically constructed bun. A huge gray hooded sweatshirt with the name of her father's university on it. Leggings and sneakers. She looked a little sheepish, a little anxious. A little tired and washed-out. My neighbor's wind chimes made their sound. She turned around to look, then turned back.

One day I'll write in advance like a normal person, she said.

I laughed. I told her I was glad to see her, and I was—in fact I was almost overjoyed. She had solved my problem for me: her arrival meant Karl would have to go, and I would be able to avoid, at least for now, having to give the speech in which I freed him to go make sure his children stayed happy.

This is my boyfriend, Karl, I said, after I'd ushered her inside the apartment.

Nice to meet you, he said, sure and direct, extending his hand with a fatherly aplomb, and again I felt the loss of never being able to belong to him in public.

This is Elinor, I told him. *She's a former student.*

Hello, she said brightly, and extended her own. So un-ruffled by the lie she could have been my flesh and blood.

28.

Elinor, at 7:00 a.m., asleep on the couch, white comforter pulled up all the way over her head, so completely buried by the drifts it was not clear whether a human lay beneath them. A copy of Iris Murdoch's *The Bell* lay tented on the hardwood floor by her head. It looked to be my copy, which she must have taken from the shelves. I bent down and picked it up to see what kind of marginalia it might contain. No notes, but a Post-it from Rose, stuck to the last page, its bright pink color unfaded, in reference to another book, one I no longer owned, that said *We can do better than this. We have done better than this!* With the *have* underlined four times. Elinor's suitcase sat next to it, thrown open, overflowing, possessions in a tumult because that's probably how she felt when she'd packed them, with travel-size bottles of shampoo and conditioner having leaked out all over her jeans, some socks, and another sweatshirt. I fished out the stickiest pieces, put them in the washing machine, and went off to buy us some expensive croissants.

While we drank coffee and ate, I suggested we drive to Big Sur. Big Sur, because scenery like that would either drive you back into your silence or crack it wide open, and it was mine, now, to show off.

What is this place? she said. Ten in the morning, fog

shrouding the ocean and cliffs along the Pacific Coast Highway. *It's like we're high up in a Chinese mountain painting.*

At every overlook she asked if we could stop; at every overlook she said *This can't be real.*

On the way to Pfeiffer Beach I lowered the windows and she turned the radio up. When we heard Taylor Swift telling us to shake it off, Elinor abruptly turned the radio down.

I'm sorry, she said. *That advice is ringing very hollow right now.* Then: *I've been reading a lot of Joan Didion.*

Haven't we all!

She laughed, which made me happy.

Is that why you moved out here?

I'm sure it's one of the reasons. I've loved her for so long I sometimes forget she's not actually my mother.

How old are you again?

Again? Now I laughed. *I don't believe I've ever told you.*

Why won't you?

It helps me feel more dignified in front of you if I retain some mystery.

Don't you think it would help me to see a woman embrace the reality of her non-youth?

I laughed. *Yes, it would be good for you, but it might not be good for me. I hate to say this, but you'll understand when you're older.*

Is there any possible way you could do better than that?

I know, and I'm just as disappointed in myself for saying it out loud to you. But—

But what?

Let's see how I feel after another day or two?

You know what my mother used to say to us? In the immortal words of the Magic 8 Ball, ask again later.

That's funny, I said, and asked her where her mother thought she might be.

Right here. San Francisco. I didn't lie this time. I mean, I didn't lie about where I was going. She has a boyfriend now. Anyway, it means she's currently not that invested in controlling our outcomes.

That's good news.

Is it? Yeah, I mean, her getting off our backs is good news. But if you mean it's good news that she has a boyfriend, I think it's just one more piece of evidence that we all secretly want some man to save us.

Once settled on the beach, we let the ocean make the conversation for a while. Elinor broke the silence first. She said: *He doesn't belong to you, does he?*

No, he doesn't.

Does he have daughters, too?

Are you pregnant? I said. I must have felt guiltier than I'd been willing to admit, if I turned the tables that quickly.

She looked at me.

There are only so many reasons someone like you would show up on a doorstep belonging to someone like me, unannounced, for a second time, I said.

Is that another way of saying that there are only so many plots?

Yes.

Please don't be mad at me.

Elinor. I'm not mad at you. I'm sure you're mad enough at yourself. I'm sorry. Just—please leave him out of this.

I wanted you to convince me not to have it, she said.

I absolutely don't think you should have it, but I wouldn't feel right trying to argue you in or out of whatever it is you think you want. That can't be my responsibility.

Well, who else are you responsible to right now? What else are you doing with all your free time? Why don't you use it to help me?

I said nothing.

I wanted you to give me a feminist sermon.

Isn't that what the Internet's for?

She groaned.

I'm sorry. I can't.

You won't, she said.

No, it's more that I don't have it in me. I couldn't even give one to myself right now.

Okay, well could you tell me why I'm in this kind of trouble?

What if I said it was because you wanted some man to save you?

She said nothing.

Do you regret it?

I regret how it ended.

How are you feeling? What are you feeling?

Strange, she said. *Bloated, pendulous, displaced from my own body, a little bit.*

Yes, I said, and wished I hadn't.

Have you ever had one? she said.

An abortion? Yes.

How old were you?

Thirty. The age Rose was, her second time.

Did you love him?

Yes.

You loved him but you got rid of it.

We were very young.

Is thirty young?

In New York it is.

That's the age Joan Didion was when she left New York. Or no, twenty-eight? She sounds like she's eighty when she's talking about it.

Two corgis tore across the sand, their pink tongues and avid black eyes visible from where we sat.

What would you say you've done with the freedom you have? she asked.

I thought about that for a little while. The real answer, in my opinion, was absolutely nothing, but I couldn't say that. Didn't want to say that. I said: *I've kept myself from slowly killing the spirit of a child or two with my ambient unhappiness.*

It's not the most powerful argument I've heard for not marrying or having a family, she said, *but you're being honest, and I respect that.*

I might have just needed a certain amount of space and time to think halfway straight. But the real question here is what do you want to do with yours?

I want it to stop mattering so fucking much, what I do with it. I don't know anymore.

Did you love him? I said.

I wrote a lot while it was happening. Does that mean anything?

I thought about the document sitting on my laptop, swollen like a river from what I'd thought was long-overdue rain, and said nothing.

Have you told him?

No, she said.

Who was he?

She didn't answer.

Was he a professor of yours?

She said nothing, and scraped the sand back and forth with a rock. At that point I knew I must be officially older and wiser, if not as good as dead, because I was in no way jealous of her realizing one of my more abiding girlhood dreams.

Is he married?

No.

Are you lying about that?

She didn't answer.

Okay, I said. *You need to get rid of it.*

Why? Her voice now insistent. *How smart am I, after all, if I can make this kind of dumb and totally predictable mistake? Everything I thought about myself must be a lie, if this is what I did with all my intelligence. Why should I protect my intelligence? Why should I give it unlimited time and space and let it keep running the show?*

Elinor.

And I have this feeling that it—I mean having her—could turn into something beautiful.

The corgis were on their way back again, tearing down the sand, the helpless mania in their faces now in full view.

But, she said, *I feel the same way whenever I sit down to write.*

I'm sure she will turn into something beautiful, I said, *if you're her mother. I don't doubt that, in the least. But he has all the power here, and you have none, because the power of creating life is in many ways no power at all. You fell right into it. I fell right into it. It happened to us. We didn't make it happen. And you're protecting him by not telling him. I'm sure at this very moment he's walking around his life making plans in blithe, unearned confidence, writing whatever the fuck it is, pardon me, he writes, typing up a syllabus, I don't know, with some tiny satisfied smile on his face, so proud of himself, thinking about what to have for lunch, while here you are spiraling out trying to decide what your own mind is worth.*

He's not smug like that, she said, coldly. *I wouldn't have done this with a person that smug.*

I know you wouldn't have, I said. *But the point is that it takes real work for a woman to sustain the creation of something outside herself that is not a child. Real will, because we are always going to be tempted in a way men aren't to wander off the road and find some place to get knocked up so we can relieve ourselves of the burden of trying to figure out what everything in life is really worth, and then, as a reward for this abdication of responsibility, get ourselves worshipped as if we'd climbed Mount Everest when all we'd done was let nature take its course. Men don't walk around with a door inside them that they'll constantly have to worry about—should I open it, should I keep it shut, does it lock, well wait, if I lock it, can I call a locksmith to get it back open, how long does it stay open, what's the data on what happens if you've left it open for a really long time, can anything get through? Should I shut it or keep it open? Shut it or keep it open? Shut it or— you get the idea. This is why men will never experience their underutilized freedom as a perversion. They don't have this inherent, latent source of power serving as a standard against which they can measure every other way they can access power, or every other dream they might have, and then run the risk of finding those dreams or that power wanting in comparison to the thing their body could do. So men will never put too much pressure on their freedom and it will never put too much pressure on them.*

My face burned.

I can always write later, she said.

That's when I began to envy her. It had never occurred to me, when I was her age, that I could write later; never occurred to me to keep my mouth shut until I'd lived enough to collect a few things worth saying. I'd wanted to enter the convent of art immediately. Elinor might want to enter the convent of motherhood in order to protect herself from further mistakes. I thought of something else.

Who knows what it could do to your sisters if you keep the baby? I said. *They could find themselves living in reaction to your decision for the rest of their lives. They could either become too careful or not careful at all.*

Oh, she said. She had not thought of that.

Please find another way to punish yourself for not being perfect.

That seemed to have hit home, too.

I'm sorry, I said. *Or you could have everything. You could have it and have everything.*

That seems unlikely, doesn't it? she said.

Prove us all wrong, I said. *But if you do, promise me you'll never write a book telling us how you did it.*

She laughed.

Later, while climbing back up to the road, Elinor said she wanted to return to the beach in the morning to do some more thinking, and we decided that if we could find a motel room we would stay overnight.

I don't mind turning my underwear inside out if you don't, I said.

That sounds delightful, she said. *Let's become feral.*

After lunch we visited a bookstore, situated in a cabin

by a creek in the redwoods, where I offered to buy Elinor a book if she saw one she liked, but she said there were so many of them she wanted it was stressing her out trying to decide on just one.

Who's that? she said, sidling up to me at the register and tapping the cover of *A Spy in the House of Love,* which I was about to buy.

Someone whose work I have actively avoided my entire reading life.

Oooh, she said. *Why?*

Oh, I'll tell you later.

Tell us now, said the man behind the register. His manner thoroughly unhurried, his eyes inquisitive and amused, and the combination lent his hooded sweatshirt the air of cashmere and turned his unremarkable face handsome. If I'd been alone I might have tried to flirt with him.

She's taken, said Elinor, with a sharpness that I sensed had something to do with mothers and their failure to protect.

The man remained unhurried as he handed me my card—as if he had daughters, too, and could not be fazed by their moods, and on the way to the car Elinor started chatting up a storm. And kept chatting, through lunch and just after, because we'd talked enough about what grieved her to contemplate, and she needed to pretend everything was fine. She talked about books she'd been reading, shows she'd been watching, the ridiculous things her roommates did, the ways her sisters pissed her off. She might not have even needed me to listen. But I didn't mind listening. As she talked I could see her sisters, see her roommates, very clearly, as if she had painted their expressions, their angles, their foibles, with words, which meant she was a writer, and I could see why someone who taught her would have fallen in love with her. My heart hurt, as I listened, and I was glad, very glad, to feel it hurting for someone other than myself, and by the time we reached Point Lobos she'd talked herself out. At dinner I asked her questions so that she would not ask me questions. Asked her what she thought of the Iris Murdoch, and that led to a very long conversation, or, okay, it might have been me giving a lecture, about how Murdoch's thoughts about fiction might have been more valuable than the fiction she could not stop writing.

Whereas with Virginia Woolf, said Elinor, and from coffee to the motel we finished that sentence together.

In the wood-paneled room we looked in the drawers to see if anyone had left anything interesting behind, and sat on our respective twin beds watching *House Hunters* until she said:

Did you ever fall in love with a professor?

Not exactly, I said.

That sounds like a good story, she said, and I laughed.

Well, it's not really a story.

Beginnings and middles and ends are completely overrated, she said. *Who was he?*

When I was in college, I told Elinor, I had what I supposed you would call a crush on a professor. Dr. K.

How many people are here because this was the only upper-level literature course available to sophomores this semester? he said on the first day of class.

No one raised a hand.

Well, he said, *I'll find out sooner or later by your shitty papers.*

Dr. K. I wished for his approval, longed for his approval, worked for his approval, and inhaled, reread, and savored the comments he left in the blue books and on backs of papers the way I inhaled, respooned, and savored Nutella whenever a jar was put in front of me. I'd reread them between classes, and again at the end of the day, just after getting into bed and just before turning the light out. When I learned that my roommate had found me asleep, curled up on my side, cheek resting on one of these papers and drooling, I stopped. I still have those papers, responses still stapled to the back—single-spaced responses printed from a dot-matrix printer, and I cannot throw them out because they made me who I am. Perfectly punctuated, full of insights into my insights that seemed to have rolled effortlessly out of his mind and onto the paper, full of a mind alive and at home in the act of analysis, words just acid enough to provide the thrill of knowing that your intelligence had been just keen enough to outwit their full acidity.

I changed the way I wrote my sevens because of Dr. K—by slashing the number through the middle with a horizontal stroke. This flourish, picked up, I guessed, while he was studying in France, might have been one of his only three affectations.

Dr. K, the crew-cutted son of Staten Island schoolteachers, stood at the podium as if it was his birthright. He projected an air of impregnable but voluble intelligence, and a happy, benevolent openness, and people thought he was handsome because of it. I remember the beat-up brown leather knapsack that he'd toss onto the table near the podium at the beginning of every class—

sometimes an apple or a pacifier or a tie would ooze out from it while he lectured—and his penchant for wearing wide-waled brown or green corduroy jackets over khakis or jeans.

Dr. K, I heard another girl once say, *made corduroy seem like one of the more sensuous fabrics you could upholster a man in.*

That made Elinor laugh out loud.

He did not have a penchant for ties, however, preferring to leave his shirts open at the neck. I would sometimes stare at the divot in the middle of his collarbone, resting there just between his buttoned-down collars, which were often plaid, and envy his wife for being the person who could legally touch her index finger to that hollow.

Which did not mean, I told Elinor, that I wanted Dr. K touching me. I would test myself with the thought, and would invariably recoil.

This isn't—hitting too close to home? I said. *Should I go on?*

Please, she said.

Dr. K looked you in the eye when you talked to him, and he very quietly turned skeptics who thought the medieval was moot into English majors with him as their advisor.

The semester I took his course—that fall semester of my sophomore year—I was also a work study for the English department, which meant I spent a lot of time xeroxing things and talking to Joyce, the department secretary, who smelled not unpleasantly of clandestinely smoked cigarettes, Certs, and Oil of Olay. Joyce schooled me on all the soap operas going on around campus. Affairs, breakdowns, suicides, expulsions, staff strikes, meningitis outbreaks, petty cash and property theft, alcohol poisoning, fraternity hazings ending in arrests. I also spent a lot of time watching girls arrive for Dr. K's office hours. I don't think Dr. K had any idea he was so beloved by a certain strain of female liberal arts major. He was a husband, a father to a new-born son, and a rising academic star, and was too busy to notice that he might appear as a much-needed instance of confident, enthusiastic authority to young women in need of better fodder for their romantic idealism than the idiot boys around them. But those boys, idiot and otherwise, looked up to him as well, because his wit and confidence created the impression of swagger achieved without re-course to brute strength.

There were other professors who were more celebrated instances of glamour, drama, and cruelty—showboaters who made everybody participate in some ridiculous group encounter on the first day of class, or shot devastating zing-ers into the unsuspecting crowd. If you liked that kind of act, you liked it, but drama and glamour and cruelty have always seemed to me a waste of everybody's time. I had papers to finish and a life to write.

A girl named Teri—the smartest girl in our class—often waited outside his office. Her clothes and her glasses were plain but just stylish enough to not draw attention, and her hair was long, but not long enough to make you wonder if she'd been homeschooled.

Teri's face was free of guile, and her smile was quick. She was smarter than nearly everyone around her, so smart she did not have to worry about people beating her out for whatever she wanted, which also made her nicer than ev-eryone around her, and as such a little bit lonelier than everyone around her. She also played the flute.

Hi Charlotte! she'd say, waving, when she saw me sitting at the secretary's desk or standing at the copier.

Hi Teri! I'd say, and smile, too, meaning it, wishing I was secure enough in my own intelligence to be a real friend to her.

No other English professor had this many girls standing around waiting for him, and it irked Joyce. Whose recipe for kolaches, which she wrote down for me on an index card, I will also never throw out. Dr. K was beloved by his male students, too, but they didn't show up outside his office. They argued with him on the way to class, waylaid him in the cafeteria in order to eat lunch with him.

God in heaven, they think no one sees them, said Joyce one day, when three girls showed up early at the same time.

Do you think he knows? I said, relieved that Joyce had not lumped me in with the Rest of Them.

Men are oblivious, said Joyce. *Didn't your mother ever tell you that?*

No, I said. *Should we hold a brown bag seminar in here about it? Get some folding chairs, some of those chocolate chip cookies from food services?*

Don't be a smarty, she said, trying not to laugh. Then she stood up from her seat, grabbed a piece of paper, wrote on it with her authoritative, sweeping, Palmer Method hand, and then thrust it at me. *Dr. K has gone home sick for the day,* it said. He hadn't, of course. She asked me to tape it to his door. I did, and those girls scattered.

Joyce came to my graduation, and I attended her funeral. And when I said that out loud to Elinor it reminded me how lucky I had been to know and love all the women

I had known and loved, and realized I no longer wanted what I didn't already have.

Thank you for spending all this time with me, I told Dr. K, in his office, after I'd clarified some thesis or other.

I have ways of keeping it short if I want to, he said. *And if you don't mind, I'd like to keep you here five more minutes so that I don't have to talk to that kid*, he said, pointing to a legendarily indefatigable loudmouth who could be seen loitering in the hallway through the door window.

I thought I might want to become a medievalist because of Dr. K, instead of a modernist, which is what I'd always assumed I'd be. And in the spring of my sophomore year he asked me to become his research assistant—he'd gotten a grant to turn his dissertation on medieval attitudes toward madness into a book. As fall turned into winter, and five o'clock became the dead of night, sitting in his office with a desk lamp the only light, and a mug of tea, microwaved in the lounge, in front of me—no roommates, no traffic, no crush of students suffocating me—I thought I'd died and gone to heaven.

When I graduated, Joyce told me that it was she who told Dr. K to give his assistantship to me, because I had once or twice mentioned being broke.

One afternoon, when I showed up to work for him, he gestured toward my earrings and said *Those are fascinating*. They were a brand-new pair of very large silver hoops I'd bought over the weekend, at the urging of friends, in New Hope, in Pennsylvania.

He said it the way he might have said that a car wreck was fascinating or the discovery of water on Mars was fascinating. I told him where I bought them, and who I'd gone there with.

Oh, he said, smiling, broadly. *Those alt-rock Valkyries you stalk about with?*

I blushed, and then laughed, because I liked that image, thought that line was a pretty good one, astonished in the way youth is always astonished when the ancients let drop that they know what goes on outside their cave of age. Alt-rock! I wanted to be seen by him, and there was pleasure in knowing he looked at me when I was not looking, and that he thought I ran with some tough chicks. I smiled.

Forgive me, he said. *I was just teasing. I'm sure they're lovely people. Would you like a coffee? I was just about to get one.*

Yes, I said, and we began to get coffee before every one of my shifts. The coffee would last exactly thirty minutes. No more, no less. I did not feel, sitting on a stool in the café, like a sexual object. I felt like a representative of my generation that Dr. K was examining for defects—like Dr. K had put me on the stool purely because of his interest in making sure the kids were all right. And I had seen him having coffee with male students in the same café, in the same spot. We would get a coffee and he would tease me, but it did not feel like flirtation, it felt familial—as if he was making sure his younger sister wasn't doing anything stupid, like falling in love with Milan Kundera or Jack Kerouac, or actually believing that the people-pleasing Democrat she'd just helped vote into office was really going to change the country the way it needed to be changed.

Of course you should go to graduate school! he said one afternoon, setting down his coffee cup so hard on the saucer that it rattled.

Did you go? said Elinor.

I went, I said, *but I couldn't stay.*

One day I came into the office and found a brand-new

copy of *The Malaise of Modernity* sitting in the middle of his desk. I turned on the desk lamp and opened the book.

For Charlotte, with friendship

I sat down at the desk, and stared at the four words, read them over and over, drank them in until I was flooded with pride, contentment, pleasure, and hope. I sat in his chair, in the mostly-dark, and wished that one day I'd have an office that looked out over a river that glittered at night with light that looked like scattered stars even though the source came from plain old streetlamps. An office lined with books, books like bricks, the wealth of them a fortress, the wealth of them a solace. The accomplishment of them, rising to the ceiling, creating a sanctuary for girls like me whose parents could not give them this kind of home. One day, I hoped, I might create that kind of home for girls myself.

It sounds like he was in love with you, said Elinor.

No, I said, *he wasn't*.

I sat there at his desk dreaming, and deepening my will. When I realized how tired I was—it was Friday, and I'd taken two hard exams that week—I placed my hands over the book like a pillow and rested my cheek on top, with the intention to rest there for just a moment. But I fell asleep in that position, and a knocking on the door woke me. Angry knocking. I jumped up, mind woozy, heart racing, and opened it. A woman stood there with a baby on her hip. She was short and elfish and a little pugnacious-seeming, and reminded me of the girls who played goalie for my high school field hockey team. She'd pulled her long, possibly bleached blond hair back on either side with gold-plated drugstore barrettes whose gold, I noticed, had begun to flake off, and wore a long teal parka, pink plaid shirt, jeans, and running shoes. No-nonsense, but clearly feminine colors.

Where's Dr. K? she said.

I looked at my watch. It was 8:30.

Do you know where he is? His wife, I thought. His son screeched in glee and grabbed at her hair.

I don't, I said. *I'm sorry.* She looked through me, once around the office, then right at me.

Get a boyfriend. The baby now screeched in bewilderment. I was too stunned to move or speak. *Get out!* she said.

Beyond the baby, over Mrs. K's shoulder, I saw Joyce hustling in her orthopedic shoes like a racewalker, chicken wings out at the side, down the hallway to the office.

Mrs. K! she shouted. *Mrs. K!*

I grabbed the book off the desk and ran out of there. I could not sleep that night from shame. I kept hearing her voice—*Get a boyfriend*—and kept seeing her livid face. I don't think my mother had ever looked at me with such furious ice in her eyes, and my mother's veins were full of it. Had her nostrils flared? They might as well have. I'd thought I was better than what she was mistaking me for, but I wasn't, I was just some girl, some thief, hanging around, trampling the garden, feeding on scraps, trying the locks.

But I felt sorrier for Dr. K than I did for myself. That wife. If I never made demands on a man or clung to him for dear life, I told Elinor, watching that woman descend into wild-eyed desperation over her missing husband was at least 50 percent responsible.

That's not the first time she's come down here, said Joyce, the next day, *with that baby on her hip like a lit torch.*

Do you know where he was?

Don't ask those questions, she said, with a sharpness that I had to wonder at, and then declined to wonder at, because I was, luckily, still an innocent, and I had papers to write and my own life to save.

Which I thought I was doing by signing up for Race, Gender, and the Birth of the Modern, taught by a woman who told me that I should go to graduate school only if I was interested in being infantilized for three to ten years. Dr. L! Who told me that I should be a writer, not an academic, because, as she said, I wrote too well to have such a gift crushed by groupthink. Who told me I had a first-rate mind save for my affection for E. M. Forster—*Empire's vessel full of ectoplasm,* she called him—but who through my testimony came to grudgingly understand what those Merchant-Ivory film adaptations had done for principled young American virgins in the 1980s. Dr. L, who, like Dr. K, was not afraid to wield sarcasm in the arena either, and, I told Elinor, when I used it on my students it was in tribute to her utter lack of fear. Whenever I tucked a vintage silk blouse into Hepburn-wide pants, or plaited my hair into pigtails, that was also in tribute to Dr. L, who never wore anything but. Dr. L, who gave very warm and bracing hugs upon hearing both good news and bad. Who, one Friday afternoon after classes ended, while we chatted in her office, introduced me to both red wine and dark chocolate Hobnobs, telling me that she always brought back five tubes of them in her suitcase whenever she visited friends in London, where she'd worked in a pub the summer before starting her PhD. *Though you'd never guess*, I remember her saying that day as we put away a sleeve of Hobnobs, *these go very well with red wine*. And then another afternoon she produced a bottle from behind a few books on her shelf, pulled a corkscrew out of a desk drawer, and began waving some colleagues in for a drink through her open door. I remember the laughter and the warmth in that office, and in the hallway that day, the day I learned that ebullient hospitality could turn the humblest of ingredients and settings—industrial carpet, disposable plastic glasses—into a glamorous salon.

I once saw Joyce and Dr. L drinking some whiskeys together at some beloved dump of a student bar—it was like catching Gertrude Stein and Simone de Beauvoir in the act of handicapping the game and shooting the shit.

Dr. L, who let slip a roll of the eyes once when I mentioned how much I loved Dr. K—a response I didn't quite understand until I began teaching, and my female colleagues and I would roll our eyes at yet another triumph achieved, or innovation advanced, by blisteringly confident male faculty members on the ascendant.

Dr. L, whom I betrayed by writing a senior thesis for Dr. K. I did not think the world needed another modernist— although who on earth needed yet another young woman writing about the covert rebellions of the oppressed sex, circa century twelve—and I thought if I wasn't just another modernist, I might have an easier time getting a job at the end of the PhD I hoped to earn. And he might feel bad enough about what happened with his wife to go easy on me, and write me a glowing recommendation for graduate school. I could not eat for two weeks between making the decision and informing her of the decision.

When I used the word betrayal in apologizing to her, Dr. L closed her eyes and said, *No, this isn't betrayal, but I am hurt.*

But, she added, after thinking for a moment, putting her hands over her still-closed eyelids, trying, it appeared, to commune with something other than jealousy, *this is about money and self-sufficiency and, I suspect, your father, a tangle of competing needs and loves that I certainly understand, so I must give you my blessing to go forth and be the Dorothea Brooke of your own life.*

She stood up and brought out another bottle of wine from behind a few books, and asked me what I planned to write on.

Heloise and Abelard, I said.

Avenge her for us, my dear, she said, uncorking the wine, the red-black plenty splashing loudly into those plastic cups, the sound of that wine-dark sea turning us into sorceresses.

Dr. K is still married to Mrs. K, who went on to have one more child bearing his last name, while he went on to become the department chair.

What happened to Dr. L? said Elinor.

A lifetime ago, when I told Rose about Dr. K and Dr. L, I said that last I knew, Dr. L had moved back to West Virginia, earned a degree in massage therapy, married the man who took over her father's veterinary practice, and had twins.

So she committed suicide, said Rose, who could not know how close her joke was to the truth. When Dr. K told Dr. L that he would not leave his wife for her, she hung herself from a bathrobe belt tied to a curtain rod that she'd bolted into the sides of a window in her apartment. I did not mention this to Rose because I didn't want to turn a woman's torment into some story I hauled out to show people how close I'd stood to tragedy. And maybe I worried that I'd always had a little too much Dr. L in me and not enough Dr. K, and hid the truth about the past in order to stay in the present, where Rose and I were writing a story that would weave a spell against losing my way to everything I ever wanted. But that worry, I knew, was a bigger betrayal than if I'd demeaned Dr. L's life by treating it like nothing more than gossip. And here I was betraying her again, telling her story because it was still too painful to tell mine or Rose's. Trying to write yet another fiction, my favorite: that I could outwit whatever had befallen all the women who had ever given birth to me.

What happened to Dr. L? Elinor said.

I didn't speak.

What happened to Dr. L?

She killed herself.

Silence.

Is the moral of this story that we should stop stealing men from other women?

Maybe, I said. *Although I didn't mean for it to have one.*

Can I turn out the light? she said.

At three in the morning, I woke up, needing to use the bathroom. Elinor had turned the lamp back on and was reading the Anaïs Nin I'd bought earlier that day.

This is gross, she said to the pages, as I passed the foot of her bed. *Like, muy stinky.*

Should we drive to the bookstore tomorrow and ask for my money back?

No, she said. *I think we should just chuck it off one of these cliffs.*

Your idea's better, I said, and shut the bathroom door behind me, thinking that I would be sad when she went back to Ohio. Thinking that, and hoping and praying she did not have that baby. When I came back out she'd turned the lights off.

Do you smell that? I said, ten minutes later, to the dark.

I do, she said. *Am I crazy or does that smell like—wood-fired pizza?*

That's exactly what it smells like.

I'm sure it's just a bonfire or something, she said, and we fell asleep.

We had no idea that wildfires smelled seductively, confusingly, like the platonic form of autumnal woodsmoke, and I had been too worried about earthquakes to remember to be concerned about the wildfires, which I also for some reason thought occurred only in Southern California. To me death and destruction smelled the way September 11 did—charred plastic and paper, seared metal and flesh.

This place has never seen a lick of fire in the fifty-one years of its existence, said the man at the front desk, while we were checking out the next morning, explaining that up where we were the fogs kept the flames from the wildfires at bay.

It's always been the ocean that'll kill you here, said his wife, and told us that a body of a woman and her daughter had been found on the beach that morning. *If people are stupid enough not to know what that ocean is about just by looking at it, they deserve to drown.*

We don't need to go to the beach, said Elinor, as we walked out of the front office. *Can we go back to the city?*

We were about halfway through the drive when Elinor said:

Why have we stolen from other women?

Because we wanted to, I said. *Because we could. Let's just stop doing it.*

29.

Elinor saw him first.

I think that's your—friend, she said.

We were standing in an aisle of the Safeway north of Market Street, arms full of frozen pizza and some other junk. She inclined her head toward the end of the aisle, where Karl stood looking up at the long wire rack full of chips. He had a habit, he'd told me, of eating through a family-size bag and chasing it with a few cans of Coke Zero after particularly harrowing therapy sessions, and I wondered if that's where he'd been.

As he reached for a bag I set the food in my arms down on the floor and walked toward him. I did not know what I was going to do or say. When I was about a foot away from him he turned. I must not have looked very happy. He did not look scared, but his face showed apprehension and concern. His eyes said *Don't* and *What took you so long?*

Jesus! he said as I punched him in the stomach and he doubled over, one arm clutching his gut, his opposite hand reaching for the wire rack. But he still looked to be in control of himself as he stared at the floor, and I still recognized him, he was still so beautiful to me, so piercing, so clear, so I accessed my core, like they'd taught us in Pilates, tensed my arm, reared it back a little, told it to do what it should have done the first time, and punched him again. He buckled and grabbed at me and I lost my balance; it sent us to the floor in a pile of elbows and knees and shooting pain. *Shit*, he said, through gritted teeth, it sounded like, as he rolled onto his side. The word he liked to say when I gave him what he wanted and he couldn't take how good it felt, couldn't believe it, couldn't bear it. *Shit*, he said again, into his hands. *Fuck you*, I said, and pounded my fists down onto his right shoulder and right arm. *Fuck you*, I said, and started to cry, as the scent of detergent rose up from his clothes and reminded me of all the times I buried my face in his shirts, his sweaters, his bare chest. My friend.

Knock it off! Karl shouted, and curled into a ball to get away from my reach, but I scrambled closer to him and kept at it and at a certain point I forgot he was Karl and thought he was Dr. K and that I was there to avenge Heloise, and Dr. L, and Elinor, and any other woman who'd learned the hard way that no matter how much a man's desire for us undid them or how cool we tried to play it, anyone who had a home they couldn't bring themselves to leave had all the power here, so it was Rose I was fighting with, too, although it was unfair to drag Rose into this when she might have wanted my help to leave, just as it was unfair to Karl to think he needed to know exactly how much it hurt, the love he said he had for me, but rage and despair tend not to give a shit about exactitude, and later I would see that it wasn't the men I was angriest with, it was with Rose and myself for deep down being nothing more than good girls, and really the person I was angriest with was myself, because I was on my knees on the linoleum floor of a supermarket crying over what I could no longer afford just like Mark's mother, on my knees seeing no other way to say no but through a raised hand just like Elinor's mother, which meant that I was the daughter of an incomplete revolution, and if I hadn't helped to push it any further then I didn't deserve my freedom and I couldn't tell Elinor what to do with hers.

She pulled me away from Karl and I fell back on my seat, then onto my side. I sensed Karl dragging himself upright and sitting back against the rack a few feet away from me. A manager stood over us, hands on his hips.

Is this the kind of thing where I have to call somebody? said the manager, clearly sick of having to say those words to people. He looked like every manager of every restaurant I'd ever worked in—dough-faced, short-sleeved, hair too neatly combed. Necktied and deficiently humored.

They're okay, Elinor told him. *They're my parents. We're so sorry. I'll get them out of here.*

If they're not out of here in five minutes, I'm calling somebody, he said, and left.

Elinor walked over to Karl and crouched down beside him.

Are you okay? she said.

Just take her home, I heard him say, as he got to his feet.

I thought you were going to teach me how to not become my mother, said Elinor, in the parking lot, as I put the key in the ignition. Or she was the one putting the key in the ignition. I was having trouble understanding where I stood in relation to the person I thought I'd been all my life. *What an idiot,* she said, and I could not tell which one of us she was referring to.

When we entered the apartment, she headed straight for the bathroom, slamming the door behind her, and when she came out, picked a book up off the couch and went out to sit on the back steps. I stayed in my bedroom, door shut, trying to read, trying to pray for forgiveness to anyone who would listen, until around 8:30, when everything that had happened that day had started to seem very funny. I went out to the living room to tell her I was sorry, but her suit-case was gone. I did not need to search the rooms to know that she'd left and was on her way to a plane back home.

30.

The smoke from the wildfires reached the city that night. It seeped through my locked windows, and over the next few days a yellowish, grayish haze the color of hard-boiled yolk filled the skies. Various authorities suggested we stay indoors as much as possible, and if we had to go outside, they said, wear a mask. There were no masks to be found in my neighborhood. I stayed inside and wrote. I wouldn't have said I was writing to exorcise pain—Rose and I used to think it was one of the worst reasons to pick up a pen, and anyone who claimed it worked wasn't a writer, they were a magical thinker of the highest order and a pretty shallow pond, if coughing up words could cure what ailed you. I missed that Rose every day. She might still exist in some form, but I was done giving people the benefit of the doubt, which meant that really I just missed my youth every day. I was better than she was: I needed to repeat it until I believed it the way people believed Jesus died on the cross for their sins. I was better than she was. Stronger than she was? For standing all by myself out on this edge of the continent without husband and children to give me shelter or break my falls. She had betrayed the girls we'd been and I owed her nothing. Or she had grown up and I might never? I was a little confused as to how I actually felt, which meant I probably shouldn't have been writing about her, should have waited until I was seventy to do it, but she and I had been a song, and I wanted to sing it before I forgot the words, and I had started to forget words, words like *iconoclastic* and *obnoxious* and *cherished* and *vulgar*. I wanted to sing a sentimental and nostalgic song before I forgot how, and if the song trailed off and grew wounded and mumbling toward the end, and if I could not produce satisfactory, valedictory attitudes toward the long painful moment where youth ends and what Elinor had called non-youth begins, and if as I wrote I could not bring myself to tell the whole truth about my life despite wishing I could cut every vein open and bleed to death once and for all and so never have to write again, I pled with Puck—if we shadows have offended—and perhaps my real offense was not against future readers but against reality, which I had insulted over and over again by expecting it to be more and better and clearer than it was. I did not want to care about future readers. I wrote for myself, or tried to. The notion of putting down sentences to please only my own mind had never made sense to me; my own mind was the thing that needed escaping, and so could not be appealed to as an authority. I wrote this instead of writing Karl, which meant that sometimes I wrote pursued by a fever. One day I would not feel it when I thought of him. I wrote for the daughter I'd never have. If she read it when she was too young she might shout, out loud, at the women in the pages the way Rose and I shouted, out loud, at Isabel Archer for her infuriating passivity, and if she read it when she was too old she'd be annoyed with the women in the pages for being too concerned with their love lives. As was

I, sometimes, when I read back over these pages. I wrote for Elinor, knowing that I really should have written her directly to apologize. I'd get around to it. I wrote for the student who'd asked me *How do you know when you've become an adult?* and I said without thinking *When you stop needing an audience*, and she said *What does that mean?* and I said *When you stop caring what other people think* and she said *But won't that take a long time?* and I said *It could, but everybody's different*, and when my student sighed, I wished I could have known what it was like to be the body sought by a small face when it was sad and lost. It had taken a very long time for that yearning to make itself known, and I wondered what would have happened if I'd been a different person sooner. If I had given in to Jimmy, or demanded more from Karl. If I stopped to think about that for too long I'd want to go outside without a mask and use that air like it was Sylvia Plath's oven, so I typed quickly, sloppily, first thought best thought, typed maniacally, a little, to outrace my regrets. What did I want? To respect my solitude. It could be soil not sand. To forgive myself for my mistakes.

31.

Elinor had decided she would name the baby Iris. *After Iris Murdoch*, she told me, when I called two weeks later to check up on her. *But also after you, in a roundabout way.*

Her news filled me with the kind of hope I'd known, for just a few moments, one afternoon, a few days after I'd told Karl I was pregnant. At the end of a school day, on our way out of the building, Lina and I heard a piano rumbling under girls' voices as we passed by the music room. They were singing a song I thought I knew by heart but could not name. "One Fine Day"? "Please Mr. Postman"? "My Boyfriend's Back"? Songs my mother and her sisters danced to in the kitchen when they were teenagers, songs my mother and her sisters sang to me in that same kitchen when I was very small. Folk songs. Hymns. I loved those songs then and I love them now.

I took Lina's hand and pulled her over. We stood looking in the window of the door to the music room, and I saw a student I loved—Claire—standing in the middle of four other girls who were singing, stopping, laughing, and starting up again. I heard the music teacher, off camera, at the piano, laughing, too.

I know you can do it! he said. *I believe in you! Let's make those harmonies happen!*

The girls shook out their hands, bounced on their toes, bobbled from side to side. The music teacher began to play again, and counted off. *One two three four*—and they stood tall, readying themselves for liftoff—*five six seven eight*—and then launched themselves into the background vocals. Claire planted her feet second-position wide, knitted her hands together and cracked some knuckles. Then she brought them toward her chest in prayer, lifted her head and sang, eyes to the fluorescent lights, in a pure, clear soprano that showed a few cracks in its crystal, the first line of "Mama Said" as the other girls' voices, with more joy than precision, more desire than aptitude, rose up and down around her like synchronized lit-from-within water fountains. Standing there looking through that window I felt, for the very first time, the weight of the life inside me in a way that did not feel like grief. Innocence and joy were possible, therefore this child might be possible, and my sadness did not have to be the only thing I passed on to her. I could teach her these old songs that always sounded new, and I could tell her of the alchemy that happens when girls stand next to each other working hard, so hard, like these students, like Rose and I did, to stun and beguile and so become much more than girls and turn into gold. Go find those girls, I could say, and you will never get lost.

Hello, little bird, I whispered to her, as Lina sang along, as the voices behind the glass effervesced. *Come meet your sisters.*

Acknowledgments

Jenna Johnson and PJ Mark once again have my undying gratitude. Many, many thanks also to Juliet Mabey and the wonderful people at Oneworld for the enthusiasm they have shown these words.

This book could not have been written without the friendship and insight of Dawn Bauer, Trish Bogle, Christine Byl, Ada Calhoun, Rebecca Carman, Donna Freitas, Tavia Kowalchuk, Amy Maclin, Ilona McGuiness, Deborah Shapiro, Emily Votruba, and Carey Wallace.

© Emily Frances Olson

Carlene Bauer is the author of the memoir *Not That Kind of Girl* and the novel *Frances and Bernard*. Her work has been published in the *Los Angeles Review of Books*, *Virginia Quarterly Review*, *n+1*, *New York Times Book Review* and *Elle*. She lives in Brooklyn.